Praise for Caroline O'Donoghue's

THE RACHEL INCIDENT

"*The Rachel Incident* offers a tender reflection on those twenty-something friendships that leave a permanent imprint. . . . She illuminates these Irish lives with a light all her own."

—*The Washington Post*

"*The Rachel Incident* is my favorite kind of novel: charming and complex, with flawed and extremely lovable characters whom you're rooting for page after delicious page. A must-read!"

—Elin Hilderbrand, *New York Times* bestselling author of *The Five-Star Weekend*

"This novel is on fire. . . . O'Donoghue deepens the familiar coming-of-age premise with riveting moral complications."

—*People*

"If you've ever avoided going home or run out of things to say to your parents; if you've ever built your life and your personality around a friend; if you've ever loved the wrong person, or the right person at the wrong time. . . . In short, if you've ever been young, you will love *The Rachel Incident* like I did."

—Gabrielle Zevin, *New York Times* bestselling author of *Tomorrow, and Tomorrow, and Tomorrow*

"O'Donoghue is a unique and exciting talent. . . . I galloped through this book, enchanted by its characters and its full-hearted vision of friendship." —Chloe Schama, *Vogue*

"Caroline O'Donoghue, where have you been all my life? *The Rachel Incident* is a transportive joy, a superhighway to young friendship. Bighearted, witty, and expertly crafted—I want to live inside this book." —Sloane Crosley, *New York Times* bestselling author of *I Was Told There'd Be Cake* and *Cult Classic*

"Smart, funny, and completely captivating. . . . In the author's expert hands readers are treated to seeing [Rachel and James] fumble toward adulthood—no matter who gets in their way."
—*Town & Country*

"O'Donoghue imbues her characters with all the complexities of human experience—humor, heartbreak . . . and the everyday struggles of holding a job and paying rent. . . . Surprising, realistic, and utterly satisfying." —KMUW Wichita, NPR

"Caroline O'Donoghue shines a laser beam on young adulthood, particularly the crazy intensity of those messy, beautiful friendships forged in the fires of romantic crisis." —Lauren Fox, *New York Times* bestselling author of *Send for Me*

"I didn't just read . . . *The Rachel Incident*. I pigged out on it. . . . O'Donoghue's novel is twisty and compulsive. . . . Good thing [it] ends or I'd still be sitting on the couch covered in word crumbs." —Maren Longbella, *Minneapolis Star Tribune*

"By turns hilarious and heartfelt, breezy and bittersweet, *The Rachel Incident* is a full-throated, bighearted romp through early adulthood." —Christina Baker Kline, #1 *New York Times* bestselling author of *Orphan Train*

"A timeless coming-of-age tale of love and betrayal. . . . *The Rachel Incident* is for the young, messy, and politically inclined." —*Nylon*

Caroline O'Donoghue

THE RACHEL INCIDENT

Caroline O'Donoghue is the *New York Times* best-selling author of *All Our Hidden Gifts*, her YA debut fantasy, which has been published in more than twenty countries around the world. She has written for *The Times* (London) and *The Guardian*, and is the host of an award-winning podcast, *Sentimental Garbage*. She was born in Ireland and lives in London. *The Rachel Incident* is her first adult novel to be published in the United States.

THE

RACHEL

INCIDENT

THE
RACHEL
INCIDENT

Caroline O'Donoghue

Vintage Books
A Division of Penguin Random House LLC
New York

FIRST VINTAGE BOOKS EDITION 2024

The Library of Congress has cataloged the Knopf edition as follows:
Names: O'Donoghue, Caroline, author.
Title: The Rachel incident : a novel / Caroline O'Donoghue.
Description: First edition. | New York : Alfred A. Knopf, 2023.
Identifiers: LCCN 2023005907
Subjects: LCSH: Friendship—Fiction. | Self-realization in women—
Fiction. | LCGFT: Novels.
Classification: PR6115.D659 R33 2023 | DDC 823.92—dc23
LC record available at https://lccn.loc.gov/2023005907

Vintage Books Trade Paperback ISBN: 978-0-593-46944-6
eBook ISBN: 978-0-593-53571-4

Book design by Anna B. Knighton

vintagebooks.com

Printed in the United States of America
10 9 8 7 6 5 4 3 2 1

To the men in my life.

To Ryan Farrell for loving me then,
Gavin Day for loving me now
and my dad for loving me always.

THE

RACHEL

INCIDENT

I WAS NEVER MY PLAN to write about any of this.

I know journalists say that all the time, but for me, it's true. Almost all of us are sitting on some big life experience that we're hoping to turn into a book one day. I swear to God, that was never my intention. The process of book-making was demystified for me at the age of twenty-one, and I've had no instinct to be in any way involved with them since.

1

ONLY EVER really talk about Dr. Byrne with James Devlin, and so I always assumed that, were he to ever come back into my life, it would be through James.

I was wrong. He came via the *Toy Show*.

The Late Late Toy Show is an annual Irish TV event whereby small children review the year's best toys and advise other children what to put on their Santa lists. It's a big deal if you're a child in Ireland, and a bigger deal if you're an Irish adult who lives abroad. It's a hard thing to explain to outsiders. This, in itself, is part of the appeal. Either you get it or you don't. You're one of us or you're not. Perhaps it's because so many people claim Irishness that we keep putting our private jokes on higher and higher shelves, so you have to ask a member of staff to get them down for you.

All over the world there are group screenings where Irish adults cheer for five-year-olds testing out Polly Pockets on live TV. I am an editor at *The Hibernian Post*, a newspaper for the Irish in Britain. It is my job to write about ex-pat movements, and therefore it is my job to write about the *Toy Show*.

"Are you sure?" Angela says. "I don't want to send you out in the cold, all the way into Soho, three weeks before Christmas."

"It's fine," I say, wrapping a long scarf up to my chin, smothering myself briefly in the process.

"I don't want to sound like *that* colleague," she says. "But in your current condition . . ."

"I'm grand, honestly." I rub at the dome of my stomach, having just recently settled into a period of relative calm in my pregnancy. The rough nausea and perilous uncertainty of the early months had made me feel like I was in the first stages of a long whaling voyage. I had, after all, miscarried before. But by month seven, I have reached a kind of plaintive ocean madness. I cannot imagine land. As far as I am concerned, I am going to be pregnant for ever.

I make my way to the Soho bar that has, for one night only, become a haven for the homesick. I used to come to a lot of these ex-pat nights out, arranged around referendums and demands for change. I cared a lot. I was invested. I was also making great money. English papers were running a lot of features on the Irish fight for abortion, and I was one of the people they commissioned to write them. I interviewed campaigners, people from Marie Stopes, people who had lost daughters or wives to complicated childbirth and a doctor that refused to act on behalf of the mother. It was a blip of a moment, where being an Irish journalist in England meant something. I went to protests and ended up at parties afterwards. My contact list heaved with people who I would drunkenly promise something to, some form of coverage that was utterly not in my jurisdiction to provide.

My phone still clings to them now, four years and an iPhone upgrade later. CLARA REPEAL, SIOBHAN REPEAL, ASHLING REPEAL, DONNACHA REPEAL. Strangers to each other, but briefly connected to a family tree of people who all wanted the same thing, and, now that we have it, have almost nothing to connect them at all.

We are glad to have abortion and gay marriage, but we are lonely for nights like this.

There are no seats, and in my current bout of ocean madness, I forget that I now have a right to a chair. A man around my own age, happily settled with a gang of friends, offers me his.

"I don't want to break up your circle." The group, so vivid in their enjoyment of the evening, strike me as mostly gay. Out of courtesy to the gay social gods, I must at least pretend to resist being the intruding straight female. I am, obviously, sweating to get involved.

He shakes his head, and guides me, gently, into his seat. "No worries, missis, no worries," he says, the Dublin accent pranging through. "What would we be like, leaving a pregnant lady to stand at Christmas?"

"What would the baby Jesus think?" says another, and because we're all now sitting so closely, I have no choice but to become an honorary member of the gang. I'm grateful for it. They make me feel large and special, like Mary hovering before the Children of Fátima.

The first ad break begins, and I feel a tap on my leg. "Sorry," he says. He's one of the men from the other side of the circle, who I haven't talked to yet. "Can I just ask—"

I miss what he says next. The host of the evening hits mute on the TV screen and turns up the speaker. "C'est La Vie" by B*Witched plays, the volume way too loud, shocking everyone briefly out of their seats. The host quickly turns it down, putting his hands up, in a *sorry, guys* gesture.

I turn my attention back to the boy.

". . . do you by any chance know what's going on with him?" he says, finishing a sentence that I did not hear.

Maybe it's because I'm among gay men, or because I'm asked about my best friend so often. Maybe it's pregnancy brain. But I really thought he was asking about James Devlin. This is the precise setting where I would normally be asked about James. He occupies a funny intersection on the fame Venn diagram: Irish famous, gay famous, social media famous, but not *actually* famous. Famous enough that, if he were here tonight, he would be stopped for pictures, but not autographs. Famous enough that, when he's one of five writers on a film, one of the papers back home will run a headline that says "Hollywood movie penned by Cork local."

"New York," I say proudly. "He's doing really well, you know, and not just on the Instagram videos. He writes for one of the talk shows."

He looks blankly back at me, and so I name the talk show. Another empty look.

He furrows his brow. "You were in his third-year seminar group, weren't you?" he says. "Dr. Byrne? Victorian Lit?"

"Dr. Byrne," I repeat, and for a second, my brain disconnects. Like a power cut. A thousand lights in an apartment building switching off at once.

"You were in UCC with me, I'm pretty sure?" he says slowly. "You were in my group with him. Fred Byrne's class."

"Yes," I reply, and despite my shock at hearing the name, I'm already conscious of the PR message my face is sending. I smooth my expression, but it's too late. I need to explain something to this stranger, but where would I start? How could you understand the year in Shandon Street unless you were there, with us, living it?

"Listen, I didn't mean to . . ." he says, realising that he has somehow put a foot wrong, but with no clue where or how to retrieve it. "I just thought, you know, you were one of his favourites, or it seemed like you were, and maybe you knew."

"Knew what?" I say. How can I subtly inform this stranger that I was not, despite popular myth around Cork at the time, having sex with Dr. Byrne?

"He's in a coma," he says, dropping the information so he can run quickly away from it. "He got some crazy brain illness, and now he's in a coma."

Being this pregnant makes me feel my body in layers—crust, mantle, core—and all of it rumbles at once when I think about Dr. Byrne. Big, strange Dr. Byrne, lover of French wine and fancy little cakes. The Portuguese tarts he brought us, still warm from the English Market. That deep yellow taste, the freckles of black-ened sugar on the top.

The music pours out of the speaker to inform us that the ad break has ended, and the *Toy Show* comes back on, and a little boy from Wicklow rides his bike around in a circle.

I need to call James.

2

T'S FUNNY that James and I turned out to be such great friends, considering that for the first two weeks of our friendship he thought I was someone else entirely.

I remember our first meeting like it's a scene from a movie about someone else. It was a Thursday in November, and I was standing behind the counter at O'Connor Books. This was 2009. It was my final year at university, and there were twenty-nine days until Christmas. Our manager, Ben, was already worried that it would be a disappointing season, and was always walking around saying things about "the industry." He talked about the book industry as if it were a dragon that was chained in the basement, and would tear us limb from limb at any moment. He spoke about that year's spate of stocking-filler books—Dawn French and Julie Walters had competing memoirs out, I believe—as if they were charred corpses that we were flinging into the dragon's throat to keep it sated.

"This will keep the industry going," Ben said, with almost touching sincerity. He had more faith in the memories of character actresses than I imagine either Julie Walters or Dawn French had when writing them down. I lifted another stack out of the stockroom, the book tower starting at my waist and sitting under my chin.

James Devlin had started as a Christmas temp the Thursday

before, which I had taken as time off so I could finish my end-of-year essays for college. James had spent his first shift with Sabrina. Later, he would say that he was so inundated with new faces and names on his first shift that they were a blur, and when I said that was bullshit, he threw his hands up and said straight women all looked the same to him.

The first shift with Sabrina must have been fun—puzzling, considering how little craic Sabrina was generally understood to be—because when James opened the wooden flap to the counter area, he was full of conspiracy.

"*Someone* here has scabies," he said, "and they left the lotion in the jacks."

It feels strange now, setting that first conversation down like this, because it does nothing to communicate how James was. How utterly charming this opener was to me. "*Someone* here has scabies." He said it like he was Poirot investigating a country house blighted by murder. Like someone who saw the inherent prejudices of our polite society and was prepared to unveil it. The second part of the sentence was a whole different thing: "and they left the lotion in the jacks." He was Cork county, Fermoy to be exact, which was strictly country to me. But he had grown up in the UK—all over it, I would later learn—and so his voice had a peculiar quality that was hard to place. I was born in Douglas, a suburban little village that was two miles south of the city centre, and I was still living there.

"What?" I said, the shock of the sentence shattering the glassy reserve that I had cultivated as part of my persona. The persona broadly known as Girl Who Works in Bookshop. "And what are scabies?"

"They're like a parasite."

"Like worms?"

"Worms are inside. Scabies are outside. Have you ever had worms before?"

"No."

"Even when you were a kid?"

I thought about it. "Ringworm. Is that the same?"

"How did you get that?"

He was genuinely interested. It made me go digging in memories that I had not remembered before, and I felt as if I had discovered a new part of the ocean floor. "We had a cat, a stray. I think I got it from him?"

"Funny how all pets were strays in the nineties," he said. He was signing in to the till, punching in a six-digit number. "You just got your dog from the middle of the road, back then."

I had a certain expectation, when I started at the bookshop, about how conversations should go inside one of them. Conversations would be about books, I thought. But we rarely talked about reading. The reading taste among staff was extremely diverse, but rather than stimulating lively debate about literature, this meant we just sat quietly with our books in the staffroom. Ben liked his Joyce. Sabrina loved Terry Pratchett and Douglas Adams and all those other sorts of writers where you were never sure whether they were joking or not. There were other members of staff who were variously fascinated by pop psychology, Freakonomics, local history, and the *Simon's Cat* franchise, but I could never find common ground with them either.

I was usually reading . . . well, novels. Mainly older ones. Books that were rancidly popular in the mid-twentieth century and therefore approved by the cultural establishment, but were forgotten enough by my contemporaries to make me feel special. I liked dead women talking glibly about society. I liked long paragraphs about rationing and sexual awakenings in France. Until I started working at the bookshop I had considered myself quite well read.

I was eager to not ask James about reading, because I had lost too many prospective friendships to this line of questioning already. I wanted to ask him something real, or what my twenty-year-old brain considered to be real. I wanted something as good as his scabies thing.

There was no time however, because at that moment a dozen

customers arrived, and we rang up their purchases side by side. I had done this hundreds of times by now: standing next to a colleague for hours, working the till, making occasional small talk between customers. I had always felt entirely on my own planet. It sounds silly to say this, or like I'm assigning huge emotions to this one late shift long after the fact, but this felt different. It felt warm, like the occasional silences on road trips with dear friends.

When our shift was over, he asked me what I was doing next.

"I'm meeting my boyfriend," I said, instantly worried that by going to meet Jonathan I was missing out on my one opportunity to be James's best friend.

James was already lighting up a cigarette. "Which way you walking?"

"Sober Lane."

"Ah!" he said, and I wasn't sure if he had burned himself or had come to some kind of epiphany. "I'm Travers Street. I'll walk you there."

We walked that way together, and despite my longing to crack open James and live in him, it seemed like there was no time for me to ask questions. James didn't really want to ask questions either. He wanted to make assumptions.

"All right, now let's see. Your father works in the bank."

I smiled. "Wrong."

"Grandfather in the bank, then. There's a bank-ish hue."

"My grandfather was in the bank, yes. But my dad's a dentist."

"See, that's it. I knew it."

"You didn't know anything!"

He waved his hand over me, as if casting a spell. "Ah, you know, I got the sort of genteel middle-class thing down. *Old* money, *old* Cork. Now your mother is one of two things, haven't decided which: fabulous thin drunk or a total wagon. Tight little mouth, like a canary's minge. Am I warm?"

I laughed, wondering how he could possibly know this. "Warmish. The second one," I said, and then felt mean. My mum worked in the practice, too, and because my father's procedures were mostly cosmetic, they had both suffered from the shifting priorities of a country with less to smile about.

"And the boyfriend . . . the boyfriend, the boyfriend, *the boyfriend*. I'm split between two again."

He had moved his hands so much while talking that the cherry had fallen off his cigarette, and he paused to relight it.

"Together since secondary school, sweethearts of your year, everyone thinks you're going to get married, you're not so sure, though. Plans to go to Thailand together." He exhaled. "*Or* older man, doing a Ph.D. or something, slightly inappropriate age gap, a bit of a dry balls, your friends hate him but they haven't told you."

I don't know why he thought it was okay for him to insult everyone I knew, both real and imagined. But he was comfortable that he would get away with it, and so I let him get away with it.

"Neither," I said, defensive of Jonathan. "He's neither of those things. He's not categorisable."

"But which one is he closer to?"

I thought about it. "I mean, the first one, I suppose." Which I only said because it was the less bad one.

I was in love, or so I thought. My trouble was getting people to take it seriously. I was twenty and I needed two things: to be in love and to be taken seriously.

Jonathan and I were both Cork kids who had grown up in the suburbs surrounding the city and felt resentful that we went to university there. There were six good pubs and three good clubs, as far as we were concerned, and we put on a good show of being jaded about Cork city while simultaneously making no effort to visit anything or do anything that we hadn't done when we were seventeen.

As a couple, we were serious to the point of dullness, and curiously conservative in our outlook. Not long ago, I had to venture into an old email account to change my password for something or other. While I was there I found one of my sociology essays from this time, the Jonathan period, emailed to my tutor. The essay was called "The Patriarchy in Modern Ireland." I clicked into it, eager to see what my young self had to say about the subjugation of women in Ireland.

Whether the patriarchy is or isn't a factor in modern Ireland is beyond the point, the opening sentence read. *The question is: why has the patriarchy been so unfairly derided as an organisational principle?*

The essay shocked me. I was being completely sincere. There I was, nineteen years old, the same girl who had used all her birthday money just two years prior to procure the morning-after pill in a country that made it purposefully awkward and uncomfortable to obtain, fighting on the patriarchy's behalf. I read the whole thing and deleted it. I then walked around London for two days, paranoid. I was paranoid the way only people of my generation are paranoid, that I was about to be publicly derided by an unseen, online mass for ideological crimes committed as a teenager. I had thought I was always a feminist. Surely I was *born* knowing that things were unfair. But no, that all came later, in my mid-twenties, when I lived in London.

But this was the me that Jonathan knew, and that Jonathan and I had created together. We would sit in pubs and invent opinions, mostly by taking a common consensus and then reversing it. Radical thought to us was hating the film *Anchorman*.

James left me outside Sober Lane. I asked if he wanted to come in and meet my boyfriend. He said no.

"I wouldn't want to make trouble for you," he said. "I wouldn't want him to think I was stealing his girlfriend."

I laughed, because James was so obviously gay, and the idea of him stealing me from anyone was ridiculous. But the laugh was too long, and loud, and the way James looked at me made my face burn. He was hurt and he was closeted, and he thought that his closet was a good one. I stopped laughing.

"He's not the jealous type," I said quickly, and a little sunshine came back into James's face.

I said goodbye to my new friend and disappeared inside the dark bar where Jonathan was waiting, kicking myself for being rude.

But James did steal me from Jonathan. Over the course of just a month, I would be colonised by James on a molecular level, and my personality would mould around his wherever there was space to do so. The official line is that Jonathan dumped me. The truth is that I left him for another man.

Here's a story that James loves telling people: *Rachel and I have had one fight, and it happened before we even really knew each other.*

And I usually say: *We had our one fight, and James still thought I was a girl called Sabrina.*

And then he says: *So really, my first fight was with Sabrina.*

We've had more fights than that, of course. Two. We do not discuss them.

It had been a couple of weeks since James had walked me to Sober Lane, and he hadn't shown the same interest in me again. I started to resent him. It wasn't fair to shine his light so harshly and then to skip away, leaving me dark and chilly with my own dull crowd. Most of my closest friends had gone away to college. The high achievers to Trinity, the aspiring teachers to Mary I. The people I was left with were either girls who I had been tangentially friendly with in secondary school or Jonathan's friends.

James was the first person I had met in years that I badly wanted to be friends with, but it seemed he did not want to be friends with me. On top of that, he had charmed everyone in management so much that he always got first pick of the best shifts.

I didn't know how to be mad at people yet, so I just aped the behaviour I had seen at home: speaking to someone in tight, terse little sentences until they went insane. It was how my mother fought with me, how I fought with my younger brothers, and how they fought with their friends. It's not that we weren't capable of warmth, as a family. But we were regularly seduced by the concept of being wronged. People were always *wronging* us. That the most recent economic crisis had devastated my parents' business and depleted their investments was yet more proof that the world was out to *get* the Murrays. We were responding, at that time, by giving the world the cold shoulder.

After a while, James sensed my new iciness and floated towards it. He kept on trying to engage me, making jokes about my ancestral bank-ishness. I was mostly ignoring him. The shifts thing really bothered me. I had come to the conclusion that James was a selfish, shallow person—a sociopath, maybe—and that I was going to keep clear of him until he realised his mistake and stopped hogging the good time slots.

After I had ignored a few of his attempts to engage me, he came behind the counter to sort out some orders. And he poked me with a pen at the back of the knee. He hit, as he would continue to do, a nerve. My knee buckled and I went down a little. I didn't fall, but the disturbance in gravity made me queasy and annoyed. I told him to stop. He laughed and slipped into serving a customer as if nothing had happened.

An hour later, he did it again. The same thing happened. The buckling, the nausea, the fury. I yelled at him to stop, and he made a big show of cowering: the tiny, big-eyed Jerry to my huge, hulking Tom. He had already sniffed out that I was insecure about my size—5'11, which was close enough to six foot that I often skipped the formality and told people that I was six foot to cut any argument about it off at the pass.

There was no one around except our manager, Ben, and the minute I turned around James did it again, and the motion was so unexpected that I went down fully. Ben laughed so hard he forgot about the dragon. I was so angry that I temporarily mislaid my suburban manners and pushed James, using the full force of my body, into the wall behind the counter. The shelf above, loaded with pre-orders put aside for loyal customers, shook and the pile toppled. The hardback thoughts of Dawn French hit James and opened the skin above his eye. He started to bleed, his flat-ironed fringe clotting around the wound like gauze.

"Rachel!" Ben yelled. "What are you *at*?"

This was when James learned my name was not Sabrina. He smiled at me while Ben ran to get the first-aid kit.

"At last," he said, laughing with an odd, fresh sort of fondness. "There she is."

I felt so bad about it that I took James out for a drink after work.

"Okay, killer," he said, grinning and wrapping his extremely skinny scarf around his thin neck. "You got a table booked at the golf club?"

James's fascination with my middle-class-ness has not changed since the day we met, and sometimes I wonder if his entire friendship with me is based on some urge to catalogue the precise livelihoods of dentists and their children. A sample question that might come at any time of the day or night: Does Bridget serve the carrots cut into circles or strips?

Strips, I will write back.

Knew it, comes the response.

At this point I would not be surprised if I found out that he's been writing a book.

It was Christmas party season, and after a few false tries at ordinary pubs we found a tapas restaurant on Washington Street that was attempting to seduce Cork into the concept of small plates by having a bring-your-own-wine option. The whole thing became accidentally romantic, and it made me nervous that James thought that I was trying to undo my earlier faux pas by forcing him on a date with me. I started loudly narrating the menu, accusing the restaurant of trying to make ham sound fancy.

James rested his little face on two closed fists, enjoying the ham chat.

"Small plates," he said. "So, if I needed stitches, would it have been large plates?"

"Oysters," I replied.

"What if I broke a limb?"

"I'm not a charity," I retorted, and he laughed.

"This is how it happens. I read the papers. The rich try to buy you off with a big gesture to keep you from suing."

"Why do you think I'm rich? I'm not rich."

He gestured to our surroundings, the chalkboard menu that said "Specials," the candlesticks in the empty wine bottles that presumably had been brought by customers from the various homes of Cork city.

"I live at home, that's all."

"Ah. You're working for pocket money, then?"

I told James to order whatever he wanted, and despite his assumptions about my wealth, he ordered the cheapest bottle of wine and a bowl of cashews. Seconds later, we were given a bottle of water and two tiny glasses.

"No," he said, pouring the water. "No one works as much as you do if they don't need it."

"Well." I shrugged.

"You work Thursdays, Fridays, Saturdays and Sundays," he counted off on his fingers. "And I think I came in once and saw you on a Monday afternoon. But you go to college as well?"

"I come in whenever Ben rings me." I was shrugging again, and was becoming very aware of how boring shrugging is, as a conversational tool.

"Look," I said. The waiter came with the wine and the cashews and asked *are we thinking about food yet, guys?* and James said that the cashews were fine for now.

"Go on," James said, once the waiter had left.

"I've had to pay my college fees," I said, trying to keep my tone frank instead of pitiful. I told him what I had not told anyone: that my parents, who had easily sent me and my siblings to private schools, were unable to pay for college.

Back during the good days, when both my family's finances and my reputation as a responsible child were intact, my father had given me a credit card. I had a regular babysitting job, but the credit card was to pay for incidentals like books, notepads and taxis home on nights out. The card was handed over, very ceremoniously, after a long talk about how it was better to have a credit card, because it meant you could build a credit rating.

It was something Jonathan found very funny. His parents were in the civil service, and having a girlfriend who had "Daddy's credit card" made him feel very earthy. But the truth is, I barely used the card. Until a few weeks into my first term of UCC, when it stopped working.

"Dad," I said, standing in the campus bookshop, having stepped out of the customer queue to call him, "did you forget to pay off the card?"

"No," he said. "I didn't forget." There was a plunge in my guts that felt like fear but in fact was the first dose of reality I had ever tasted. Since the crash, my parents had stopped travelling, stopped going to restaurants, and stopped buying new things. I thought they were being prudent. I had not realised how broke we were. It was on this call that I was told that, in addition to the credit card being cancelled, I would also have to find a way to pay my college fees.

College fees were quite nominal in Ireland back then, a few grand a year at the most, and everyone I knew had their fees paid for them. This goes some way to telling you how stratified my world was. My father was ashamed and I was embarrassed for him.

"We'll have to figure out something between us, Rachel," he said, as if he were sating an angry bookie. He did not want me to get a student loan. His trust in banks was too damaged for that.

"Of course," I said quickly. "I can work."

"Right," he said. "And it would be . . . *between* us. The boys don't need to know."

I had kept it between us. But now it was between me and James, too. I felt bad about breaking my father's trust, but I wanted to lasso my new friend in with confidences. Luckily, it was working. James felt the drama of the situation very keenly.

"This is very . . . I don't know. It's like *a play*."

I burst out laughing. "It is not a play."

"It's very a play," he said sternly.

"It's not so bad," I said, wary of attracting pity. "I've paid my fees for this year and I'm not doing a master's so now I'm just . . . flush." I gestured at the table. "We should order some actual food," I said.

"We should live together," he said.

"What?" I choked on my wine. "You don't even know me."

"I know that your name is Rachel," he said, and at the time it felt like a joke, because I did not know about the Sabrina thing yet. "And that I like you.

"Anyway, I don't love my gaff, as it is." He examined a cashew. "And I think we'd have a laugh, don't you? There's some nice places up by Shandon Street. Which I know is technically north side, but you'll get over it, won't you? South-side princess falling on hard times, on the wrong side of the tracks? Very theatre. Very *a play*."

I looked at him cockeyed. "You've found the gaff already, haven't you?"

"Yes."

"And whoever you were *going* to move in with has dropped out."

"Yes," he said, without contrition.

"And I'm your last resort."

"No, no, Rachel! No!" He looked at me aghast. "It just occurred to me now, in this minute. You're the random flight of fancy *before* I consult my list of last resorts."

"Oh."

"Well, think about it."

We moved on, chatted all sorts of bollocks, and when I came home on the 11 p.m. bus my parents were both at the kitchen table. The man who owned my father's office building had drowned himself in the Lee. It was in the *Evening Echo*. Dad had never met the landlord, had always worked through a lawyer. My parents were worried about whether the man's widow would raise the rent or sell the building.

In the years since, I've asked other Irish people if they remember the suicides, the businessman suicides that happened around this time. They all say no, not really. Maybe I'm asking the wrong people, or everyone's just forgotten. Maybe Cork was hit worse, or the recession was just an idea, not a real thing that everyone talked about every day.

"I'm moving out," I announced, and my mother looked at me like I had smashed a jar of pasta sauce on the floor and was now hopping over it, with the excuse that I had a taxi waiting outside.

"With who?"

"A guy from work."

The tactlessness. It makes me want to climb into a car and set myself on fire. It makes me want to scream at my own unborn child, *Don't you fucking dare abandon me like that.*

"You guys have been talking about downsizing anyway," I said. Which was true. We had five bedrooms: theirs, mine, Christopher's, Kevin's, and a little spare room that we used for a study. There was a hot tub, outside, that was a present from my father to my mother on her fortieth birthday. They talked about selling the house constantly.

"In a few years you'll all be gone," my dad had said. "And this house will be worth even less."

My mother would interject here. "Or more," she would say. "We don't know what's going to happen."

My mother was glaring at me. Hating me for collaborating in the downsizing scheme. But it was too late, and I had made up my mind.

I came home, with laundry, for Christmas. I remember thinking that they looked older, but no one could have aged that much in ten days. The truth was that I had been extremely sheltered. I thought of my parents as heads on Easter Island, and it took moving two miles away to realise they had been people all along.

"Twenty is late to realise that," James says. He's probably right.

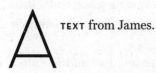

3

TEXT from James.

How are the poos babydoll??

Month seven has made me constipated, and the only people in the world who know are my husband and James Devlin. I am not, generally, a poo-talking sort of woman. But there was never a version of this pregnancy where I didn't tell James every movement, every phase, every symptom.

Shandon Street is historically a poor part of Cork city, but is strangely picturesque. It's full of old houses, but also modern riffs on ancient architecture. A pantheon-shaped theatre; an old market hall known simply as the Butter Exchange; a church with real bells and a big fish on the steeple.

The house itself was a cottage, built to house the tubercular families of the 1930s, and the only bathroom was downstairs, through the kitchen. There were two boxy bedrooms upstairs, each big enough for a queen-sized bed, a pine wardrobe and a chest of drawers. In my head, there was no "better room." James, however, had lived in more places—fifteen homes by that time, and he was only twenty-two—and knew how to take an instant inventory. He saw things I didn't, like where was bound to get the best of the morning sunlight and which had a window too close to the head of the bed.

"Do you want the room nearest the stairs?" he asked, in a way that made it seem like the stairs room was the best room and he was being chivalrous in offering it to me.

"Sure," I said, and tossed a black bin bag full of clothes on the bed, where it exploded like an overcooked dumpling.

The radiators in our bedrooms worked, but downstairs just had a bricked-up fireplace and a collection of space heaters under the stairs. The living room was a grand big space, two couches and a dining table that could seat six, with a sweet kitchen and a little yard. There was even a herb garden leftover from the previous tenant.

I couldn't believe that we were only paying six hundred euro a month between us. I understand now that the house was incredibly run down, that only two working gas hobs out of four is unacceptable, and that moving into a mostly unheated house in the dead of an Irish winter was unwise. These things would matter to me now, but they didn't then, and even though I spent most of the following year drunk and malnourished, I sometimes wonder if I was maybe better off not caring.

James had an iPod, one of those big clunky ones that was old even then, and he let me choose what our move-in day song would be. I ran my finger around the tricky circular dial, terrified of getting it wrong, not realising that this was all James's music, and therefore it was kind of impossible to get it wrong. It strikes me now that, if James was really invested in me thinking he was heterosexual, he would never have let me go through his iPod. The selection was an odd mishmash: somewhere between a middle-aged straight man and a middle-aged gay one. Cher snuggled next to the Creedence Clearwater Revival, the Eagles next to Elton John. The only thing even slightly of our generation was Britney Spears.

I settled on "Cecilia" by Simon & Garfunkel. I had no reason except for the word "jubilation!," which was repeated throughout, and was exactly how I felt, although I was far too shy to admit it.

We propped the iPhone speaker in the corridor and went to our rooms. I suddenly felt extremely self-conscious, awkward in my movements, like I was unpacking in the *Big Brother* house and aware of how the public would interpret my knicker folding.

The feeling lasted two minutes and fifty-five seconds, wherein "Cecilia" ended, and immediately started again.

"*Cunts*," James shouted, and marched out to the speaker. The screen had frozen, leaving "Cecilia" on repeat. "It does this sometimes," he said, and a thin blush crawled up his neck. "Fucking useless *shite*." He hated having a bad thing. It's a good job James is rich now because being poor never suited him at all.

"It doesn't matter," I told him.

So we listened to "Cecilia" again. And again. We started singing along, our voices bouncing off the cheap plaster. By the eighth time, we were running into each other's rooms to elaborately lip sync, our limbs in all directions, grabbing on to the song fiercely. If it were a phone book we could have torn it in half.

By the sixteenth "Cecilia," James and I had given birth to our relationship and it wandered around the house like a sticky, curious foal. We picked up each other's belongings—bad T-shirts, pretentious books, preserved concert tickets—and accompanied each with the same question: *What the fuck is this?*

"What the fuck is this?" I asked, discovering a collection of bandanas.

"What the fuck is this?" he asked, picking up my copy of *The Pumpkin Eater* by Penelope Mortimer.

"What the fuck is this?" I retorted, finding the top half of a Subway uniform.

"What the fuck is this?" he announced, finding a packet of Femfresh wet wipes that had come in a Student Health kit and I was too suspicious to use and too frightened of my own vagina to throw away.

What we were actually asking, of course, was: Who are you? Who were you? Are you okay if we have the kind of house where I slag you off for reading? How did you get fired from Subway? Are you really the sort of girl who washes her vulva with a deodorised wipe?

We were so busy falling in love that I had forgotten completely about Jonathan, who I had asked to call over around five. One of my main motives for moving out was sex. We had both lived at home for most of college and were still relying on house parties, parked cars and our parents' schedules to have it. It was also getting exhausting, having sex at college. Doing it in a campus bathroom is exciting the first time, but there's something depressing about asking your boyfriend to meet you at "*our* bathroom."

He rang the doorbell and wandered into a maternity ward for private jokes. I wrapped my arms around him, giddy and sweating, excited to drag him into my new world, purely so the new world would have a witness.

"This is James!" I announced. They greeted each other warmly enough, but as I looked between them I felt an instant flash of revulsion for my boyfriend of two years. He had no features. He had eyes and lips and a nose but I felt like they had all been made by the Bauhaus, obsessively streamlined to perform a function and no more. Whoever had put James together had at least tried. He was sort of runty, with big eyes and big black brows on a face that was either elfin or bloated depending on the week he was having. He had a nose like an old man's, with deep indentations at his nostrils. James had a look that most of us described as "emo" but really just meant his clothes fit him and they were from Topman.

I hugged Jonathan again, doing a show of devoted girlfriend-dom to drown out my new feelings. He seemed grey, like a mushroom. He kissed me on the forehead. "Give me the tour, then!" he said, and the tour lasted thirty seconds before we went upstairs and I showed him my room, the sheets not yet on the bed, and then I took my shirt off. It was mostly because I had been sweating and I didn't want him to smell me.

There's something about sex with a long-term partner at the age of twenty that makes it the most depressing sex of your life. At least in your teens, everyone is prepared to eat humble pie together. Everyone's embarrassed, no one knows what they're doing, there's slightly more *is this all right?* and *does that feel good?* In a way, the sex I had as a teenager was more mature than anything between the ages of eighteen and twenty, where the boys were so certain that they had found a winning formula. Jonathan had one girlfriend before me and had told me she fainted when he went down on her. This meant I was supposed to faint also, or at least come close. I was so annoyed at myself for not enjoying it more. The whole thing felt very ticklish and lonely.

It's tempting, when you're talking about your sex life as a young woman, to slip into little melancholy asides about how you gazed heavy-lidded at the ceiling while a dull brute pummelled away at you. Sadly, I don't think I can say any of that and get away with it. The sex was unsatisfying but I couldn't have been more obsessed with having it. I was always on top, moaning away like a stuck pig. If someone told Jonathan tomorrow that Rachel Murray said he was a bad lay, he would laugh and tell them to get fucked. I don't think he'd entertain it for a second.

"How are you getting on with your man?" Jonathan asked afterwards, as we lay on the bed.

"James? Great." And then, carefully: "I think we're going to be friends, you know."

"Are you going to become one of those fag hags?" he said. "Like Will and Grace?"

(Have patience: this was considered to be an extremely witty thing to say in 2009.)

"Do you think he's gay?" I asked earnestly.

He looked at me, not even bothering to argue. Just a raised eyebrow that said, *Oh, come on.*

"What makes you think that?" I pressed. Ever since my faux pas at Sober Lane, I was fascinated with what made a person *seem* gay. Neither of us had any gay friends at that point. There were certainly gay people, acquaintances and people you would just know to see around, but for some reason we hadn't ended up being friends with them.

We were completely cut off from gay culture, and yet we both had perfect confidence in this assumption about James.

"I have eyes," Jonathan said simply, and he left soon after that.

We ordered a pizza for dinner and James plugged in his TV and DVD player. The only DVDs he had were three seasons of *Frasier*.

"Your boyfriend thinks I'm gay," he said, without emotion.

I waited a second before answering. "No."

He paused the DVD on Kelsey Grammer's contorted face, ranting about Seattle spa memberships. "Listen," he said, as if he were about to lay down an important house rule, like no shoes on the carpet. "I'm camp as a row of tents, I know that, but I'm not gay."

I laughed awkwardly.

"Don't you think if I was actually gay, I'd go ahead and just *be gay*?"

I nodded. It made sense. If you walked around with Cher on your iPod then you had probably thought more seriously about whether you were attracted to men than the average rugby-playing alpha male. I saw James as extremely advanced, a person who had interrogated all sides of his soul. He was too emotionally intelligent to get stuck in the doldrums of what music or behaviour seemed gay or straight.

In that moment, he wasn't just a person to me. He was the future of people.

The truth was that he was terrified.

"What was your endgame?" I asked him once, years later.

"To wait until I could move away," he said. "And then go somewhere where no one would know me."

Which he did. Which we both did.

But I'm getting ahead of myself, because before any of that happened, Dr. Byrne happened first.

4

D R. BYRNE was the only other man in my life whose opinions I cared about. When I wasn't hanging off James's word, I was clutching on to Dr. Byrne's. I must have cared about Jonathan's thoughts at some point. But student relationship dog years being what they are, any deep respect I had for him had long since worn off. We were already behaving as though we were in a years-old marriage, functional but surly.

Dr. Byrne dressed like he was impersonating a university professor. In my memory he has patches on the sleeves of his coat. It's possible that I'm inventing that detail, but everything else about him suggested coat patches. The first time I saw him he was ten minutes late and sweating. He seemed angry at us, the first years, for having the gall to attend a 9 a.m. class.

He was horrible at mornings, which I related to him being a very big person, 6'5 and extremely wide, a farmer's build. I've had this idea in my head since I was young that a person's body is a factory, a big Edwardian job, and that you need every worker comfortably sitting at their station before the day's work can begin. The bigger the person, the further the workers have to travel: trudging up stairs, turning down corridors. This was my own explanation for being bad at mornings and I was happy to extend the kindness to Fred Byrne.

"Right," he began. "The Victorians."

He nudged his brow with the heel of his hand, trying to stop a bead of sweat before it fell on the lectern.

"Who knows Sherlock Holmes?"

He knew that most of us would drop out by the end of our first year. That's how it is with Arts. People love it for the variety but can't handle the droopy uselessness of it, and when the hangovers and the depressions kick in around February, it's hard to justify dragging yourself out of bed for Cronus eating his babies. Dr. Byrne was passionate about his subject but he also did not like to waste energy, so he spent those first few classes giving us just enough information about the Victorians so that it might one day be handy in a pub quiz.

He repeated his question, after it was met with silence. This was pre–Benedict Cumberbatch's reign over the BBC, so it was a dry time culturally for Mr. Holmes, and we didn't know a lot.

"Detective," someone said.

"London," another.

A long silence.

"Drugs," one boy said, finally, and there was a titter because we were eighteen and imagined ourselves to be the inventors of drugs. "Wasn't he on drugs?"

A few people in Dr. Byrne's factory sat down at their machines just then, and he suddenly erupted in talk, talk so fevered that it was at first hard to tell whether he was mad at the boy for saying "drugs" or very happy. He talked about opium, laudanum, morphine and cocaine, which were legal in Victorian England at the time. He noted that non-white writers don't tend to put out exploratory Drug Books with quite the same tenacity, and was that because they had bigger things to say about drugs, such as how they destroyed their communities. He talked about spending five years in America as a younger man, about how the war on drugs there was merely a feeding tube for the private prison system. He argued with himself, representing both the pro- and the anti-drugs side, his face reddening as he did so. He was thirty-eight in 2009, which I suppose makes him fifty now.

"Right," he said, at the end of his spiel. He always ended his classes the way he started them: with the word "right."

We loved it, of course. We thought of him as the Drugs Guy. We would later learn that Dr. Byrne didn't really care about drugs so much as he liked having a subject that was old and could be argued from a lot of directions. Incest, sodomy, abortion, prostitution: anything that had been around for two thousand years and had always been controversial. I suppose he liked the Victorians because they tried to put rules on things, and he loved debating whether or not those rules should exist. He was everyone's favourite lecturer, which I sometimes think was not down to his brilliance but to the fact that the English faculty was mostly women. We already know that I was something of a misogynist. So was everyone else, I suspect. I also think there's something in the fact that most English teachers at most secondary schools are women. Having a large man teach you about a book felt exciting, like *Dead Poets Society*.

I had been in several of Dr. Byrne's classes by the time I met James, at the end of 2009. At this stage in Dr. Byrne's career he was so popular that he was allowed to have any stipulations he wanted for his seminar group, and everyone who signed up was asked to write an essay about any aspect of the Victorian sensibility that was still present in culture today. The group would run from January to April, my final term of university. There were only fifteen places, and something like 150 of us had tried to sign up. I would be surprised if even twenty people wrote the essay.

I received an email to meet him at his office, which was situated in a department-owned house on the college road. This sounds seedy. Are all colleges like this? Faculty members being outsourced to tiny little houses that smelled of old radiators? Anyway, he wanted to discuss the essay I had written. It was very exciting for me. Sitting in his pokey little office, I thought what I always do when I'm in a small room with a man I'm not related to, which is: *Are we gonna fuck?*

I don't know why I think this. It's never happened. I've had one-night stands, of course, but they were always an extension of a date or a night out. But I've never been in a lift, or a stockroom, or in library stacks with a random man and then suddenly found myself wrapped in his arms. Despite this, I am always poised for it to happen. I could be standing next to a seventy-year-old man in a lift and think: *I hope he doesn't want to have sex; I'm still on my period.*

Dr. Byrne was obviously different: I really *did* want to have sex with him. It wasn't just that he was a random man in a small room. I had been nursing a quiet crush on him since my first year, a crush I only kept private because of how annoyingly obvious it seemed. I didn't really talk to the girls in my year but I was pretty sure we were all hoping to fuck Dr. Byrne. He was huge, and passionate, and he was the only man under fifty in the English department.

Most tantalisingly of all—oh my *God*—he had a wife. But not just that.

That wife *had been a student.*

Despite being so uninvolved with college, I was very aware of the situation with Dr. Byrne's wife. Crushes are like that. No matter how checked-out you are, there's always one microphone left switched on, and it only records information about your desire. He and the wife had been married four years, had met six years ago. *When she was an undergrad?* We counted on our fingers. No, came the answer. She had been a master's student. She had been well into her twenties. This was less good, but still exciting. It proved it *could happen.*

So I sat in the little room and looked at his face. He had what James would later call "baby dinosaur features." The broad brow, wide nose, heavy-lidded eyes all came together and made you think of a brachiosaurus lazily eating leaves out of a tree.

"Right," he said. "Rachel Murray."

He was reading my name off my essay paper, then looked up and smiled, as if he were glad to finally be putting a name to a face. I had been in four of his modules by that point.

"Hello," I said, motioning to close the door behind me.

"No, no, leave it open," he said. "Have a seat."

I must have looked agitated. I have a thing about sitting in rooms with the door open. It makes me fidget. *Were you born in a barn?* etc.

"We have to keep it open," he said absently. "In case I try to pounce on you."

I looked at him, shocked. He did not bother to meet my gaze.

"It's unfortunately rather common at third-level education," he said gravely, and I thought, *Don't kid a kidder; I know how you met your wife.* "Anyway. Pyjamas. Explain your notion."

"I've written it in the essay," I said.

"I know you have, but I want to hear you explain it. I want good chatters in my group. Go on."

I had written an essay about pyjamas, based on the idea that in the Victorian period young women started buying negligees from France for their bridal trousseau. It had caused a great moral panic about what young brides were doing in bed with their husbands, and whether they were adopting cheap whore's tricks. I related this to modern sensibilities, because at the time there were a lot of *Daily Mail* headlines about women wearing pyjamas to the supermarket. Morality and pyjamas. I felt quite clever about it. But explaining this back to Fred Byrne, I wondered if writing the essay was the cheap whore's trick. It was all so embarrassing and intimate, talking about garter belts and lace.

"And really," I said, my throat dry, "the design of Victorian undergarments would go on and be part of more cultural movements. Like the flappers. Their outfits were just slips, really, and this thing of underwear as outerwear, it was like . . . it was a *sig*nifier, of the growing independent female population in urban areas. The private made public."

It went on like this for a while. Signs and signifiers. He started to glaze slightly, the way a lot of clever men do when the discussion is getting altogether too feminine, too fussy, and too preoccupied with bits of lace.

"Why aren't you doing film studies, if you're so into all this? Or fashion?"

I should have said something twee, like, *Because I simply love the novel*, but I knew this would not truck with him.

"English feels like a better way of keeping your options open. There are no jobs in film or fashion."

"Have you heard the news?" He smiled. "There are no jobs anywhere."

"No," I reasoned, "but it feels like the whole world is filled with bits of text, doesn't it? Brochures and signs and things. Something is bound to come up."

"Brochures and signs and things. And that's why you're pursuing an English degree?"

I didn't know what to say. I chose English, originally, because I liked to read. But even then what I liked most about reading was that I was good at it. I had taken to it quite quickly as a child. In the absence of any other discernible gift, it seemed like a fine thing to pursue, if only to receive more praise.

There was a knock on the open door, and I turned around to see another girl waiting to discuss her essay and potentially to be fucked by Dr. Byrne. *Don't bother*, I wanted to say.

I got an email the next day to say that he was delighted to welcome me to the seminar class. It was a form letter, my name just filled in at the top, and no personalised sign-off or PS whatsoever.

I printed it off, though. I still have it somewhere.

5

O N 14 JANUARY 2010, Jonathan dumped me outside the Crawford Art Gallery with the explanation that we were growing apart. I asked him how. He murmured something about how I "seemed fake" and then bounded off towards Patrick's Street before I could ask him what that meant.

Of course, I now know what that meant. I was living with James, working with James, and talking like James. I can't really hold it against Jonathan: I was being extremely annoying. The thing that drove him the most crazy was that I was now obsessed with describing whatever situation I was currently in as though it were a movie or a TV show.

Some sample dialogue.

JONATHAN: I think it might rain.

RACHEL: Are you sure?

JONATHAN: The forecast said rain.

(Beat)

JONATHAN: *(looking out the window)* I think it's starting to rain. Maybe we should stay in.

RACHEL: *(giddy)* I feel like I'm in a French
film and we're two lovers who are trying to will
it to rain so we can stay tangled in ze sheets.

(Silence)

RACHEL: Ah, monsieur, doesn't ze sky herself
want us to stay indoors? Enjoy ze ways of ze
flesh, ah-haw-haw-haw?

JONATHAN: Okay, so, I'm going to go.

It wasn't really fair on him. We'd had a straightforward and fond relationship up until that point, and our jokes had been mostly taking the piss out of other people. I couldn't just expect him to start playing silly games, the kind me and James were now doing, when there was no pretext for it in our relationship.

The only reason I remember the date is because I was working that afternoon, and Dr. Byrne came into the bookshop.

Dr. Byrne had come into the shop before, of course. All of my college professors had. We were a big bookshop, and we carried a lot of stuff from the smaller, Irish-run presses. I often got a nod from faculty members of UCC, people who weren't necessarily my tutors but who recognised me and were willing to make small talk about the holidays. But now it was different. He had hand-picked me to be in his seminar class of final-year students, so he knew me.

It was a Thursday night, the weather bitter cold outside, and the shop was set to be quiet until it closed at 9 p.m. Processing my grief, I started marking down a stack of literary-themed calendars on the counter. WAS: 9.99 / NOW: 4.99.

"Rachel," Dr. Byrne said. "I didn't know you worked here."

"Hello!" I said brightly, stumbling into that young person's problem of never knowing how to address your professors, your parents' friends, or your friends' parents. "Yes!"

"Any recommendations?" he asked politely, which is something people always ask if you work in a bookshop. I could never remember the title of a single book.

I looked down at his stack: a reissued book of poetry by Irish revolutionaries and a snow thriller. I wanted desperately to recommend something tense, lean and masculine to show him that I understood men.

". . . Hemingway?" I threw out, uselessly.

"Ah," he said, without emotion. "Batman for fat, bookish boys." Then he looked down at himself: "I'll take two."

I burst out laughing. I hadn't grown out of the schoolgirl giggle habit. I was always nervous and I was always laughing my head off.

"Like Dorothy Parker," I said, "is Wonder Woman for depressed girls."

I couldn't believe I had come up with a line like this so quickly. He laughed instantly, caught my eye, and I thought: *Fuck me and I'll say more things!*

He tilted his eyes skyward, trying to remember the verse. "Guns aren't lawful; Nooses give; Gas smells awful . . ." He trailed off.

"You might as well live," we said together, and then we smiled. With perfect conviction I realised that I was going to rebound from my ex-boyfriend with my college professor. How chic!

"She went bull-fighting with him once, you know," he said. "For a magazine. I think they wanted her to be appalled by him, but she couldn't have been more charmed."

"Me neither," I answered. And then: "About Hemingway, I mean."

He looked at me, perplexed at this half-flirting, but not altogether uninterested.

"I wonder if I might trouble you"—he pointed at the computer at the end of the counter—"to check a book for me."

"Of course," I said, stationing myself at the creaky PC. "What do you need?"

"Well, ah, it's a little odd."

He coughed, and I had a painful fear that he was about to open our affair with a red-faced request for *The Joy of Sex* or something. I considered whether I would still go through with our relationship even if he did this. Surely not, Rachel?

"I was wondering if you had, on pre-order, a book called *The Kensington Diet* by . . ." He rummaged in his pockets, and looked at the emergency exit sign. "By, ah, Dr. Frederick Byrne."

"Oh," I replied, strangely embarrassed for him. "Right! Okay!"

I started to type. "On pre-order, did you say?"

"Yes," he rushed. "It's not coming out until February."

"February eleventh," I said, reading the screen. I named the publisher. They were famous, and Irish, and famous because they were Irish. They discovered a lot of authors that would then abandon them for larger contracts in the UK.

"I wanted to know how many the shop had on order," he asked. "Bit pathetic, but this is my first time publishing outside of an academic press, and I'm hoping more than four people might read it."

I saw that the order selection was zero.

"Fifteen," I said. "Fifteen copies."

"Oh," he said, surprised. "Quite a lot, then."

"Yes," I answered, trying to suppress the blush that always accompanies my lies. "We're very excited about it."

He cocked an eyebrow, wary that I might be making fun of him.

"I mean, obviously we're excited about it, if my manager is ordering in copies. What's it about?"

"Irish writers during the famine, the artistic response to Victoria starving us out of it," he answered. "Very cheerful stuff, I assure you."

I remembered the Eavan Boland poem that I had done for the Leaving Cert. She and Adrienne Rich were the only poets I liked at school.

"What is your body now," I said, quoting her. "If not a famine road."

"Very good," he said, and the atmosphere was tense again, too much like teacher and student. He was growingly conscious of how vulnerable he was, enquiring about his book like that. That particular poem also had a certain relevancy to his personal life, but we'll get to that later.

James came over and started scanning a stack of books he had just recommended to an old woman. James didn't read much but he was constantly watching films, and for that reason he was always selling *Notes on a Scandal* and *Perfume: The Story of a Murder*. He had the best sales numbers of anyone on our team, which is why Ben kept him long after his Christmas-temp term was up.

"What's the craic?" he said cheerfully. James would never judge you for talking to a friend at work, and you could always count on him to cover if someone popped in to see you.

"James, this is Dr. Byrne," I said. "He's one of my lecturers."

"Well, how do you do?" James said. He didn't go to college but loved talking to people connected with it like this. It was somewhere between a piss-take and genuine admiration.

"Very well, thanks."

Dr. Byrne moved quickly, as if realising that he had been lingering too long. I wanted to dive across the counter and keep him from escaping out of our private world filled with little poses and sexy jokes about literature. But I could not do this, so he paid for his things and left.

The rest of the shift passed quietly. Now that we were living together, James and I loved arranging our shifts so that we were both closing. We pulled down the shutters ten minutes early and blasted our own music through the speakers as we tidied up.

I, however, was taking longer than usual.

"What are you at?" He put his head on my shoulder, gazing at the monitor. "Who's Dr. Frederick Byrne?"

"My college professor. The one who came in earlier? And this is his book."

"And who's Moira Finchley?"

"She's an ex-customer. She died a few years ago," I said. "She's also one of the people who's ordering his book in."

"What? Why?"

"Because I stupidly told him we pre-ordered a load of his books. We haven't ordered any, but if Ben thinks that customers are ordering it in, he'll order some."

"Okay." James began to nod. "I have a question."

"Why am I doing this?"

"Yes."

"Because . . . I don't want him to be disappointed. He's so excited about his book."

James practically leapt into the air.

"You *dirty bitch*!"

"Shut up."

"So, what? You're charging some old dead lady for a book she won't read because you're horny?"

"No! It won't charge her. No one will pick up the book, and then I'll just put it out on the shelf."

"Who else are you going to make order it in? Who else is dead?"

"The rest I'm just inventing," I said bashfully. "I'm making new customer profiles on the system."

He looked shocked at what he perceived to be the first real insane behaviour from me.

"Jonathan broke up with me today," I said, hoping that he would interpret my crazy behaviour as a kind of noble grief.

"He broke up with *you*?" he replied, in disgust. "I thought, the other way around, maybe."

"Why! I loved him!"

"Rachel. Come on."

"We went out for two years."

"Well, I'm glad he's gone."

The fact that he could talk to me like this, after a month and a half of knowing each other, still shocks me. There are people in my life I've known years who I would hesitate to tell their clothes tags are showing.

"Well, Ben will know something is up if you don't change the dates on the orders," he said, pointing to the screen. "They'll all say January fourteenth."

So we stayed an hour after closing time to invent back-dated pre-orders for Dr. Fred Byrne's book on Victorian Ireland during the famine. I realised that I had never been in love with Jonathan, after all. I had known the love from my parents and the strange affection of a college relationship that was somehow both stale and naive. But me and James and the pre-orders: that was love.

———

It worked better than we could have possibly expected. Late the following week, Ben was gazing into his A4 printouts and asked, "What the fuck is *The Kensington Diet*? Is that like Atkins?"

I may have been young, but I had been working in a bookshop for almost three years. Even then, I had serious questions for Dr. Byrne's publisher, who had the gall to release a book with the word "diet" in the title so close to the New Year.

James picked up the baton straight away.

"Christ, Ben, did you not hear them on about it on Fergal O'Riordan's show? They had that brilliant doctor on." James was clicking his fingers, as if trying to recall. "Rachel, you know the guy, don't you?"

"Dr. Byrne," I said, trying to sound non-committal.

Ben looked at his form again. "There's a lot of buzz around him, I gather."

"He teaches up in UCC," I said. And then, in a fit of genius, "We could ask him to do a signing here."

"Or a launch," James chimed in. "A Cork launch, on his whistle-stop tour of the country."

"It would be very good for the shop," I said, nodding at Ben, like he had suggested it.

Ben tapped a pen on his teeth. "The industry is in a bad way," he said. On top of the recession, there was also a lot of anxiety around the Kindle and what it would do to bookshops. Getting an author in might make a case for the shop's own relevancy.

The seminars I had with Dr. Byrne were every Wednesday morning and ninety minutes long. They were intensive. He burned through material. Nothing he was teaching us was particularly mind-bending. It was a lot of dead Irish people through the eyes of dead English people then reinterpreted through Irish scholars who, like Fred Byrne himself, needed to write a book about something.

Every week, fifteen badly groomed children sat around in near silence while their odour suggested they were being pickled from within. I was no better. I had given up on becoming enlightened and was just getting drunk all the time. James and I were going out three nights a week, usually with the other Christmas temps from the shop, sometimes just by ourselves.

Dr. Byrne didn't mind us being hung-over, but he wanted those hangovers to fuel us, not mute us. I think Dr. Byrne liked the idea of a crowd of stinking drunks arguing about Trollope. What he couldn't abide was silence. On this particular day, he was raging at a Kerry boy called Elliot about *The Playboy of the Western World*.

"Elliot, in your opinion, was the controversy around *Playboy* an inappropriate response?"

Elliot blinked. "Yes."

"Mr. O'Donovan, your own father is a farmer," Dr. Byrne said. "Are you telling me that you find no problem with a global vision of Ireland where people kill their fathers by bludgeoning them with a spade?"

"No, that's bad," Elliot answered. "That's like, that's stereotypes."

Dr. Byrne moved on, disgusted. There were always a few people who had done the reading and were willing to argue, and the majority of the class relied on them to do the heavy lifting. I was becoming one of those hot young arguers, high on my own ability to plagiarise an opinion. I picked up the thread, and blathered something from Yeats, butchering a quote I had read on JSTOR about when a country creates a genius, the country is always mad at the genius for not reflecting the right idea of the country itself.

(Which, oddly enough, was a line I repeated to James years later when a tweet he wrote went Bad Viral.)

Dr. Byrne was pleased with the Yeats quote. He obviously knew it himself, but was glad I knew it, too.

After the class I hung around for Dr. Byrne and told him that my manager wanted to know if he would like to launch his book at O'Connor Books.

James and I had planned this conversation carefully, and in all versions of it, Fred Byrne would be delighted. In some hypothetical eventualities, he took me out for a drink afterwards.

But he was just confused.

"I don't understand, Rachel," he said. "It's not exactly going to attract a big crowd. It's mostly still an academic text, even if it has some crossover appeal."

This was not a conversation he was having with me, but a repeat of a conversation someone else had recently had with him. An agent or a publisher or maybe his wife, trying to temper expectations.

"No, no," I said. "We're very excited about it."

"Do you get authors in a lot?"

"All the time!"

Which was true, but they were mostly fiction writers. On the last Sunday of every month we invited a children's book author, of which there were seemingly an endless supply, to read to kids.

Dr. Byrne eventually agreed to the launch. I said I would email him about it, and introduce him to Ben. "Hang on," he said, tearing a piece of paper out of a jotter. For a brief, brilliant second, I thought he was writing down his phone number. "Make sure you include Deenie on the email."

I looked down at the email address he had written down. Aideen .Harrington80@hotmail.com.

"And who is . . . ?"

"My wife," he answered. "And, well, my publisher."

My face was turning red. "Oh, of course," I said.

6

ONCE, on a press trip to Iceland, I was stuck on a broken-down coach an hour outside of Reykjavik. We were on our way back from the geysers. The geyser was beautiful, and it splashed everyone, and the splash was so happily received that it felt like a version of Sea World for people who read *The New York Times* on their phone. But on the way back, the water stuck to our skin and froze there, as we waited, and waited, for roadside assistance. The whole time I stamped my feet and ate my frigid packed lunch and thought: *But is this as cold as January in Shandon Street? No.*

It was so cold that we couldn't be downstairs any more. We went down for food and to use the bathroom, but we lived in James's room, both duvets stacked on the bed, the radiator going, the space heaters choking us with rancid air. We brought the TV upstairs and watched season boxsets of shows that we found in charity shops.

James was far more housebroken than I was. He washed his sheets every week, ironed them, and had specific ideas about fabric softener. I had never done my own laundry. I had no perception that clothes could go stale in the washing machine if you left them there too long.

"You smell like a troll," he said one day.

I sniffed under my arms, surprised my body was even warm enough to sweat.

"No, I mean, like you live under a bridge. Your clothes smell like dirty water."

And it was up to him to show me how laundry worked.

I was unusually stupid about household things, my mother having pampered us all without any of us realising. I thought because I unloaded the dishwasher at home that I knew how a house worked. In my defence, James was advanced. He'd had to take care of himself early, and had lots of rules about housekeeping. He also had an obsession with magazines, and would pick up *GQ* or *Take a Break* or *Hello!* whenever he went to the shops, like I might pick up a chocolate bar.

I once asked him why this was, and he said: "They were my toys."

"What?"

"My mum would sometimes come into our rooms and say, 'We're going tomorrow,' and we'd have to fill two carrier bags. You can fit a lot of magazines into a carrier bag."

Nothing in his tone sought to arrange the information as though it were tragic backstory. Sometimes he would just drop these things into conversation and I would have to force him to backtrack, ask him all the questions he asked me about my dentist father, except James would get bored of answering and move on.

Over the first month of living together, I had learned the following: that James was born in Manchester, that his father was an addict, and that he was periodically in prison. He had two older sisters, and a mother he loved very much. On release, his father would often try to track down the family in an attempt to reunite with them, wherein James's mother would move them on. She didn't do this because she hated James's father. She did it because she loved him, knew that she couldn't say no to him, and that if she said yes, the lives of her children would become worse. She was trying to recover herself. When James was nine, she moved them to Ireland, where she quickly met his stepfather, and he had been in Cork ever since.

His English accent was mostly gone, but he still peppered his speech with words like "minge." He called college "uni," which I liked because "Rachel's off to uni" made me feel clean and jolly hockey sticks about my education.

I told him about my conversation with Dr. Byrne while under two duvets eating a chow mein that came in a bag from the freezer section of Tesco and whose water chestnuts never properly defrosted. Your teeth would slide through them, particles of crusty frost landing on your tongue.

"Oh my God," he said. "We'll have to make it really glam."

"What? How?"

"Let's make it black tie."

"James! No! It's a book launch, not a gala."

"Okay, but wear a skirt. Oh! And you have to give him an introduction."

"An introduction? To what?"

"To his reading. You stand at the lectern and say, 'It is my great honour to introduce . . . ,' blah blah blah."

"Is that normal?"

"Very normal, yes."

I have now been to enough book launches to know that sometimes the bookseller might give a short introduction, and so in a sense, it is kind of normal. But honestly, if James told me that it was normal to take your top off while working the register, I probably would have believed him.

We spent the rest of that evening researching Deenie Harrington, who was thirty years old and a senior editor at Dr. Byrne's publisher. There wasn't much else to "research," except for a few grainy photos of her at publishing events.

"Christ," he said, zooming in on her face, "you can tell he's into the Victorians."

It was easy to see what he meant. Deenie had shiny black hair and the kind of eggy eyes you see in portraits from the era. She had a sharp nose, a rounded chin, and the pretty look of someone academic yet slightly in-bred.

But even then, I could tell that she was a nice person. She was always smiling in photographs, a warm and nervous smile, and she had a weakness for seventies-style silk hairbands in an array of jazzy patterns.

"She seems a daft bitch," James said, "daft" being another English-ism he had kept from childhood.

James had no love life himself, so he was prepared to throw a lot of energy into mine. I think I would have put the crush on Dr. Byrne aside if James hadn't been there, spurring me on. He wanted me to have a glamorous, exciting rebound after Jonathan, but he was also keen for the drama. He wanted to arrange the whole thing like a photo spread in *Heat* magazine.

"I've been thinking," he announced, a few days before the launch. "Once the drinks bit ends and everyone leaves, we make him stay."

"How?"

"We make him sign all the copies of his book. Stick him in the stockroom. Then you can seduce him."

This was a seduction technique stolen from *Empire Records*, a film we watched a lot because it was about young people in retail.

"In the *stockroom*?"

"You've never fantasised about fucking someone in the stock-room?"

Of course I had. James knew that, too, so I'm not sure why he was asking. We were already at a stage where I had told him about my obsession with strange men in enclosed spaces.

On the morning of the launch I got an email from Deenie Harrington asking if it would be okay for her to come by the shop an hour early to drop off the wine. I told her of course.

I felt like a child whose imaginary friend was starting to bite people. The game had already gone too far. The game had always been just that. A thing to keep James and me entertained while we waited for our frostbitten January to end.

I didn't actually want to start an affair with my professor. It was a ridiculous notion. There was also the unavoidable fact that Dr. Byrne hadn't showed the remotest bit of sexual interest in me.

———

When I got to work that afternoon, Ben was behind the counter with two big boxes of *The Kensington Diet*.

"Rachel," he said, "this is about, like . . . history?"

"History and literature," I answered. "The history of literature."

"Right," he replied. "Not about diets."

The cover had a picture of a young Queen Victoria on it, as well as a political cartoon of a starving person. It did not look compelling.

"I never said it was about diets."

"You said it was written by a nutritionist."

"I said it was written by my literature professor, Dr. Fred Byrne. Where did you get nutritionist from?"

"I don't know. I thought it was, like, Dr. Gillian McKeith. Why . . . why are we launching this?"

"There's a lot of buzz," I said, and whisked myself away.

But I couldn't stop asking myself the same question all day. How had this got so desperately out of hand? James and I hadn't the faintest clue about book launches. We had printed off some fliers and had them all over the shop, fliers that neither stipulated nor clarified whether *The Kensington Diet* was an actual diet. We put "free!" on the flier, and now I was beginning to worry whether my adored professor was about to be humiliated by a crowd of people looking for advice on carbohydrates.

Deenie came at 4 p.m. She asked for me by name. Eggy eyes aside, she was very attractive in person. I was holding a stack of *The Help* by Kathryn Stockett.

"Hello," she said. Her approach, in all things, was a strange mix of timid and self-assured. It was like she was confident about being shy. "I just wanted to say hello. I'm Fred's wife."

I'm Fred's wife. Why wouldn't she say that she was his publisher? She hadn't taken his last name, so it was negligible how much stock she put in being visibly married.

"I was hoping you had some kind of kitchen where we could keep the wine chilled," she went on. "I've brought a few mixers, too, as you can always bet on someone being pregnant."

"Can you?" I asked.

"Oh, in publishing, always." She smiled. She had very small teeth. "Also, I wanted to thank you for putting this on."

"Ah, well." I shrugged, plopping *The Help* down on the floor. "The shop had already seen a lot of buzz around the book. I just joined the dots."

"Right," Deenie answered. "And when did you first notice the buzz?"

She did not attempt to sound convinced. While I was able to explain the book launch to Dr. Byrne by appealing to his vanity, I would never be able to fool Deenie. As his wife, she might *think* he was the greatest author of his generation, but as his publisher she probably had a stack of printouts proving that he was not.

"Well, I hadn't known about the book at all," I said, trying to stay casual, my guts turning to sludge. "Not until Dr. Byrne came in asking about it, and I saw we had lots on pre-order. All customer ordered."

"Customer ordered," she repeated. "That's so interesting."

"Everyone loves his classes up at college. He has a lot of fans."

Deenie Harrington scanned her eggy eyes over me and tried to puzzle out my interest in her husband. There are too many clichés about male English professors and their adoring young students for her not to have been on the alert. She had been in his class herself, albeit as an MA student.

This is what it's like to love an unreliable man, or to have an untenable job, or an unsteady parent, or an ill child. It is the outfit you constantly dress up and down, accessorising it according to what insecurities hang well, what caveats are the most slimming. But we were close in age; but I was still his student; but we are in love; but what's to say he won't fall in love again.

"Working together must be fun," I said lamely.

"It is," she replied. "On the days he can bear to be edited."

She rolled her eyes slightly, and then smiled to confirm this was all in good fun.

"Well, I'll see you later," she said. "It was nice to finally meet you."

The "finally" rang out between us, deadly little aftershocks of a natural disaster. I took a step backwards and she left the shop. It was four o'clock. The launch was to start at six thirty. I would host it while James worked the front till for the late-night shoppers.

Deenie wanted to figure out whether I was the kind of girl who has ill-advised but unrequited crushes on her professors, or the kind of girl who orchestrated bookshop launches in order to seduce them. I don't think she found an answer. I was odd and tall and I was not skinny. I was nothing at all like her. But maybe, she must have figured, he was approaching his mid-life crisis and maybe part of that was wanting an ingenue that reminded him mostly of himself.

If she did find an answer that day, I don't know what her plan was. I don't think she would have threatened me. She was, before anything else, an extremely kind person.

WHEN YOU'RE YOUNG you tend to live in absolutes. In my head, there were only two ways for the book launch to go. Either it was going to be abysmal and a profound humiliation or it was going to be the best book launch in the history of small, un-catered events.

The truth was, as always, somewhere in-between. It rained badly all afternoon, which mentally made me cut at least ten people from the guest list. We sold a few copies that day, the table we dedicated to the book having conferred a sense of importance on it, and we were sure to tell everyone who bought a copy that the author would be doing a reading that evening. Ben, having gotten over his disappointment that the book was not by Dr. Gillian McKeith, was starting to talk about the night as a "trial run" for other launches, and was talking enthusiastically about developing a "relationship" with Deenie and her publishing house. He went out to buy crisps from the big Tesco in an attempt to cement this relationship. He refused to call them crisps. He would only call them "refreshments."

I didn't talk to James much that day, which I was grateful for. I knew he would make a lot of jokes about this being "the big night," and I didn't want to tell him that the plan was never really on. I wanted us all to pretend that this was a normal event for a local author and that life would quietly resume afterwards.

Dr. Byrne came in just after six. He was wearing a dark grey sports jacket and a pair of tan brogues, and both were splattered with rain. He looked handsome and wilted, like a tough flower that was gallantly surviving despite over-watering. I realised then how much my crush had developed, even though I had decided to do nothing about it. I admired Dr. Byrne when he was my fiery, huge professor. He made me feel better about studying English literature in a recession, because he was a professor who acted like professors in films acted. He added heft to the grand pointlessness of mooning over set texts. But over the last few weeks, my hero worship had crusted over into something more knobbly, more textured. He had been so happy to believe me about the pre-orders. I wanted to protect him against the world's many disappointments, guard him with my body like I would a baby or a small dog.

On top of all that, he was the only man I'd met who made me feel petite, and to feel protective over someone who physically towers over you is a hell of a drug.

"Oh my God," James said, when he saw him across the shop. "I bet he's hung like a chandelier."

"Shut *up*."

"Do you have clean knickers on?" he prodded. "You don't have your under-the-bridge-troll knickers?"

"I'm not discussing this here."

"No one holidays at the swamp."

"James!"

"I'm just saying."

It was the kind of thing we found hysterically funny at home but James would sometimes drag into public life, where I was still trying to be Bookshop Girl. I wanted to be caught in a beam of sunlight looking elegant and melancholy, possibly writing a poem at the same time. I tried this for years and it took me until my midtwenties to realise that it's strictly for short women.

But all the same, I *was* wearing nice knickers.

I approached Dr. Byrne from the side, as if not to spook a horse, and he had a wide, nervous smile for me. He smelled like rain and cigarettes.

"Hello," I said. "You just missed your wife."

"When?" he answered.

"Oh . . . two hours ago." I bumbled around. "She seems nice."

He merely nodded, and I thought: *What right do I have to tell this grown man that his wife is nice?*

"We're really excited about tonight," I went on. "Everyone at the shop."

James came over, proof that other people worked there. "Hello," he said. "Can I just say, your book is fantastic. I started reading it on my lunch. I'm already on chapter two. Unreal."

Fred Byrne smiled gratefully. "Really?"

"Yes. And I'm a useless reader. But, like, I grew up in England, and they get taught none of this stuff over there. It's all the Empire this, the Empire that, no one would be able to hold their knife and fork if the Empire hadn't taught them to."

"Quite right," Dr. Byrne said, his lecture-hall confidence starting to come back to him. "And when did you move here?"

"Nineteen ninety-seven. My mum married a farmer."

"Whereabouts?"

"Fermoy."

"Ah."

"I know. Don't worry about it. I have nothing good to say about Fermoy either."

"It's not so bad."

"Nowhere's too bad if you have a DVD player in your room."

"God, if only we had that when my family moved to Canada."

With every word spoken I felt like I was becoming more and more invisible.

"You lived in Canada?" I asked, my voice oddly strangled.

"For a few years," he said, and at that moment Ben came over with a bowl of refreshments.

About thirty people came, in the end. Twenty-two of them were friends, family or work colleagues of the Harrington-Byrnes. The rest were drifters, or people sheltering from the rain. I delivered a short, burbling introduction that was adapted from the press release that was written by his wife. Afterwards Dr. Byrne read the introduction from his book, and I remember feeling that his writing was nowhere near as compelling as he was. The book teetered between big statements designed to provoke a headline in the culture section of *The Irish Times* ("in all Irish art, whether it's Yeats or The Corrs, the long shadow of the famine still lingers") and long, drifting asides about how the Irish were not just literally starved but continue to be starved by the British on a soul-level. Dr. Byrne almost sounded like he thought the famine was a good thing. He seemed to think most worthwhile books and paintings sprung out of the potato blight, and I wondered if Deenie ever told him to calm it down a little.

I've wondered how *The Hibernian Post* might have covered such a book, or whether we would cover it at all. Since being made editor I've thought about whether Dr. Byrne would reach out with subsequent books, and what I would say if he did. I think I would have run a review, slipped it in on the weekend edition, five hundred words long and written by yours truly. I think I would have been generous, used phrases like "tour de force," and justified it to myself by saying that there was a much bigger market for cultural reflections on Irish oppression now. We're feeling confident the last few years, and open to hearing about the ways we were wronged.

There wasn't so much of an appetite for it then. Our opinion of ourselves was very low. I remember going home one Sunday to parrot Dr. Byrne's theories about the famine as an attempted genocide, and my father folded down his paper to look at me. "What were they supposed to do?" he said, meaning the English. "We were the ones too stupid to grow anything else."

After the reading, Dr. Byrne was set up at a table that we usually used to stack the toilet books on. His friends and colleagues queued up to speak to him. A photographer from the *Evening Echo* was there to take pictures for the social diary. He was ushered in by Deenie, who seemed to know him, and Dr. Byrne posed for shots, holding the book in different positions. The photographer fulfilled the same role as a clown might at a child's birthday party. There was a sense that, without him, it was just a bunch of adults who knew each other and were willing to participate in the role play that one of them was famous for a day. It seemed a revolutionary act of kindness, like the Make-A-Wish Foundation but for well-liked men nearing forty.

It was all over by nine o'clock. The friends decamped to a pub, and Dr. Byrne, without any prompting from us, said that he was going to stick around the bookshop to sign the excess copies. Deenie kissed him, getting up on her tiptoes to do it, and said she'd see him at the pub. I felt annoyed by the tiptoes, the gauche expression of tiny-ness from her. Teenie Deenie. *Fuck you,* I thought. *I'm going to shag your husband just for that.*

As usual, I was getting ahead of myself. Ben wanted me to clean up the shelves first, which had been put in disarray by all the browsing friends of the author. Hardback Fiction was in bits. James put on music, plugging his old iPod into the aux cable. More Paul Simon. "You Can Call Me Al" was our big clean-up, home-time song, belting the lyrics across the stacks. It felt weird, having Dr. Byrne there for our clean-up song. He seemed to enjoy it, though, signing his books on the counter and humming along with us.

Ben made me put the table back to its original spot, and we piled the toilet books back on top of it. We argued whether *Pride and Prejudice and Zombies* belonged in Humour or Fiction. Then he took the tills upstairs to start counting the day's takings.

"Under African Skies" started playing and I realised that I was alone. The floor was clear, each book neatly slotted back in its place. The shop lights, which operated by motion sensor, had gone out on the rest of the floor. I was standing in half-darkness, only one fluorescent bulb awake above me.

I wandered the floor confused, like a girl lost in a parallel world, its differences not yet clear to me. Eventually, I decided that Dr. Byrne and the remaining staff had gone ahead to the pub without telling me. Or perhaps they had told me, shouted it over the speakers, and I hadn't heard.

There was half a box of *The Kensington Diet* that would not fit on the shelves, so I gathered them into my arms and nudged my way into the stockroom. Where Dr. Byrne was, and where James looked so small in his arms that it took me a second to realise that he was not alone.

8

F YOU WANT TO KNOW how long I stood watching my professor passionately kiss my best friend, I would say that it was just above "glimpsing" and just below "gazing." Time slowed down, and allowed me to take in details that I would have never noticed otherwise. The fact that Dr. Byrne's hands were in James's shaggy brown hair, and that his hands were so big one covered James's left ear entirely. That he seemed to be gripping James with such intent that it looked like James's head was a cantaloupe that was threatening to roll down a hill.

Even if the kiss hadn't been a betrayal, I would have still been captivated by it. If the kiss were happening on the street, I would have slowed down to watch it. It wasn't just that they were men. It was that they were both so inside the kiss that they were mutually trying to prevent the other's escape. Fred Byrne, with his hands firmly on James's neck and skull, and James pushing his body so hard against Dr. Byrne that it seemed he would have to physically peel James off if he wanted to stop kissing him.

Which he didn't.

They must have heard the stockroom door banging behind me. No one followed or shouted at me to wait. I stood on the shop floor for a few seconds, and then grabbed my bag and bolted home.

It was a sixteen-minute walk from the shop to our house on

Shandon Street. On the journey home, I told myself what I would do the moment I got inside: put the kettle on, get into my pyjamas, and fall deep under the bed covers to cry. It had stopped raining by that time but the streets were covered in puddles. I was so dazed that I kept treading in them, and by the time I was home I was wet to the knee.

But all I could do was stand in the kitchen and shiver, eating handfuls of cereal out of the box. When my mouth started to get dry I opened one of the cans of Diet Coke that James always kept in the fridge and drank the whole thing in three swallows. I wished, desperately, for someone to talk to. There was no one. I had created a sea of problems for which James was the only navigator, because he was the only person who knew about my crush on Dr. Byrne. And there was no one to tell about James's betrayal of me without also betraying James at the same time. Even then, in my fury, I was aware that James could find an equally interesting housemate tomorrow, but for me there was only one James.

I wondered whether this was the first gay experience he had ever had. I worried whether my hurt feelings were in fact repressed homophobia; then I reasoned that, had James been a girl, I would have been much more furious.

When he finally came home I was still shivering in the kitchen like a spooked poodle. James dropped his keys on the hall table. I waited for an additional pair of footsteps. I heard none.

"Rache," he called. He repeated it, calling up the stairs. "Rache!"

There was no door from the kitchen to the living room. The kitchen was more of an alleyway that led to the bathroom than a real room. He stopped when he saw me.

"All right," he said.

"Is this it, then?" I replied, not meeting his eye. "Are you out now?"

"What do you mean?"

"I mean I don't see the point of you being in the closet," I snapped, "and me telling people that you're straight, if you're going to fuck my professor."

"What does you *telling people* I'm straight have to do with any-thing?"

I found a vein of anger, something other than my own shame at losing Dr. Byrne, to tap into. "I *vouched* for you," I said. "People asked me if you were gay and I said *no*."

"Did you believe it?" he said calmly.

"No!" I exploded. "But you were my friend. I was *being* a good friend."

He looked down at my sodden socks. "You're freezing," he said. "Come on, let's go upstairs."

We climbed the stairs like an old married couple, hands on the banister. James changed into pyjamas. He gave me a pair, too, knowing that all mine were hanging on a drying rack downstairs. They were soft and smelled fresh, the way everything he owned did, and the way I've never been able to replicate no matter what laundry trick I've tried since.

I got into his big grey T-shirt and the big grey trousers in my room. As always, my room looked like somewhere a night porter might sleep in-between room calls. Clothes just fell as I stood, and the bedspread was permanently rumpled. There was a chipper down the road from us, and one night while we were waiting for our fish I noticed an empty, industrial-grade mayonnaise bucket behind the counter. "Can I have that?" I said. James couldn't believe it. I took it home and used it as a laundry basket. To this day, he refers to this period of our lives as the Mayonnaise Bucket Days.

"Are you coming in?" he called, and I padded into his warm, clean room, and got into bed with him.

"I'm sorry," I said, once the light was out.

"No, I'm sorry," he said. I could feel his breath on my face. "He was yours."

"No, no," I replied. "He was never mine."

In the years since, I have heard about the night James was first kissed by Fred Byrne so many times that I feel like I was there, experiencing every beat of it. I feel this way about a lot of James's life. I pass certain stations on long train journeys and I think: *Sandhurst. When have I been to Sandhurst?* And then I remember that I have never been there, but that James lived there for a year in the nineties.

At some point while I was arguing with Ben about *Pride and Prejudice and Zombies*, Dr. Byrne made a crack to James about being under no illusion that the many signed copies of his book would sell. He asked if the shop would be out of pocket; he wondered whether he should feel guilty, times being what they were.

"Never feel bad," James had replied. Then he named a memoir by a disgraced politician that was currently taking up half the stockroom. The politician was one of those brown-envelope guys who were apparently responsible for the downfall of the country.

"He signed every copy, so we can't send it back. Now we just use it to stop the water coming in on wet days. It's like a dam."

This being a wet day, Fred Byrne asked if he could see the dam of political betrayal. At some point, James felt a hand on the small of his back. Just a graze, the warm palm of plausible deniability. He turned his face, and there he was. Big and handsome and feeling, probably, like he deserved a glamorous treat on his big night. While I was trying so desperately hard to be Bookshop Girl, James was effortlessly being that rarer, more beautiful thing: Bookshop Twink.

I've often asked James why he didn't come out sooner. Shame and terror aside, he just didn't feel like he *needed* to. Coming out, he reminds me, is a political decision and not a practical one. At least for gay men, anyway. He was part of a culture that had been both highly sexual and deeply underground for hundreds of years. "Coming out" only really started after AIDS. There have always been enough men who simply *got it* without having to be told. Fred Byrne was one of those men, but there had been others. There had been bathrooms and staff kitchens and, yes, stockrooms before.

I was amazed by this. I, Rachel Murray, had spent my short adult life disappointed that random men didn't want to have sex with me in random places; meanwhile James was getting it constantly.

"Not constantly," he corrected. "Not even frequently."

At twenty-two, he had fewer than ten of these experiences to his name. But they were sexy and sustaining and you could never quite tell when the next one was going to occur. Only one thing was certain: when they did happen, you didn't say no.

"You can always say no," I said, thinking this was a consent thing.

"No." He shook his head. "You're not understanding me. I mean me, personally. James Devlin. I *cannot* say no."

He looked genuinely sorry. "I know he was yours, Rachel, but let's be honest, you were never going to actually go there and we both knew it."

"Yeah." I sighed. "I wasn't."

James was too nice to say: *And he would have never gone for you anyway.*

I was desperate to know more information about Fred Byrne. I thought that the two of them fucking for twenty-five minutes in the stockroom of O'Connor's after closing meant that James had downloaded Dr. Byrne's entire autobiography into his head.

"Does he do this a lot, then?"

"I don't know."

"Is he secretly gay? Or just, you know, openly bisexual?"

"No idea."

"Does his wife know?"

"Not a clue."

"You didn't talk about his wife at all?"

"Funnily enough, she never came up."

I only learned a few facts about Dr. Byrne that first night, and they were thus: that he was, indeed, hung like a chandelier. That he wore boxers. And that, after they were done, he was not drenched with shame and distance, the way many married men were. In fact, as he had been led out of the stockroom, he had kissed James, very softly, on the back of the neck.

9

N IRELAND, spring begins on 1 February. It's a pagan thing, I think, because it's certainly not a climate thing. Most Februarys are overcast, frigid, and with only a few green shoots visible through the gates of Bishop Lucey Park.

That spring was different, though, because James and I were the hopeful green shoots, pushing up through frozen earth with brand-new velocity.

James was now officially out to one person and that one person was me. It opened up things. There is a photograph of us on a Facebook page somewhere, attending a burlesque night at a gay club. Me, in a red corset and black jeans, breasts reaching towards my ears, white fat slipping over my waistband. Him, dressed as the emcee from *Cabaret*, if the emcee from *Cabaret* had to dress for winter. If you were to look at the photo now you would say he was dressed as a mime, the white make-up is that thick.

When I started doing his face, he was sitting on a hard wooden dining chair in our living room, and we were each drinking from our own bottle of a four-euro wine called Marqués de Léon. It was available only at the big Tesco, and when it was warm it tasted like piss and when it was very cold it tasted like nothing. We drank it with a lot of ice and very quickly.

I swept rouge on his face, drew black lines over his eyes. I filled in his top lip with liquid liner.

He looked in the mirror of my compact. "Rachel, no," he said. "I still look like me."

"I don't know what you want me to do. I'm not a make-up artist."

"More white," he said. "Like a mask."

I started painting it on with a pastry brush that came with the house and smelled like sunflower oil.

That night we danced to "Coin-Operated Boy" by The Dresden Dolls, and "Babooshka" by Kate Bush, and yes, songs from *Cabaret* itself. The burlesque dancer had a Hula Hoop and for a few minutes it was on fire. At some point, James peeled off, his sweat dissolving the clown paint, and ended up glued to some boy in the corner. I don't know what I did. I don't remember ever being bored, or lonely, or like I was an accessory to his sex life. I was starting to come out of myself, too.

Hell: *I was wearing a corset in public.*

Most often, I was in the smoking area with another young gay guy, or a group of them. I began to realise that everything I had ever really loved as a child—*Death Becomes Her*; the concept of Bette Midler; pulling the neck of your T-shirt around your shoulder and then posing in the mirror, slightly kissing yourself—was all very *gay*. I had a camp mindset. I picked over certain quotes, certain women, certain micro-moments in pop culture. My quote-reeling had been dimly appreciated by Dr. Byrne ("what is your body now if not a famine road?") but was embraced enthusiastically by the random men I met out. "He doesn't look any bigger than the *Mauretania*," I said once, to a boy who was pointing out a huge man on the dance floor that he wanted to sleep with. He grabbed my hand and laughed, and we reeled off *Titanic* quotes for the best part of an hour. "Best part" in that it was the majority of the hour, and best part in that it really was the best part. For me, anyway.

I look at the photo from the burlesque night a lot. I attach a lot of memory to it, memories from other nights out that we attended together but do not have photos of. Themed queer-adjacent nights with specific costume prompts, gay bars that paid for guest appearances by the Vengaboys, parties held by the drama students at UCC in order to fundraise the props for their next play. Every now and then I would see a club photographer propelling around James and whatever boy he was kissing, and I would tap him on the shoulder and politely ask him to fuck off.

"Just come out," I said, on the walk home once. We were eating chips, cheese and garlic sauce. "Why are you even bothered? Most people assume you're gay, anyway."

"My mam," he said. "She'd find it very upsetting. I think she worries about me a lot as it is."

This felt like a lame answer to me. His mother, after all, had married a drug addict, a criminal. She knew about the world. "Have you considered that she might already know?"

He scowled at me. "I just don't want things to change."

"But they are changing," I insisted. "They *have* changed."

We didn't just go to queer nights. We still went out with our friends from the bookshop, who had somehow managed to expand and morph into our friends from the music shop, friends from Topshop, friends from HMV. Without realising, I collected the names of roughly a hundred people aged between eighteen and thirty who were working part-time jobs in Cork city, each of them with boyfriends or girlfriends in bands, on campus radio or working as bookers at live music venues.

There were a lot of gig tickets going around. UK-based bands who had hung Cork dates on the end of their tour like stray socks on a clothes line. Glasvegas, Dirty Pretty Things, The Pigeon Detectives. And others, ones who you wouldn't even remember. Bands that are kind of a punchline now, a shorthand for short-lived fame and flat-ironed fringes. But they occupied a delicious role for us, a magical sweet space between celebrity and accessibility. Despite the fact that I have lived in London for almost ten years, which is supposedly the land of the desperately clutching wannabe, I have never known fame clutching like the kind I knew in Cork in 2010. I'm sure all regional cities are the same. You're so far away from it all that even a fragment of notoriety can make you high.

James got off with someone in one of these bands. I'm not being discreet. I literally don't remember which. We were at their gig and he disappeared, then texted me an hour later to meet him outside. James and I had an agreement that we were allowed to vanish but never on one another. He would never go home with someone if it meant me walking home alone, and vice versa. We either put the other person in a cab or made sure they were en route to a house party somewhere.

I met James outside the Savoy, freezing in front of an open minivan. "Are you coming?" he said, stamping his feet. I had no idea where we were going. Inside I could see four skinny English boys, jittering away like dashboard nodding dogs. "Of course," I answered.

In the long dark cab ride to the Vienna Woods in Glanmire— preposterously out of the way, at least a thirty-minute drive from the city centre—I was allowed to choose which of the band, if any, I was going to get off with. There was one girl in the van already. Balanced, predictably, on the knee of the singer. James was with the guitarist. The bass player and drummer were mine to destroy, a fact which would have made me feel more powerful if they weren't constantly asking me: "Do you have any mates, love?"

I went with the drummer.

I had been studying literature for almost three years at that point. I had read about the Bloomsbury Group, and Paris in the 1920s. But despite all that I was blind to the emergence of a scene when it was happening right in front of me. I never considered that the bands I saw, the things we wore or the people we slept with were the edges of a larger circumference, the makings of a circle. I suppose it's because none of them ever became famous. Or never stayed famous. Maybe fame is what confers importance, and not, as my essays for college would suggest, the other way around.

The drummer had one of those faces where the skin sits very close to the bone. Maybe a year of touring had thinned him out somewhat, not in weight but in essence. We kissed, foreheads together, on one of the twin double beds in the room he shared with the bass player. James was in the next room.

"Is it true what I've heard about Irish girls?" he said. He was Northern. Leeds, I think.

"What's that?" I whispered.

"That you all swallow?"

I kissed him to make him shut up but I left quickly after. James came with me.

As for Dr. Byrne, the whole thing was dissolving into the past for us. It was the catalyst for this new life together, this breakthrough of sexual frankness, but we didn't discuss it very much. In many ways, I was glad it had happened. For the first few weeks of me and James, I was always slightly confused as to why he was so bothered about being friends with me. Now that I was his secret keeper, I felt like I had a role in his life. I put this to him once, drunk and years after the fact. He was lightly horrified. He said he loved me always. And despite saying crazy things like this, loved me still.

The only time I ever had to think about it was in my Wednesday seminars, where Dr. Byrne had not acknowledged my presence for weeks.

I have read a lot of books about the lasting trauma of young women and their dastardly, corrupt English professors, and what happens when they fuck you. I have read nothing whatsoever on the trauma of when your English professor decides *not* to fuck you. Fred Byrne, who had briefly considered me a sparring partner, now preferred to skip over me in tutorial discussions, and only nodded when I spoke. I understood that he was embarrassed, and aware of the thin line of secrecy that I represented—I had his wife's email address!—but I still felt it was extremely unfair. I had done nothing wrong. I hadn't even *tried* to sleep with him, except in my own head. Sometimes, during those long seminars where everyone in the class got shouted at except for me, I wondered if Dr. Byrne had understood the plan all along. Maybe he felt sorry about not being attracted to me, and about fancying my housemate instead.

Still, I thought sniffily. That didn't mean he had to deprive me of an education.

I tried to shrug it off. By April I would be finished with classes for good, and in May I would sit my final exams. The time for knowing Dr. Byrne was starting to pass. College was mattering less and less to me, if it had ever mattered at all.

But the law of small cities meant that we bumped into Fred Byrne anyway. It's not as if Dr. Byrne was out cruising. He was too married for that. But there was an older class of arty Cork person that he belonged to, and those people sometimes touched the outer edges of our groups. He was still in his thirties, and childless, so he and Deenie socialised a lot. We ran into them at a Goldfrapp gig. They attended it the way I go to gigs with my own husband now—fun, dinner first, home by eleven, something to do. There's only a short stretch in your life where you can attend gigs with spiritual commitment.

"Hello!" I said, too loudly, over the music.

"Rachel," they both said at once, and then they nodded at James, Deenie not remembering his name, Dr. Byrne not wanting to appear to.

I didn't want the interaction to last any longer than a pleasantry. I was still angry at Dr. Byrne for snubbing me in class the way he did. James wasn't feeling so shy.

"You both look so elegant," he said baldly.

Deenie smiled widely, so instantly charmed that I knew she must not have a clue about her husband's other life. "Stop!" she said. "I'm still getting over a cold; I didn't even want to use the tickets tonight. A friend at Red FM gave them to me."

Did anyone actually buy their gig tickets back then? Is this why the economy was in bits?

She held up a balled tissue in her hand to prove herself, and it looked like a white flag of surrender. She winced. "My head is actually pounding."

"Rachel has paracetamol," James blurted. Everyone was looking at me.

"Yeah," I agreed, "I do. Do you want some?"

"Rachel is the pill girl," James went on. "Paracetamol, Solpadeine, ibuprofen. She's a walking pharmacy."

It was true. My handbags were full of half-empty pill packets, bought from the all-night Centra on the way home from a night out, my fear of hangovers great but my desire to get drunk greater.

"Solpadeine," she said, her eyes lighting up. "Christ, can I have some?"

"I only have the sachets," I said, waving one around. It looked, in the dark, like a condom packet.

"I don't mind, I'll get a glass of water from the bar." She laughed, shook her head. "I'm so rock 'n' roll."

"Rache, it's your round," James said, holding up his plastic cup of melting ice. "Bacardi Coke?"

"Sure," I said, realising what he was doing. I was walking to the bar with Deenie Harrington, tying ourselves in the queue's thirsty knot.

"How's the shop?" she asked brightly. I said it was fine. She said that she regretted having never worked in a bookshop, that most people in publishing had, and that sometimes she felt left out. "It's funny, most people in the music industry haven't worked in an HMV, but everyone in books has worked in a Waterstone's."

"How *do* you get into books?" I asked. I was keenly aware that in a few months I would be another unemployed graduate with an English degree, and no one at the college had given me any hint as to what I might do with it. There were no job postings for brochures and signs and things. I had looked. Books seemed like a natural next step, but apparently so natural that no one was willing to offer directions.

"Oh," she said, "it's about who you know."

We surged forward in the drinks queue.

"Sorry," she said, after a moment's pause. "I just realised how absolutely fucking useless that was, as advice."

"Ha! No, not at all."

"My dad," she said. "My dad was in the business."

"Like an author?"

"A poet," she said. "Not famous. But known, in a way. Alistair Harrington?" She raised her eyebrows briefly, searching for recognition. I shook my head. "That's okay," she said. "He's the kind of poet a normal person hasn't heard of but, like, Seamus Heaney has."

"A poet's poet," I replied.

"Yeah," she agreed. "A poet's poet. It gave me an edge at the interview, I think."

The bartender was putting out cups of water on the bar. I reached to grab one for Deenie.

"I'm sure you were great at the interview."

I wish I knew then what I know now: that it is vanishingly rare for a person working in the arts to admit that a blood connection secured their place within it. Particularly so quickly after meeting someone. Deenie's admission, which I saw as being polite chatter then, would have endeared her instantly to me now.

"I don't think so. I give a terrible first impression."

I thought about her at the bookshop two hours before her husband's launch, and how suspicious she had been of me. Maybe she felt bad about it. More than that: maybe she was sorry. She had observed me that evening, in all my goofy largeness, and thought: *My God, why was I so frightened of that poor stupid girl?*

She was so bewildered by how unthreatening I was that she missed James, operating right under her nose.

10

J AMES THOUGHT ABOUT Dr. Byrne the way other people think about puppy farms. It was bad, but the puppies were there, and some nice family had to take them. He didn't want Fred Byrne to cheat on his wife, but there was no doubt that he was going to, so why not with James?

We didn't spend any more time with the Harrington-Byrnes that night. We drifted away, talked to our own people, did our own thing. But James's heart wasn't in the night any more. And because he couldn't get into it, I couldn't either.

"I might go," I said, at around eleven. "I have a class in the morning."

"Same," he said, and we headed for the door.

As soon as we were clear of the venue, James blurted it all out.

"I gave him our address," he said.

"Our *what*? Why?"

"Rachel, this is awkward to talk about, but the man was the best ride of my life."

"Stop," I said. "No, he wasn't."

I suddenly felt like he was talking about my dad.

"He was. I feel like . . . I don't know." He spat on the ground. I was so shocked that I watched the spit travel. It was such an odd thing for him to do. "Like I'm just snacking, all these empty calories, but it all tastes like nothing because it's not what I want. What I need."

"The guitarist from last week? He was *empty calories*?"

"I just . . ." His face was twisted, his hands were in his hair. "You saw the kiss, Rachel. You know."

I did. I knew. It was kind of making me crazy, too. I had never been kissed the way James had been kissed in the stockroom, and now that I had seen James kissing several people, I knew he hadn't either.

"So is he going to . . . ? What? Come to our house? Abandon his sick wife?"

He did not come to our house that night. He came the night after.

I was in bed with James when the doorbell rang. We were watching *Absolutely Fabulous*, season one. The window in his room looked down onto the street. He craned his head out, then went white.

"Get out," he said. "Sorry! But! You need to get out."

"To my *room*?" I said, as if I was saying: *To prison?*

"Take my laptop! And my headphones!"

I had never seen him like this, so flustered. I finally twigged who was outside.

"Dr. Byrne?" I whispered. I was holding a tub of ice cream. It was starting to leak onto the sheets. "Here? Now?"

"Jesus, just go to your room, will you?"

I went, lugging a space heater with me.

I lay in bed and shivered, listening to the sounds of my professor moving around my tiny house. I heard the murmurings of polite conversation.

I kept thinking of the different incriminating objects that populated our downstairs: the weed grinder, the unfinished can of Diet Coke, the clothes horse that I would never dismantle fully, instead just taking knickers down as needed. What was even more embarrassing was the thought of him looking at my bookshelves. The books that I had arranged so proudly—the Haruki Murakamis, the Mary Wesleys, the heavily underlined *Brother of the More Famous Jack*—were now getting a thorough inspection from someone whose job it was to read and criticise books. What conclusions was he drawing about me down there? Did he notice that none of the books I read in my spare time were Victorian?

Dr. Byrne's voice moved to the kitchen. I heard a clatter, two cups knocking together, and then the sound of James's weight on the kitchen counter.

Who was I kidding?

Why on earth would Dr. Byrne come to my house in the middle of the night to criticise my bookshelves? He had probably already forgotten that I lived there, too. I still thought I was the centre of this story, the main character, just because it had started that way.

I begged myself to fall asleep before any real noise started. James had brought a couple of people back to the house in the last few weeks, but always after a night out. I was a sleepy drunk. I was out for the count before anyone even made it upstairs, and they were usually gone by the morning.

I heard them talk again, their words indistinct but their meaning very clear. Dr. Byrne had a nuzzling kind of voice on, a coaxing, flirty timbre I hadn't ever heard him use. Bee-loud, like Yeats said. I could tell that James was trying to keep his head straight. He didn't want to bring Dr. Byrne upstairs, not while I was still awake.

I went under the covers with James's laptop, the headphones stuck so far into my ears that they were tickling my brain. It was only eleven o'clock. James and I didn't usually go to sleep until at least 1 a.m., even on the nights we stayed in.

Since Jonathan, I had not slept with anyone. I know. Aren't you disappointed? There was kissing; there were bodies pressed up against the various walls of Cork city night clubs; there were hands in my knickers. There were boys—cute ones, nice ones—who had walked me home after the club kicked out, their jackets draped around my shoulders, their hands laced through mine. But whenever they would imply that they had walked me home for sex, had understood that I wanted to have sex also, I acted all disgraced.

"You think I'm that easy, huh?" I said to them, feigning shock that a twenty-one-year-old boy standing without a jacket in February at two in the morning might have an ulterior motive. I would send them packing, triumphant, then I would go inside and feel depressed, stupid and horny.

I don't know who I was trying to impress. I did not want a boy-friend; I did want romance. I wanted passion; I did not want to be someone who was known as easy. I was desperate to be touched; I was terrified of being ruined.

All I can say in my defence is that I was developing at a kind of crossroads of female messaging. I think about it a lot now. Puberty in the 2000s was Paris Hilton's sex tape and Britney Spears's crotch shots and Amy Winehouse drunk on *Never Mind the Buzzcocks*, and if any of that happened now we would have found a way to celebrate it, but then it was disgusting. We thought a lot about the abortions we weren't allowed to have and the locked-up girls of the Magdalene laundries. We swore to each other, at my girls' school, that we had never masturbated and we accused each other of doing it on the sly. On top of that: everyone knew each other. Cork was beautiful and anarchic, but you could fit it all on the head of a pin.

Maybe that's why the Fred Byrne fantasy had been so appealing to me, as a rebound option. Something that *had* to be kept a secret and that guaranteed touch, stimulus, novelty.

There was a DVD still in the disc drive. More *Ab Fab*. I put on a jumper over my pyjamas and watched it until I fell asleep. Feeling like Edie, longing to be Patsy.

The next morning, I woke up to a breakfast roll wrapped in clingfilm. It landed on my head, the French baguette clunking off my temple. James was in the doorway.

"There you go," he said brightly. "Thanks for being a sounder last night."

"Is he gone?"

"Yeah," he replied. "I walked him to the station."

"The *train* station?"

The station was at least a mile away, and back then we never walked anywhere further than college or the bookshop. I sat up, and pulled at the curtains next to my bed. The sky was still morning blue, the trees dark.

"What time is it?"

"Just gone seven thirty."

"*Seven?*"

Dr. Byrne was going to Dublin that morning, to some kind of conference relevant to his book. He had told Deenie that he was taking the last train the night before, and used the opportunity to hit up James instead.

"Are you coming in?" he said.

I thought about it. "Have you changed the sheets?"

"Good point. Give me ten."

I padded downstairs barefoot, feeling like Santa Claus had been. I was awake too early, I had been brought a snack in bed, and someone familiar yet simultaneously mysterious had visited my house while I slept. James had cleaned up the living room, and a new bottle of orange Tropicana and some chocolate buttons were on the side.

I took a long, confused wee. Food was James's love language, and this much of it indicated that he was feeling at least a little guilty. I didn't know whether he should. It was too early in the morning to have my thoughts straight about it.

But on the whole, I was curiously unbothered. Not because I was this divinely liberal, unselfish twenty-year-old. I was quite self-obsessed, but I was also used to being passed over. I had learned not to take it personally. I had been almost six foot tall since the age of fourteen. Living with my partially closeted gay friend while he romanced my adored professor was new to me; having a friend fuck my crush was not.

James threw the old sheets down the stairs and the smell of

Dr. Byrne fell in waves around me. James never smelled of anything but deodorant and clean cotton; Dr. Byrne had a denser mix of male odour. There was something in it that pinched at the base of your nostril, like nutmeg or cinnamon.

He peered down at me from the top of the stairs. He was already getting back into his sweatpants.

"I know," he said, watching me sniff the air. "Old Spice. So typical."

We got into bed.

"What was it like?" I asked.

"Hot," he said, biting into his breakfast roll. "Did you hear anything?"

"No. Not really."

He swallowed hard, and a chunk of hash brown stuck in his throat. He swigged some Diet Coke and coughed. "That was my first time," he said at last. "My first time it not being a first time."

"You mean it was your first time riding someone for a second time?"

"Yes."

This was crazy to me. I was a boyfriend girl. Casual sex was still a thing for famous people and girls I was jealous of.

"What did you talk about?"

He raised his eyebrow.

"Come on, you must have said something to each other. He was here hours."

James looked dreamy and coy. "He said he wasn't able to stop thinking about me. Since the launch."

A spike of jealousy. I smoothed it down. "What else?"

"He got his first blow job in Canada from a boy at the farm next door."

"Wow. Okay."

"And then he lived in America for a bit and sometimes went to gay clubs."

"Why won't he just *be gay*, then?"

James shot me a look.

"Okay, sorry."

"He likes women too, though, he said that a lot. I asked him about his wife."

"Deenie."

"Yeah." He bit into his roll again, ketchup smearing on his chin. "He really loves her. She has no idea."

I felt defensive of poor Deenie. "He can't love her that much if he's keeping secrets from her. If he's *cheating* on her."

James started rooting through the plastic Centra bag for paper napkins. He wiped his face. "This is the first time he's ever gone to a guy's house. In Ireland, anyway."

"*What?*"

"Yeah." James looked dazed, like the weight of the responsibility was too much. Then he shook it off, literally shaking his head from side to side. "Which is probably a lie."

I replayed the conversation I had seen them have in O'Connor's in my mind. I was baffled. After all the posturing I had done, Dorothy Parker and the rest. All of that trying, and the man was willing to break years of heterosexuality after a casual chat with James.

"Are you telling me," I said slowly, "that Dr. Byrne was willing to put his marriage on the line for some random bookshop chat about DVD players and Fermoy?"

"Lust at first sight, I guess." It was a very un-James statement.

"He told you that, didn't he?"

"Let's watch TV," he said, and we put on *Ab Fab* until we both fell back to sleep.

11

THE MAN at the *Toy Show* had nothing else to say about Dr. Byrne, he only wanted to know if I knew, and I went home as soon as the broadcast was over.

I arrive home and say hello to my husband, who has rather gamely been sleeping in the spare room while my ocean madness plays itself out. He insists, however, that I wake him up to say goodnight if I've been out late.

"You seem a bit funny," he says, stroking my body dozily. I am tucked under his arm, a very big little spoon. "Spooked."

"Knackered, more like."

After Shandon Street, I didn't live with a man again for another eight years. But it all came back. James trained me well. You don't start big conversations at one in the morning. Men don't get energised by chat the way women do. I wait until he falls asleep, and then I get up again to eat things and to think.

I met James Carey in April of 2010, and the moment he told me his name I said: *Sorry, I already have one of those.* Because I did. The affair with Dr. Byrne was in full swing by then, and yet I saw very little of it. It was still the James and Rachel Show. I was in the library all day, studying for finals, and Dr. Byrne had only his office hours to attend to. He dropped by our house in the afternoon, usually between two and four, usually twice a week. When I got home

I always knew that he had been: sheets in a pile at the bottom of the stairs, and a relic of his bougie, late-thirties life left behind as a tribute to our poverty. A bottle of good wine, custard tarts, some fancy meat and cheese selections from the English Market. It was like he knew he couldn't pay James to fuck him but he wanted to contribute anyway. To be polite.

My classes with Dr. Byrne were over, with never an acknowledgement between us about him having once used my towel after a shower, the smell of his Old Spice on it the next time I used it.

James Devlin was still my number-one person. James Carey didn't have a hope of a first name, so it was Carey from the start.

I met him outside The Bróg after kick-out time, when people usually hung around, smoking and eating chips on the pavement. He was smaller than me, so I ruled him out for romance straight away. I don't mind shorter guys, but they seem to mind me. They always piss about with me, do the whole "one of the boys" routine, and say things like: *Wouldn't want Rachel on the wrong side of me in a fight!*

Carey was Northern Irish, and if there's one thing you can say about those men it's that they know when to shut the fuck up.

I came up to him, looking to bum a cigarette. I never bought cigarettes, but I always wanted them. He said he'd roll me one, if I had the patience to wait. So I did. He kept the filter between the gap in his front teeth, his hair all red and blond.

"What's your name?"

"James."

"Oh, no, sorry," I replied, "I already have one of those."

"Your boyfriend?"

"My *best* friend." I pointed to where he was, chatting to some girls we knew from Topshop. "My housemate."

"Where do you live? With your housemate?"

"Shandon Street."

"By the big fish?"

"By the big fish."

"If you already have a James, what are you going to call me?"

"Do you have a last name?"

"I do, but I can't be telling you that."

"Why not?"

"You'll be going around, writing all over your pencil case. Your first name, my last name. Your last name, my last name hyphenate. What's your first name, anyway?"

I laughed. "Rachel."

"Rachel Carey," he said. "See, that sounds too good, now, and you're going to drive your mother demented, writing it all over the place."

He licked the rolling paper and sealed my cigarette, giving it to me. I waited for the light, and he gave it to me without being asked. I took a long drag.

"You can go now, if I'm annoying you. Now is an opportune time to leave. Sure, you have your cigarette."

I exhaled a long plume of smoke over his right shoulder. "What if I don't want to leave?"

"If you *don't* want to leave?" he asked, puzzled. "I don't know, I suppose we could go for a walk, talk some more shite."

"Yeah, I could talk some more shite," I answered.

He extended his arm out, like someone from the past. "I've not been in Cork long," he said. "I've not seen the big fish yet. In person, I mean."

James caught my eye. "Are you off, Murray?" he called.

"Yep!" I said. "See you at home!"

"Rachel *Murray*," Carey said. And then, sadly: "Murray-Carey will never work."

Thirty minutes later I was pressed up against the stone wall of the old Butter Exchange while Carey went down on me from the inside of my coat. He had pulled down my tights so they pooled around my ankles, restricting my movement so much that I needed to keep my palms on his skull for balance.

I hobbled on my heels, the cold whipping at my face, the pleasure excruciating. My hands travelled down the nape of his neck, feeling out each notch of his spine. I must have looked ridiculous—knees buckling, bent over the man like I was trying to make a lower case n shape.

It was, as you know, not the first time a man had gone down on me. But this was not lying on my bed while a boy fidgeted about, my breasts getting cold as my mind became full of errands. For years straight women talked about men never eating them out, and now that they do it all the time, none of us want to admit that most of them are bad at it. They sucker on to your clitoris like a fish at the side of a tank, or they randomly poke about with their tongue. With Carey I felt like a shrine. He was going at this not like a person with a plan, but a person with a calling.

"My house," I breathed, when he finally came up for air. "My house is like . . . three minutes away."

"Why aren't we there, then?"

"I don't know," I said, nuzzling my lips into his neck. "I don't know."

My attraction to him came on like food poisoning. We were walking up Shandon Street, arm in arm, chatting about Derry ("Carey from Derry!") and what he was doing here (working at Apple) and how he was finding it (fine). I showed him the Shandon Bells, and he asked me if they woke me up in the morning. I said sometimes.

We looked up at the big fish, this strange landmark of north Cork, and we ran out of things to say. He put his hand on the small of my back, looked at me sideways. His eyes grey-blue. Mischief.

And then I was kissing him, holding *his* head like a cantaloupe, and his hands jumped around me in surprise, not knowing how to keep up.

I took him back to the house, my first real *gentleman caller* since Jonathan and I broke up. James wasn't home, and I went through the exact steps I had heard him go through weeks before: flicking on the kettle, getting two cups out, making small talk about how long we had lived there, how much the rent was. Then he came up behind me, hands on my hips, mouth on my ear.

"You're a fucking stunner. Did you know that?"

The clatter of the cups being pushed back, my bum on the counter, tights off. The counter was a great height for this kind of carry-on. It was far and away the best sex I had ever had, yet I couldn't stop thinking about James and Dr. Byrne. The fact that they had been in this room—probably in this position, more or less—and that I had been upstairs trying not to overhear. I wonder if having them in my head made the sex that bit more extraordinary. It was an orgy while still being extraordinarily intimate, and exclusively me and Carey.

He was still wearing his jacket, a black pea coat that smelled badly of cigarettes, and I shuddered into the collar, my fingers digging into the lapels. I remembered what James said about this being his *first second time*. This was a first time for me, too. It was my first time having sex with a stranger, and it was the first real orgasm I'd ever had with another person in the room. Life felt very full, and very funny. There was a whole life of first times to have, first times I hadn't even considered yet!

"Jesus," Carey said, and I was relieved. He looked haunted. He was older than me, and obviously more experienced, but it hadn't been an ordinary thing for him either. "Jesus. Fucking hell, Rachel. What was all that about?"

He said it like we were old friends, and I laughed, and dragged him up the stairs. There were Portuguese tarts left over from Dr. Byrne's last visit, and I took them to bed with us.

Crumbs in my hair, sweet custard coating his mouth, I decided I would never again judge Fred Byrne for what he needed to do, regardless of his wife. It was easy, now that I understood passion properly, to see why you would move heaven and earth to secure it.

12

THE THING ABOUT me and Carey is that we were both dirty. By which I mean: we were both perverted, and we were both unclean. I bled on his sheets and the stain remained for the duration of our relationship. He met me from the bus once wearing sweatpants, a string vest, and swigging from a pint bottle of full-fat milk. He smelled like sweat and like someone who had been digging outside, though he had no garden. I loved it all. When we had sex I could taste the day on him. I walked around with my nose in my collar afterwards, catching pockets of his smell on myself.

Things got weird with us quickly. Not kinky exactly: we didn't have the money for that. Kinky to me was suspenders and small, dishwasher-proof vibrators. But intense. We had a very soft way of asking each other to do obscene things.

"Let me run this knife against the inside of your leg, will you, Rache?" he said once, us both lying on his couch. The big kitchen knife was sitting on his coffee table, having been used to crumble up a small brick of hash the night before. He kissed me tenderly, his left hand stroking my hair, his right holding the cold blade against my skin while he moved inside me.

"Shh, shhh," he said. "Don't be frightened."

It was, quite simply, fantastic.

Carey lived with two other guys near the Mercy hospital. My experience of them was having them suddenly arrive home while Carey and I were being degenerates. If we weren't eating chocolate mousse from a vat intended for catering, we were having loud, odd sex. I should have been more embarrassed. There were previous iterations of my personality that would have been. But with Carey I discovered new depths of shamelessness, and I liked it. We didn't need regular meals, or real sleep, or date nights. Our love had short fingernails. It was clawing and mischievous and it wrapped us in spit. I couldn't pull myself away from it, so it amazed me when he could.

This was the problem. I could stay with Carey for as long as I wanted, but as soon as I left, it was hard to get back in again. Like a Grimms' fairy tale, or a reverse Hotel California. Once, I spent three nights at his house, and when I ran out of underwear I finally moved to go home.

"Ah, don't go," he whined, wrapping his arms around my waist, his head on my stomach. "Who will I chat to?"

"You've got two perfectly good housemates."

"They're *nerds*."

"Look, I'll go home, get some new clothes, and come straight back. Okay?"

"Promise?"

"Promise."

I went home, packed a new bag, chatted to James, and was back by dinnertime. I picked up chips from the chipper, ice cream from Centra. I rang his doorbell, and waited. No answer. I rang it again. I listened to the bell echo around his house, leaning on the buzzer again and again, until his next-door neighbour came out of her house to say I was waking up her baby. I sat on the doorstep, ate the chips, and went home.

When I got hold of him, two days later, he said he had fallen asleep. Which wasn't surprising, considering how late we were staying up, and how much weed we were smoking. "Well, you *did* say you'd come straight back," he said defensively. "How was I to know that meant two hours?"

It seemed churlish to me that someone who didn't know whether it was Wednesday or Thursday could get hung up over a stray sixty minutes. But he was firm, keeping to the letter and not the spirit of my original statement, and the more I argued with him the more he drifted away from me.

April is a dangerous time to get obsessed with a man who is harder to pin down than egg whites. It was supposed to be my study month, and I should have been working on my final essays. Instead, I was either dazed from a night with Carey or sure that he was dead. He went days at a time without talking to me. He was always concerned, after he turned up, to hear that I was so upset at his disappearance. But he was concerned the way your friend is when you tell them that the NHS won't book in your mammogram for another eight weeks: *Oh no! What a badly run system?! Too bad it's the only one we have, eh!*

James, who was going through a similar thing with Dr. Byrne, asked me if I thought Carey was sleeping with other people. Eleven years later, and with the benefit of hindsight, interrogation and a greater knowledge of men, I still think no. I think he just couldn't get it together. And by "it," I mean "life." He called in sick because he missed the bus. He couldn't be bothered buying salt ("I don't need a whole *thing* of it"), so he shoplifted small quantities when he was in Tesco, pouring it into an empty envelope. He was a person who did what he wanted, when he wanted, and if you weren't directly in his eyeline you became part of the smoky ether.

"The thing about Carey," James said once, when we were up late and commiserating over our hopeless men, "is that he would walk over hot coals for you, but he won't commit to lunch plans."

I believed it. I believe it still. He met our friends. When we were together, whether it was alone or in mixed company, I felt his eyes follow me around the room. He cornered me in kitchens at house parties, his hand up my dress, and he was constantly telling everyone about something funny I said the other day. He would read my essays for college while I was in the shower, and when I got out would start reading them back to me, smoking in my bed.

"I feel like I'm riding Noam Chomsky," he said. "This is great stuff."

When he was good he was very good, and when he was gone he was very gone. A lot of this, I now realise, was down to texting. There were six years between Carey and me, a gap I rarely felt unless it was regarding phone use. Courtship, to me, was about text messages. It was about sending someone a good-morning and a good-night message. It was ending every text with an x, or three x's, or a long line of them when you were really pleased. It was about withholding x's when you were moody, and then they would notice, and ask you what was wrong. These were the rules of love I had learned from my all-girls school, and it confused me when someone didn't play.

I tried to hold off as long as I could on texting him in the morning, then break at around noon. I would make sure they were questions, things he had to answer to, like: Are you still coming round on Thursday? And: Remind me of your birthday, again? When he didn't respond, I sent a barrage of "funny" messages that were supposed to read as Nancy Mitford but instead made me sound depressed, cranky and eighty years old.

I simply cannot abide the smell of Subway sandwiches

I've smelled fresh bread and frankly,
that's not what bread smells like

"Sandwich artists." Get a grip!

I would send so many messages that the things I really wanted to hear back about would get lost amid my babbling nonsense, forcing me to contend with his mysterious, rare responses.

like the meatball

And then nothing, for days.

I turned twenty-one on 30 April. It was during one of his quiet spells. James, who was borrowing his mum's car at the time, drove me out to my parents' house for a dinner. They liked James a lot. I expected them to be shocked by my moving in with a gay man I barely knew. Truthfully, I wanted them to be shocked. I wanted to be their troublesome eldest who was spurning the family's conservative values for a big, queer city life.

But my parents were cosmetic dentists and had been relying on middle-aged moneyed gay men for years. They're the ones who pay for veneers. That evening, they couldn't have been more glad for James, who ate and drank everything gratefully and with a charming stream of narration. "God, wouldn't you go mental without paté?" he said brightly, smearing it on a cracker. "And do you know what else I've realised, Bridget: I actually love blue cheese."

He was a bright spark in what I now know was a miserable time for them. Chris and Kevin were both in exam years, doing the Leaving and Junior Cert respectively, and swallowing the stress like pills without water. There was very little money coming in. The landlord's widow had announced a rent hike, and my parents were considering moving their practice to another, cheaper part of town where they had no client base. They were only in their early fifties, but they were nodding more slowly, sighing more, and acting as if misfortune's vision was based on movement, so they better not budge.

The fact that I was obviously unhappy didn't help. My mind was fixed on Carey, who there hadn't been a peep from in days, and I kept on hoping for an eleventh-hour appearance. My mum was worried about me. She never heard from me unless it was a crazy midnight phone call asking how she knew when Dad was "the one."

"Any thoughts on what you're going to do after exams are over,

Rachel?" my dad asked. It was a fair question. Unfortunately I was not in the headspace for fair questions.

"No," I snapped. "There are no jobs."

"Brian Hegarty says there are jobs out in Bishopstown. Tech companies."

Brian Hegarty was my dad's best friend and was always referred to by his first and last name.

"Call centres," I corrected. "I'm not killing myself at college to work at a call centre."

But I wasn't killing myself, that was the problem. I was torturing myself over a Northern Irish man who was six years older than me and shoplifted individual grains of salt. College I couldn't gather the roughage to give a shit about. Classes were over but there were still end-of-year essays due, and I didn't know where to begin with them.

"So what are you going to do?"

"Publishing," I said. "I think I should work in publishing."

I had run into Deenie Harrington recently, while I was with Carey. We were having a coffee near campus, and Deenie was there, a stack of pages in front of her. She was running the nib of her red pen along every sentence, making circles and notes as she went. She saw me, cackling on a high stool in the window. She waved. Her smile big and, crucially, real.

I left my stool and went over. "Hiya," I said. "Nice to see you."

Now, aged thirty-one, I would feel much more awkward about saying hello to the woman whose husband was spending random afternoons at my house. But I had accepted then that this was an arrangement that worked for everyone: Dr. Byrne was happy, James was sort of happy, Deenie seemed fine, the fridge was full of cheese.

"Rachel!" she said brightly. "How are you? Gosh—do you want to sit down?"

"I can't," I said. I pointed to Carey, pouring sugar into his coffee. "I'm with my . . ."

We had not talked about whether he was my boyfriend yet. The closest we got to talking about it was the second time we had sex, when he said: *Rachel, why on earth don't you have a boyfriend?*

". . . I'm with him," I finished.

"Ah," she said, and seemed tickled at this early-twenties problem of having a man in your life whose role you cannot name. "Well, lucky you. I'm stuck in line edits."

"What's that?"

"It's like the last edit before it goes to the copy editor."

"And who is that?"

"The person who looks for grammar mistakes, factual errors, that kind of thing."

"You don't do that?"

"No, I'm more policing the general story, whether the plot works, the vibe."

"I would like to police a vibe," I said.

The conversation had stuck in my head. It sounded like a great job. I loved to read, or I used to, before my main hobby was getting drunk. And Deenie had said that publishing was all about who you knew, and I knew her. I knew her in a weird way, but I knew her.

My mum put a bowl of crab linguine in front of me, then dusted parmesan over it. "I don't know if there are jobs in books in Cork," she said.

"There aren't jobs in anything in Cork," my dad replied.

"There are jobs," James said. "Just no good ones."

By May it became clear that I had, quite frankly, fucked myself.

We had a party at the house on the night of my twenty-first. My parents kindly gifted us two big bottles of Smirnoff vodka on our way out. Our cottage was bursting with people, thirty-five bodies jumping away like hot fleas. I never remember any neighbours from that time. They must have existed, but we never saw them. Carey had known about the party, had been invited, and of course had not shown up. When he was gone, he was very gone.

My heart was shattered. I left a long voicemail for him at one thirty, telling him that I deserved better than a boyfriend who forgot my birthday. I left an additional voicemail to say I knew he wasn't my boyfriend. Then I left another to say I was sorry.

At 3 a.m., I grabbed hold of a boy who worked at the Opera House and dragged him by the collar into the shower. The bedrooms were full of people. James turned the water on and ran out, laughing manically. I slipped and my heel went through the wall, knocking three tiles off. We never fixed them.

I slept the rest of the weekend. I didn't go to college on Monday. On Tuesday, I received emails from three of my tutors saying that my end-of-year essays were late, and that in accordance with faculty rules, they were going to dock my marks: 10 per cent if I got the essay in this week, 20 per cent next week, and after that they would not accept the essay at all.

One of the emails was from Dr. Byrne. It was another form letter. It asked me to *kindly submit* my essay before the new deadline, lest I be *docked further*.

I left the library there and then, knowing precisely where Dr. Byrne was.

Kindly!

Submit!

I did not simmer down on the walk home. The grief at losing Carey so quickly after finding him, the fact of college ending with so little to show for it, the prospect of a call centre on the horizon. The bookshop was not doing well. Ben used to call me at least once a week to pick up an extra shift; now he never called about extra days, and my bank balance was starting to show it.

And then there was Dr. Byrne. He had been doing this thing with James for almost two months now, and it was driving my poor friend insane. Fred Byrne's well-established vanity had morphed into a deep anxiety that James was seeing other people, something he could not forbid but was desperate to know both everything and nothing about.

The routine, according to James, was this: Dr. Byrne would come through the door at lunchtime with treats and poetry. They'd spend a while on the couch ("round one," James called it, "the appetiser") then eventually move up to the bedroom ("mains"). After which, Dr. Byrne would ask terse, loaded questions about our nights out, what we did together, what I thought of him, where the gays were. He found it all very hard. Not just the thought of James with other people, but the thought of gay clubs and queer nights going on without him. He would get mad at James, for some answer that didn't meet his needs, and then make James figure out what it was that had annoyed him. He often left under a cloud of silence, and it drove James crazy.

Fuck this guy, I thought. *Who the fuck does he think he is?*

I put my key in the door with no regard for whether they were on main course or appetiser. We had a little corridor before the living room, so they had time to put their trousers on or cover their dicks with a blanket.

Still, I was relieved to find everyone dressed.

"Hello," I barked, looking at Fred Byrne. "I want to speak with you."

"Rachel," he said. He looked sticky, like he'd just been for a run.

James was scowling at me. "Rache, what are you doing home?"

"You can't just threaten me!" I started crying. "You can't ignore me in class and use my house as a fuckpad and then treat me like I'm some normal student."

It was the first time I had really spoken to Dr. Byrne in months. Since the book launch, probably.

"Okay," James said, getting up. He was sweating, too. "I'll put the kettle on, will I?"

Fred Byrne looked like he wanted the ground to swallow him. I sat down heavily into the armchair that faced the couch.

"It's not fair," I said, hiccuping through my tears. "I've cut you a lot of slack; it's the least you can do to cut me some."

He coughed and sat up. "Right," he said. "Right. Is this about your essay?"

I nodded, pushing the heel of my hand under my wet eyes. "It's not that I want special treatment," I said, though I did. "It's just, I think there should be a bit of grace, you know, given the extenuating circumstances."

At "extenuating circumstances," I started to cry harder, because I was thinking about not just *these* circumstances, but all of them. I was in love for the first time properly, and he didn't want me, and it was eating my organs.

"If," Fred Byrne began, "there's been a death in the family, or something, you know what I mean, we can say there was a death. I can waive the—"

"I just want you to acknowledge what's happened," I continued, and I was talking not so much to him but to Carey. James and I spoke so much about these two men, compared their traits and so on, that one was kind of a facsimile for the other. "Everything's different now. I'm different now."

Fred Byrne looked over the armchair to James, who was coming back from the kitchen with the mugs of tea.

"You've not been very nice to Rachel, Fred," James said, like he was mediating a divorce. "I don't know if you've behaved sensitively."

Here is something that I love about James: he lets people have their own connections. He will never try to convince you to feel differently about someone. He will not be the delivery boy for baggage from one person's relationship to another. However, when it comes down to fights between friends and lovers, he will put the friend first.

"Right," Dr. Byrne said again. "No, you're quite right, James. I thought I had compartmentalised something that I don't think can be compartmentalised. I'm sorry, Rachel."

His voice was soft and masculine, and James's eyes filled with affection at the humility he was showing. Him, a man of almost forty, apologising to a twenty-one-year-old girl. He squeezed Dr. Byrne's leg, and Dr. Byrne patted his hand.

A new flood broke over me, seeing the two of them so clearly in love. They had everything in the way of their relationship: orientation, marriage, age. But they were making it work. They had found a space for it to thrive in. I, meanwhile, couldn't make love work with someone single and straight, purely because he could not be bothered with me.

James sat at the armchair, rubbing my back. "I'm sorry, Rache."

"Is she okay?"

"Boyfriend," James said.

"He's not my—"

"He was here three nights a week. He met all your friends. I call that a boyfriend."

"What happened to him?" Dr. Byrne sounded genuinely interested.

"Invisible Man," James answered.

Dr. Byrne tutted with his tongue. "Rough," he said.

He leaned forward and put his big hand on my knee. "Right, Rachel, let's sort this out, will we?"

He said he would fix things. He would put the word out in the faculty that I was very ill and had shown him a doctor's note. Something serious but not deadly or visible. ("Heart murmur?" James suggested.) That would get me off the hook for my essays for a while, without any penalties being applied. It would give me a clearer runway to focus on my exams, which started next week.

He said all this gently, not like he was patronising me, but like he cared.

"You don't have to do all that," I sniffed. "I shouldn't have shouted at you. It was my own stupid fault for not doing the essays."

"Don't worry about it."

"It's like nepotism, though, kind of."

"It's favourable treatment, but far less hard-working students get it all the time, so we won't worry."

"Are you *sure*?"

"Rachel, come here," he said gravely. I moved from the armchair to the couch. He put his big arm around me, somewhere between a dad and a friend. "We've all had our hearts broken, and we've all had someone cut us some slack because of it."

He opened his messenger bag and took out his laptop. I remember being surprised he was connected to the wifi already. Had Dr. Byrne been working here? James and I sat on either side while he tapped out an email to the department head. We decided that I wasn't sick, but grieving, because it was true. He said that I was afraid of approaching the whole department because I was conscious of my lack of blood connection to the dead. He stipulated that, given Rachel Murray's previous dedication to her studies, she should be given an extension until the end of May.

"Now," he said, opening another tab on his browser, "pizza."

Dr. Byrne ordered and went to the bathroom. I snuggled next to James, my head on his shoulder. "He *is* nice, though," I said, exhausted from all the crying, "is the thing."

And now I'm crying again, because he was a nice man, a really nice man. Is a nice man? So hard to know, when all you know about a person is that they are in a coma.

———

I had thought Dr. Byrne would stick around for the pizza he had paid for at least, but he made his exit as soon as it arrived.

"No, no, you two do your thing," he said, which I liked. I appreciated when any adult acknowledged the validity of me and James's "thing."

"Rachel, my dear," he said, sliding his laptop back into his messenger bag. "I just wanted to say . . . sorry again. I'm so fond of you, you know. I didn't want to embarrass you. In class, I mean."

"It's okay." I shrugged. "It's over now."

This didn't sit right with him. He knew that he had not done enough. "Is there anything else I can do? With the department, I mean. Name it."

This was my only chance, so I went for it. "I want a job."

"You have a job," James said, aghast.

"I can't . . ." Dr. Byrne began, equally tortured. He couldn't excuse my essays *and* give me a job. It was too suspect. He was already a man who had married his student.

"No, no," I said. "I want to work in books. In publishing."

He was a little alarmed. "With Deenie?"

"An internship or something. I want to work with books, and they say it's all about who you know. And, well, she's the only person I know."

"Fair enough," he said. "I'll put it to her."

The word "blackmail" never crossed my mind. Although it may have crossed his.

"I would never say to her . . ." I said, groping at the unsayable.

He put his hand up. "I know. Sort your essays first. Do your exams. I'll talk to Dee about setting something up in June."

There is a thing among middle-class people in Ireland, and it is called "contacts." There are contacts everywhere, of course, and in England most of all, but in Ireland it works differently. In England it is smooth, filtered, insidious. In England favours are exchanged through a vast web of privilege, shunting nice girls and boys down narrowing corridors of expensive schools and cultural capital. In Ireland it is overt. You refer to people as your "contacts"; you ask other people about theirs. Even now, my father will call me and ask about my "contacts" in the Irish press, because he wants to get a story out about dodgy dental businesses in Turkey and the long-term effects of a cheap tooth implant. It comes from a culture of mass immigration, I think. The practice of rocking up to a street halfway across the world with the address of someone you don't know but who went to school with your florist.

So the conversation with Dr. Byrne about a job didn't seem sneaky or underhanded. It is just how Ireland works. Or how I thought it worked.

I got through my essays, and my exams. The Carey thing still tortured me, but I was able to eat the dull gruel of it every morning and get on with my day. I stayed mostly sober for the month, and felt the sense slowly come back to me. I listened to a lot of Joni Mitchell.

I thought about the knife on my leg, the head in my coat, the milk at the bus stop. I felt ruined for other men.

We were struggling for money. Ben had cut our Thursday- and Friday-evening shifts, and instead called either one of us at 3 p.m. to say whether he needed us. He tried to be fair to both of us, alternating phone calls. We started to take his proclamations about the industry more seriously.

"Why don't you ask Fred?" I said one day, when we were counting up couch change. "He can spot you a few hundred."

"How much do you think lecturers make?"

"More than us!"

"No. I'm not going to be a prostitute."

"There's a twenty-euro bottle of wine in there that says different."

"That's not the same."

"I just think it's mental that we're drinking Côtes du Rhône and eating fish fingers."

I was too busy with exams to look for extra work, but James found a job at a cloakroom. It made him miserable: it was deeply lonely, and he was always the last to go home. He wasn't even invited out with the bar people afterwards, not that he could afford to go.

I was home one day, studying on the couch, when he came down from his room with his laptop.

"I've had enough of this!" he said. "Enough!"

"Enough of what?"

"Waiting for my life to start. We're going to write a TV show."

He opened his Microsoft Word to show that he had already started writing one. There were two characters talking, one called "Alice," one called "Michael."

"It's about two hot twenty-somethings in a struggling bookshop," he said. "He's gay and she's the only one who knows."

I looked at him sideways. "Are you serious?"

"As cancer."

He had switched the font to Courier New, the typewriter lettering, and had centre-aligned all the text to make it look like a real script. He had written two pages.

INT. BOOKSHOP. DAY.

MICHAEL, 22 and metrosexual, stands behind the
counter of a bookshop. He talks to ALICE, 20, beautiful
and studious.

"Metrosexual!" I squealed. "Beautiful! Studious!"

"Just read it," he said, sounding defensive.

We read it out loud, together. I don't remember much of what was in the script, but it was funny and warm, or maybe it just felt that way because I was with my best friend and we were playing.

"What happens next?" I said.

"Well, they say that you need a big event towards the end of the pilot, something that sets up the idea for the whole show," he said, wrinkling his brow. I was amazed. James and I both worked part-time hours at O'Connor's, but it never occurred to me that while I was going to college every day, he was learning about screenwriting.

"Where have you learned all this?" I asked. "Since when do you say words like 'pilot'?"

"The DVD extras on *Frasier*," he said. "The commentary."

James was often shy about his lack of education. He had got a Leaving Cert, barely, and went straight into retail and service jobs after school.

"You could make it about you and Fred," I said. I was trying to call Dr. Byrne "Fred" around him, to show that I was okay with it, even though he was always Dr. Byrne or Fred Byrne to me.

"No, no." He shook his head. "I want it to be a comedy. Not, like, a drama."

"But sitcoms need to have some drama, don't they?"

"Drama like Alice putting books under a dead person's name to shift copies of her crush's book. That's how dramatic I'm willing to get."

I laughed. "But why would anyone care about that?"

He rolled his eyes at me to show that I didn't understand comedy. I looked at the top of the page and saw the title of the show. *Michael & Alice*.

"I think people are going to think of *Will & Grace* straight away," I said. "Especially if it's a man and a woman's name, separated by an ampersand."

"They don't *own* the ampersand," he said. We had a very complicated relationship with *Will & Grace*. People brought it up with us a lot, wherein James would remind them that he wasn't gay. Though the longer the relationship with Fred Byrne was going on, the less he jumped to defend himself.

We got high and paranoid that our co-workers would sue once we were famous, so we changed the setting to a movie rental place. Money being tight, we stopped going out three or four nights a week. We were now down to a paltry—and in our eyes, borderline antisocial—two. We made up for it with trips to the legal high head shop, where a bag of synthetic cannabis cost a tenner and lasted us a week. My essays had finally been handed in, and college was over. We had endless hours to smoke the dense, giggly herbal blend.

Dr. Byrne, who was supposed to be working on his next book, sometimes dropped by to declare his disapproval. He was less nervous of me now, and treated me like a younger sister.

"I wish you two would smoke ordinary weed," he said.

"What are we? Millionaires?" I said, then James shushed me, eager that Dr. Byrne wouldn't feel sorry for him.

"What's your book about, Fred?" I could only call him Fred when I was high.

"The Big House novel in early-twentieth-century Irish fiction," he said. "Gothic tensions, figurative ghosts versus the real ghosts from the . . ."

"*Famine?*" I said, and then spluttered with laughter.

Dr. Byrne, to his enduring credit, saw the funny side. "I know, I know, me and the famine."

"What is it?" I giggled. "What is it with you and the famine?"

He sighed, and did something extraordinary. He took the horrible joint of synthetic weed from James, and inhaled. "Honestly, Rachel? I think it started because I wanted to be thin."

James sat up, affection for Fred Byrne suddenly washing over him, clearing the hazy high. "Oh, no," he said. "Oh, babe."

They went upstairs soon after. I fell asleep on the couch, face first in a copy of *Take a Break*. When I woke up, it was two hours later, and Dr. Byrne was shaking me. It wasn't even dinnertime.

"Rachel," he said, "I'm off, but I forgot to say: Deenie has a job for you."

I had drooled so much that my face was stuck to the pages of the magazine.

"Doing what?"

"Lord knows, but she thinks she has something for you. Fifty quid a week."

"For how many days?"

"However many days she needs you, I suppose."

I was confused. "So I could work one day or five days and still get fifty quid?"

"It's an internship, Rachel Murray, and you're lucky to be getting anything. She says to email her." He patted my leg. "Don't be high on your first day."

I emailed Deenie, and she told me to come in on Monday. Four days away. She gave an address. A quiet, residential street near the college.

My guts crunched. When I asked Dr. Byrne for his wife to get me a job, I imagined myself in a big office, where I would be dropped off in the post room by Deenie on the first day and then left to make a name for myself. I did not imagine myself going to her house: *their* house. How was I going to work with Deenie, all day every day, and come home to the sweat-soaked bedsheets at the foot of the stairs?

I was so nervous about the whole thing that I took myself into town the next day, and searched up and down the high street for an outfit. I needed something that said I took the opportunity seriously, but also, that I was willing to be covered in printer ink if the occasion called for it. I ended up in the Barnardo's on Prince's Street. I bought a black knit vest for four euro, and a white shirt to go under it.

I decided to cut through the English Market on my way home, for no reason other than it brought me joy. The high ceilings, the stone walls, the smell of raw meat and briney olives. The nobility that came from it being the only place in the county where you could buy both a cream cake and all four of a pig's trotters without having to do a full turn.

I wandered through, feeling sentimental, heavy and trapped. For the first time in my life, there was nothing to get ready for in September. I was used to entering a summer knowing that the season was a set amount of time to enjoy myself. In a few months, my results would come through, and I knew already what they would be: a not-particularly-high 2:1, from an ordinary university, in a useless subject.

What on earth would become of me? Usually, I worked full time at O'Connor's over the summer. Now it wasn't even worth enquiring about. The customers just weren't there.

"Rache," I heard someone call. "*Hey!* Rachel!"

There he was. Standing at a bread stall. Carey.

He grinned like there had never been a cross word between us. Which, I suppose, there hadn't been. He just vanished, as was his well-established custom, and then I sent all those voicemails.

I couldn't fake that I was happy to see him. Neither did I have the confidence to tell him off. I stood there, breathing hard, my nostrils warm like a dragon's.

"Two minutes," he called. "Give me two minutes."

He was working at the bread stall. He was sliding two sticks of French bread into a paper bag, his hands coated in flour, smiling at a woman while she paid him. His red-blond hair had grown out too long, not down but *out*, spikes of it pointing this way and that.

The blood ran into my face. I couldn't wait for him, even if it was two minutes. Any length of time was an insult. I left, and heard his voice calling after me.

On the street, the sun was shining brightly, and sweat poured from my armpits. The synthetic weed did that to me. It was fun when you smoked it but had all kinds of strange side effects the next day. I sat down on the stone wall of the Unitarian church, and waited for him. I prayed that he wouldn't find me, and thought I might walk into traffic if he didn't. I put my face in my hands, my breath short, my panic increasing.

"Sweetheart, what are you doing out here?" he said, and put his arm around my shoulders. "Come on now. What does Rachel Murray have to be upset about?"

The accent still killed me. The curious, amused flatness of the Derry voice. I hated myself for being Irish, and for being suckered in by an Irish accent.

"Fuck you," I said, my face still in my hands. "Don't do that. Not after everything."

"I know," he said, in that tone he used for when he knew he had acted badly. His *goddamn this NHS* voice.

"Don't just say *I know*!" I said, raising my voice so loud that the pigeons fluttered away. "Say you're sorry, at least."

"I *am* sorry."

"You're not."

"Let me buy you a coffee."

"No."

"Actually, you're dead right, I can't buy you a coffee, I'm at work."

He considered this for a second. "We close in an hour, though. Do you want to hang out with the bread while I tidy up?"

"No, I do *not* want to do that," I said, though I did.

"Listen," he said, and jangled his pocket change, "I've got pain au chocolats for days in there. Go round to Gloria Jean's and get us both a drink. Then come back and you can eat pastry and drink coffee while I finish. If at any point you decide I'm too much of a shit to stay, you can leave, and you'll have got a coffee and a cake out of it."

"Fine."

He gave me a fiver in change. I went to Gloria Jean's and got us both a small black coffee. When I came back he had found a stool from somewhere, and dragged it next to the counter.

"Sit yourself up there, now, missis," he said. He gave me the pain au chocolat, as promised, and then left me alone.

I drank my coffee and watched him serve customers. The last time I saw Carey he was a customer service rep for Apple. He wasn't earning very much, but it was a respectable job, and there was talk of him progressing. Talk from who, I don't know. He was obviously a terrible employee. He was for ever skipping out on work to spend time with me, and I wasn't even important enough for him to wish me happy birthday.

I picked up that rage, and held on to it; I needed to remind myself why I hated Carey, because watching him lock up the bread shop was far too entrancing. The smell of pastry, the chocolate melting on my tongue, the bitter black coffee. I needed to remind myself of my anger, so I didn't inadvertently mix up good snacks with a good man.

James says there are three kinds of Irish male body types: tennis, rugby and hurling. James was tennis: lean frame, long bones. Dr. Byrne was rugby: thick-set, a tendency towards chubby, and would look large regardless of how much weight he gained or lost. Carey was hurling. He was slim and small-ish, but compact, square and muscled. "Built like a Jack Russell terrier," he said of himself. "And every bit as common."

He took a long stick, and reached up to pull the shutters of the bread stall down. He got on his tiptoes in his banged-up grey trainers, the kind most men now wouldn't even wear to the gym. And I watched his stomach.

Another thing about Carey.

He had the most beautiful stomach of any man I had ever been with. Before or since.

Without even trying, he had one of those stomachs that low-slung jeans were invented for. Hip bones like ivory. Abdominal muscles that slanted in a V-shape towards his crotch. Faint golden hair under his belly-button. He had no awareness about any of this, I don't think. He was completely oblivious to how much I was objectifying him, while remaining mute on my stool.

"Thank you for staying," he said. The shop was shut. I was once again in an enclosed space with a man.

He looked, for once, genuinely sorry.

"The thing about you, Rachel," he said softly, "is that you make me insane."

"Fucking hell," I blurted out. "Is that it?"

"It's true! And I make you insane!" He picked up his phone. He still had a Nokia, not the 3210, but not much more advanced than that, either. "I have the tapes."

I tried to swallow my shame about the voicemails, and to stay angry.

"Oh, for fuck's sake, Carey."

"Pet, listen to me. I'm twenty-seven."

"So?"

"Twenty-seven is very old to be dossing off work to stay in bed with a teenager."

"I'm twenty-*one*, Carey," I spluttered. "Which you would *know* if you came to my *birthday party*."

He let that one hang there.

Northern Irish men.

They know when to shut the fuck up.

"I'm sorry I didn't wish you a happy birthday," he said carefully. "But, I don't know. Things got very serious, between us."

"No, they didn't!" I practically shouted. "We literally weren't even calling one another boyfriend and girlfriend."

For some reason, everything out of my mouth made me sound like a disgruntled four-year-old.

"Seriously un-serious, I think is what I mean," he clarified. I narrowed my eyes at him. "Listen, Rache. I'm a dosser. A born dosser. I've been dossing around all my life. I've dossed in Derry. I've dossed in Belfast. And when I moved down to Cork, I thought, *Okay, real job, real life, real flat. You've got it together, James.*"

I looked around, as if James had just appeared, and then I remembered that I was the only person who called him Carey.

"Then I met you, and Jesus Christ, girl, if I didn't piss it all up the wall immediately."

I couldn't believe how he was spinning this. In all the conversations I had imagined with Carey, I had never once thought of this.

"I never asked you to call in sick," I said. "Or wear the same clothes for four days in a row."

"I know you didn't, pet," he said. He touched my face, grazed it with the back of his knuckles. My rage flowed away and I pressed my cheek into his hand.

"But you're very young," he continued. "You're still doing the student thing. And why not? It's a laugh! But it takes so little for me to slip back into that. Sleeping till noon and all the rest of it. I've no self-control."

Neither did I. I wanted him to grab me, then and there, to screw me next to the focaccia.

"When did you lose your job?" I asked.

"About two days before your birthday," he said, looking ashamed of himself. "And you know, it was a wake-up call. I said to myself: *Listen, this is what happens, running around with younger girls.*"

The age difference had never come up before, and I was immediately suspicious.

"Suddenly I'm a twenty-seven-year-old who can't buy his college girlfriend a birthday present," he said glumly. "I had to have a word with myself. I went home."

"*Home* home? Derry?"

"I knew if I stayed, my dick would drag me back to Shandon Street."

He sighed, as if his dick was always doing that.

"You could have rung," I said.

"I know," he admitted. "I'm sorry."

"I really hate you for that."

"You *should* hate me," he agreed. "But I knew if I heard your voice . . ." He gazed off into the distance, looking sorrowful.

"Oh, *come on*," I snapped. "Stop acting like that."

"Acting like what?"

I groped at the air with my hands. "I'm just some dumpy chick who works in a bookshop, Carey, you could have rung and broke it off with me without it becoming the dance of the seven veils."

He was furious at me then. "Rachel, you've got a body like Wonder Woman; don't give me that shite."

I kissed him. Not because of the Wonder Woman thing, which I still think is bollocks, but because I had lost the will to *not* kiss him. He held me close, kissed me hard, and the smell of sweat and bread swept over me.

After a terrible and beautiful few minutes, I reached for his belt buckle.

"Now, now," he said, taking my hand gently. "Not here."

"Yes," I said. "Here."

"That's old-life stuff, Rachel," he said. "I *need* to be a grown-up now."

He sounded hopeful and sad, like Peter Pan. I kissed him on the forehead and tried to hide my disappointment.

"Then I'll be a grown-up, too."

13

THERE'S PLENTY OF LANGUAGE, now, for what Carey did to me in April of 2010. Women I'm friends with would describe it as ghosting, as psychological manipulation. As gaslighting, even. The only credit they would give him would be the fact that he rightly assessed his situation. That he was too old for me, that the relationship was doomed, that he was too childish, and that he needed to grow up and get an age-appropriate girlfriend. He *did* need to take life seriously. And if that involved keeping a wide berth of me, then so be it.

But none of this rationale changes the hard facts of the case. We were mad about each other. And in the name of this madness, we really tried, and for a time succeeded, to be grown-ups together.

Our version of adulthood was this: we bought bagels at night.

"Have you bought bagels for the morning?" I would say, calling him on the way home from the bookshop, proud of myself. I was doing four days at the shop, and two with Deenie. Those bags of American-style sesame bagels were apparently the only thing that could get us up before 8 a.m. On the days Carey wasn't working, he went to the library to fill out job applications for real jobs.

He started showering every day. I started hanging up my clothes. We said "girlfriend" and "boyfriend" fanatically, adding them extraneously to our sentences, like the word "Father" in prayer. I heard him on the phone.

Me and Rachel will be there, my girlfriend . . . I went there on Thursday, with my girlfriend . . . You want to go out to Douglas? Rachel, my girlfriend, is from there.

I learned more about him, and the painful gap of time when he pretended I didn't exist. We gave ourselves a pre-midnight bedtime for weekdays, and yet never fell asleep before two. I twined myself around his terrier body and collected facts.

"I was very poorly when I was a little boy," he said, and I shrieked with love at the use of the word *poorly*, when everyone I knew would just say *sick*. "Extremely poorly."

He was the youngest of five, with four older sisters, and had an array of mysterious symptoms that were eventually diagnosed as lupus. I had heard of lupus. A contestant on *America's Next Top Model* had it.

"Aye," he said. "Mercedes."

He was a surprising person that way. I didn't know whether he knew about Mercedes because he watched *Top Model* or because he knew everyone famous who had lupus.

"It's fine now, but I don't know, I think I was babied a lot," he sighed. "Between Mam and the girls, I could do no wrong."

He had done two college courses, dropped out of them both, took out loans to go travelling, wandered. He was bailed out of endless jams with the explanation that he had missed out on a lot of his childhood. There was always sympathy, and he had constant charm to meet it with. The first wake-up call came the previous year, when his father pulled strings to get him the Apple job in Cork, and told him that it was the last thing the family was ever going to do for him.

I nodded in the darkness and tried to put aside my own rejection in favour of the bigger picture. I tried not to see Carey's actions as good or bad but as in keeping with who he was.

If I was uninterested in my family during Carey's first tenure as my boyfriend, I had almost forgotten them by his second. Knowing I wouldn't come home of my own free will, my mother chased me down for coffee dates in town. Thinking about those coffees, even now, burns my guts. I wanted to completely reset the parameters of our relationship, and I had no interest in giving her time to adjust. I tried to rush the parent-child relationship into an adult-adult one, and I did this by drinking only black coffee, rolling cigarettes at the table, and then—most mortifying of all—sliding the rollie behind my ear.

It drove her crazy. It's a set of memories that I always witness in the third person, as if I'm a film director: my too-long hair, my cheap dresses, my tits pushed up too much. I had one black Wonderbra, and I wore it to death, until the black straps were practically falling to my elbows. My mother squinting in disbelief, even burying her forehead in her palm. "*Rachel*," she'd scowl. "Rachel, for *God's sake*." They had worked so hard to send me to a private girls' school, to tennis clubs and pony camps, to end up—with what? With a daughter who keeps cigarettes behind her ear. I came home from those coffees and threw myself on the couch, waiting for attention from James.

"My mother," I would say, "just can't *stand* that I'm self-sufficient."

My brothers I forgot about, and I assumed that they forgot about me. There wasn't a firm pecking order in our house. Chris and I played together when we were small, but once Kevin came along and I started school, they became a separate entity to me. They were *the boys* and I was Rachel. I was a child who liked reading, and writing to auction houses to request that they send me their catalogues, and being treated with dour respect. I was a kid who put "cameo brooch" on her Christmas list. The boys lived on Boy Island. I think my lost precociousness was part of my mother's misery that I was becoming such a stupid, tarty adult. There were only a few times when I still felt like the eldest sibling, and Carey was there for one of them.

We were in bed together and heard a thump coming from the yard outside. It sounded, at first, like a cat knocking over plant pots. Then the cat made a human, moaning sound.

"Stay here," Carey said. "I'll look."

I followed him, of course. I was too turned on by the notion of a man protecting me *not* to follow him. I remember him so clearly, half-lit by the bulb above the oven: gingham checked boxers, no shirt, and the most incongruous gold-rimmed reading glasses that he kept near the bed.

"Who is it?" I rasped. "A robber?"

"A *robber*. Jesus. As if you have anything worth robbing."

"We have a TV!"

"It's some drunk lad."

"What's going on?" a bleary James said, from the top of the stairs. "Are we being robbed?"

"We *might* be," I said. "We *may* be."

"It's just some waster," Carey corrected. "Rachel, throw me a hoodie and I'll go out to him."

"What if he hits you?"

Carey gave me a withering look. He had that strange, straight-boy thing of not being afraid of physical confrontation.

He put on a purple hoodie of mine, too snug to zip up more than halfway. He stepped outside, and James and I looked at each other as if Carey had just shot himself into space. I heard Carey, gentle but firm.

"You all right, mate? Had a bit much, have you? Do you need a cup of tea?"

"A cup of *tea*?" James hissed. "Is he going to offer him my room, too?"

I heard a mumbling, staggering voice, but the bass of it was still recognisable. I ran out into the yard.

"*Chris!*" It was my brother. Six foot three, seventeen years old, and his jeans soaked in blood. "What *happened*?"

I sat him down on one of our kitchen chairs. He smelled not just of drink and blood, but of something strong and medical.

"That's my sister," he said crossly to Carey, tilting around in his seat. "That's my big sister. Who are you? Are you guys fucking? Are you banging my sister? Rachel, what happened to the last guy? Long face. Long sad horse face."

"Christ," James said, already bored. "He's on meow meow."

"He can't be on Mephedrone," I snapped. "He's a teenager."

"I just need to hang out here for a while," Chris said. "Until it wears off and I can go to sleep. I'll go first thing in the morning. Please, Rachel, please, don't send me home. Come on. Be sound."

"Is Mum expecting you?" I said, my back ramrod straight. "And why are you *bleeding*?"

"Don't be a gowl, Rachel." He turned to Carey. "Dude, do you have a cigarette?"

He showed Carey the cut on his leg. He got it climbing through a broken window in a squat house where they had all been taking the stuff. I worried whether this meant my brother was a drug addict, but the more he spoke the more I realised that he was playing at this the same way I was playing at black coffee. He had made some kind of realisation about the diminishing fortunes of our family, and was trying out new lifestyles. His previous summer had been spent on a family friend's boat in west Cork, and this summer was about squats.

Carey found tweezers, an old pillowcase and a bottle of vodka. Chris refused to take off his jeans so Carey carefully cut a hole with kitchen scissors around the wound, which pleased Chris very much. "People *buy* jeans with holes in them," he kept saying. "But I got this *fairly*. Through *noble* means."

He still seemed so much like a baby to me. His big soft face and sandy hair, looking like a toddler's impression of James Dean. Carey picked glass out of Chris's leg, shard by shard, with the tweezers. Chris chatted to Carey the whole time, both of them smoking, Carey with his gold-rimmed spectacles on. James went to bed. I sat on the couch, a background character, as Carey cleaned the wound with vodka and wrapped it in torn-up strips of pillow case. I had nothing to add, but I couldn't take my eyes off the scene. I felt like I was in the 1930s. Nothing so male had ever happened in my house, unless you count the great number of men fucking other men.

At some point, Chris's high softened and conversation became more normal. We, in that way siblings do for outsiders, tried to make a travelling circus out of our childhood. Stories about old holiday rentals and falling out of trees. Carey was a generous audience, asking us questions, laughing at the right time. We eventually went to bed at around five, leaving my drooping brother on the couch.

"Thank you," I said, reaching out to touch his arm. "You were so good with him."

"He's a nice lad."

"You don't think he's a junkie, or something?"

"Nah. Brother of yours? Never."

"I don't know what we would have done without you."

He sighed a strange, tired sigh. "You can do anything without me."

He fell asleep then. Leaving me to bask in the oddness of the comment, and to wish that he had stopped at the word "anything."

At this point in our relationship, I was so obsessed with Carey that I had to stop myself from constantly comparing him to famous movie stars. I complimented him vividly, begged him for sex, hung on his every elusive statement. And yet he would still come out with statements like these. Melancholic, nocturnal comments that implied I would outgrow him, or see him for who he truly was. He was wonderful, but he didn't have a great deal of self-esteem. He was a dosser, after all. A born dosser.

My parents had always taught me that what mattered most in a person was direction. Which is another way of saying: it doesn't matter if they have money now, as long as they plan to have money later. It became clear to me that Carey had no direction, but I didn't mind. He was kind, and he was mad about me, and while he probably should have thought more about his career at the age of twenty-seven, I was quietly glad that he didn't. It gave him more time to focus on more important things. Namely, me.

The year in Shandon Street did a lot for me, but it did this most of all. It detached me from any kind of inherited moral system. I stopped sizing others up in accordance with the values I had been taught: who was a loser, who was closeted, who was cheating on their wife. I learned the value of context, and of people. It came in handy later on, when I became a journalist.

At 8 a.m., I went downstairs. Chris's eyes flew open right away.

"Sorry," he said.

"It's okay. Tea?"

"Yeah. Tea."

He got up, all long and teenage, looking like he had extra hands and feet. He followed me into the kitchen.

"I think Dad is depressed," he said. "Capital d."

I had spent a lot of time worrying about our parents, in the years I spent living at home during college. As far as I was concerned it was Chris's turn to carry the burden. My job was keeping out of their hair. It is amazing to me, now, how convinced I was that my emotional debt to the people who had raised me was paid, simply because I no longer lived with them.

"If it ever gets too much," I said, "just come here. You're always welcome."

But it was sentences like this—*you're always welcome*—that erected an invisible wall of formality between us. I needed Carey to come downstairs, to treat Chris like he was any old bloke on the street, to help me build a bridge between the Boy Island my brothers were on and the grubby glamour of me and James. But Carey did not wake up for another four hours, and by that point Chris was gone. He never came back to the house on Shandon Street.

———

Just as it was the summer of Carey, it was the summer of Deenie, too.

The Harrington-Byrnes' home was a ground-floor flat in an old house in Sunday's Well, on the other side of Fitzgerald's Park, the only decent green space in Cork city. The house was Edwardian, with big bay windows you could sit in, and bookshelves and strange rugs in every room. It was the most beautiful house I'd ever been in. At that age, you've only ever been in family homes or student houses. The home of two artsy professionals in their thirties is a magnificent thing to behold, more enchanting than an old Russian palace.

It had three bedrooms. The one they slept in, the one Deenie worked in, and the one Dr. Byrne worked in. The living room was a tiny, cosy red room with a small TV and a green squashy couch. The kitchen was huge and full of sun.

I found it hard not to hate Deenie, for the first hour I was in her house. She seemed to take it all for granted. She opened the door wearing a pinafore dress with a black roll neck underneath, and her headband was the same colour as the dress. I knew that she dressed like something between a primary school teacher and Daphne from *Scooby-Doo*, but the fact that she looked like this in her own home was too much. She led me through to the kitchen, shoeless in black tights. I felt enormous next to her.

"How are you?" she asked, as if I had just popped by socially. "Are you still with that lovely-looking boy I saw you with that day?"

I don't know whether she really thought Carey was lovely looking. Not everybody did. James used to say a lot of sly "eye of the beholder" stuff whenever his physical appearance came up. What I did see, however, was that she wanted to check if I had a boyfriend.

"Carey," I confirmed. "Yeah, he's back on the scene."

"Was he off the scene?"

"Oh, yeah." I shrugged. "We fell out of contact for a bit, there."

"God, I wish I was as lucky with men as you when I was your age. I was so dweeby, like a little worm. Didn't have a proper boyfriend till I was twenty-three."

This was startling from a number of angles. If Deenie was going to be my boss, then this was a lot of personal information from her. Also, lucky? With men?

I must have looked confused, so she clarified. "I was just thinking of that night we saw you at Goldfrapp, with that other nice-looking guy."

It made sense for Deenie to have zero gaydar, considering who she was married to.

"James," I said.

"He wasn't serious, then?"

"Just a friend," I replied, and made it sound like I was being discreet.

She poured the coffee. "Sorry," she said, shaking her head like she was reprimanding herself. "It's just, all my friends are married or pregnant or whatever. Whenever anyone has, like, an exciting romantic life, I'm all over it."

Exciting romantic life! When I couldn't even make Carey shag me in a bread shop.

We drank our coffee and eventually got around to talking about work. I learned that Deenie's publisher let her work two days at home, because it was hard to get editing done in a busy office, and she often worked well into the evening. There was a certain number of glamorous lunches involved in her job, but not nearly as many as you'd think. She named some of the books she had worked on, and I was surprised to hear that I knew almost all of them. I hadn't read them, but they had climbed up the bestsellers chart at the shop, and I had looked at their blurbs.

"Do you get a percentage?" I asked. "For all the books you worked on that did really well?"

She laughed drily. "No," she said. "I wish."

Deenie added, with a note of conspiracy, that having books that had sold very well could have other benefits, allowed you to pull rank on certain things. Her eyes flitted to the nearest bookshelf, where five copies of *The Kensington Diet* sat.

"Ah," I said, "I see."

We both laughed then, a laugh that was all fondness, because we both loved Dr. Byrne and supported his right to write useless books.

She gave me my duties. She wanted me to read through her slush pile of manuscripts, mostly sent by unpublished authors, and keep a spreadsheet of my notes on them. She showed me the Excel spreadsheet she had been keeping since she started working in books. It was hundreds of rows long, alphabetical, and colour-coded. Green meant excellent. She would try to acquire all the green books. Yellow meant "shows promise." Red meant absolutely not. The spreadsheet was mostly yellow. Within yellow, there was more coding: books that weren't quite right, authors who weren't quite ready, subjects that were slightly out of fashion. Each entry had one sentence, summing up the book and its writer. "Civil war epic, goes on a bit, he knows a lot about the skerries."

Some of the yellow entries were from years ago, and a few of those books had gone on to be bestsellers. One author, who had won a national short story award that year, was summed up as "strange little man: loves dogs, hates women."

As she explained all this, I could feel myself becoming jittery with excitement. It was the first time I had ever seen behind the curtain of the world I had been annotating diligently for years. I imagined my favourite authors showing up on one of Deenie's spreadsheets, or on identical spreadsheets across the world. Donna Tartt, Toni Morrison, Richard Yates, Barbara Trapido, Haruki Murakami, Edna O'Brien. Intellectually, I knew they all must have been rejected by publishers, and had read interviews to that effect.

But the notion that they could have once lived in the mediocrity of the yellow list was so refreshing to me.

I would have a certain number of manuscripts to read a week. I could read some at home, and some at her house. I was also in charge of her public work inbox, of sending one of her templated rejection emails to all the hopeful writers who wanted so desperately to be published but apparently not so desperately that they were willing to learn Deenie's name. "Dear Sirs" was the most common way she was addressed.

On the whole, we had a good time together. I remember thinking, several mornings while we quietly read and sipped coffee from burnt clay mugs, *If this is work, then sign me up*.

For the first few days of my internship, James was waiting at the door when I came home, desperate for intel on the inner workings of his lover's home life. I didn't know what to tell him.

"She's lovely," I said, with a note of apology.

"Does she suspect anything?"

"Well," I replied slowly, "she thinks you're straight."

"Oh."

He looked stunned, like someone who had made a monkey's paw wish that had come true, but in all the wrong ways.

I described their house to him, the bright rugs and the seats in the window, and he hated it. "Tell me how their marriage is," he said desperately. "Do they seem happy?"

"He's never there!"

And he wasn't. College was out and the summer literary festivals had hit, so Dr. Byrne was still doing his best to shill copies of *The Kensington Diet*. He had found some momentum with his new book, too, so his mid-afternoon visits were beginning to dwindle.

James was trying to convince Dr. Byrne to let him tag along to one of the literary festivals. To say he was an assistant. Dr. Byrne was firm: absolutely not. The people at the festivals were Deenie's people. The risk was too great.

I feel a twinge of guilt, looking back on those months now. I was either at work, under a stack of manuscripts, or with Carey. I had sworn off the synthetic weed, but James was still smoking it in bed, miserable in front of *Frasier*.

"I'm your best friend," he snapped once, when he saw me circling and underlining a manuscript, the way Deenie had taught me to. I had graduated from her slush pile and was now doing some light editing. "You're supposed to love me the most."

The baldness of this. It was something neither of us would say to a boyfriend, terrified as we were of admitting raw and open need. But we could say it to each other.

"I *do* love you the most," I said, throwing my arms around him. "But I need to compartmentalise. I can't be a spy for you. She's my friend, sort of."

I had a new flush of sympathy for Dr. Byrne, who had got through his own clashing loyalties by blanking me. I understood the temptation.

"How's the TV show going?" I said. We had given up on saying that I was co-writing it with him. I hadn't opened the document or written a word in a month.

He didn't reply, and just went to take a shower. His second of the day.

Some days later, James took three buses to Dingle, eight hours in total, and gatecrashed a festival that Dr. Byrne was speaking at. It was a profoundly stupid thing to do. Dr. Byrne ignored and dodged him at the festival, sent him a terse text message to meet him at the hotel, and then they argued all night. I don't think James actually wanted Dr. Byrne to leave his wife. He just felt like he deserved more respect, more time, a small pied-à-terre and a marabou dressing gown. He wanted the affair to be Frencher, if at all possible.

James knew all this was impossible, but he was reaching the same space that I had hit in May. He was starting to wonder what was going to become of him, too, except his case felt more drastic than mine. He didn't even have the mediocre degree from the mediocre university.

One morning in July, he came into the kitchen, where I was toasting bagels. Carey was in the shower.

"What are you doing up?" I asked.

This was three days after the Dingle trip, and James had been sequestered in his room ever since. He had the ironing board out, and was going through both my clothes and his.

"I've decided to get a grip," he said. "I'm going to give up Fred."

"Wow," I said. "Well done."

Just as I had been willing to accept that James was straight when we first moved in, I was prepared to allow for this fiction also. My suspicion was that Fred Byrne had finished with him in Dingle.

"I'm going to get another job. I'm sick of being poor. And I'm going to finish the TV show."

I nodded. "I'm so pleased, pal. That's great."

I was relieved that we didn't have to officially discuss my no longer writing the TV show with him. I had lost all interest at that point, but it felt rude to say.

"I'm twenty-three in November, Rache."

"I know."

"I want to have a plan by then. Not just a plan. But, like, prospects."

I hugged him. Carey came out of the shower with my towel around his waist and his famous stomach on display.

"Carey, can I come to the library with you today?" James asked.

"Course, mate," Carey replied, grabbing a plate. "What are you at?"

"I'm going to become a screenwriter."

"Quality," he replied, leaving the room with his bagel.

Carey had no idea about James and Fred Byrne, and had no concept of Fred Byrne outside of him being my ex-professor and the husband of my boss. It's amazing to me now, how many secrets I kept from him, but it just never seemed to come up. He never asked questions about James's sexuality, although I'm sure he assumed. Equally, I knew he didn't care. Not that he was making a conscious choice to be accepting; but that it literally didn't figure on his radar.

There were many, many things that did not figure on Carey's radar. The longer we were together, the more I could tell that everyone who knew him was frustrated by the way he existed. His eldest sister, Cate, had started calling me when trying to find him. I had never met her, but she understood that we were locked into the same fate and had to find a way to work together. "Rachel, how are ya?" she began every call. She did not wait for a response. "Listen, James needs to charge his phone and call Mam. She's not well again. And it's Dad's birthday on Saturday. Can you tell him?"

Our chats, short as they were, always felt like two people who were managing a child after an amiable divorce. Sometimes it was a lupus thing. Carey would never say it, but there were days where he just had to sleep, or to stay still, and he refused to call me on those days. It was the only thing I ever saw him be embarrassed about.

But mostly, it was just him being a flake.

"Why can't you just charge your phone?" I would say to him. "Why can't you just . . . ?"

"I don't know," he would answer, equally mystified. "I just don't know."

For as many things that didn't figure on his radar, there were many quite wonderful things that did. Once he rang me from a payphone outside the library, having once again forgotten to charge his mobile.

"Rache," he said, "listen to this. Back in the whaling days, eighteen hundreds or whatever, they figured out the best oil was in the sperm whale's brain. They called that the junk. And they would lower someone down, with a winch or whatever, into the whale's skull, and he would have to, like, scoop out the brains. Did you know that?"

"I did *not* know that."

"What do you think *that* smelled like?" he asked. "We're talking a brain that's as big as your house."

I heard a faint tapping sound on his end of the line. "What?" Carey said.

"Sir, you cannot take books from the library if you've not checked them out."

"I'm only reading this to my girlfriend. Rachel, are you still there? The oil was called spermaceti. Because it *looked* like cum."

"You need to bring the book back inside, sir."

I howled with laughter, gasping so hard that I had to explain it to Deenie. In those moments, I didn't care about Carey's fundamental flakiness, or the fact that he was supposed to be in the library filling out job applications. But the fear always came back. I had long, paranoid nights of wondering whether he had died. There were days when I didn't hear from him. But I was learning that this was part of love, or of loving him anyway.

"If he was anyone else in the world," I said to James one night, after looking at my phone for the fiftieth time, "I'd tell him to go fuck himself."

"But he isn't anyone else in the world," said James, warm sadness rising in his throat.

I laced his fingers through mine. It had been weeks since he had seen Dr. Byrne.

14

N JULY, Ben called a meeting and said he had to cut our pay. Up until that point I was on 9.50 an hour, and James was on nine. The extra fifty cents reflected the two years of seniority I had on him, plus the fact that I had keys to the till and could do cash refunds. We had time-and-a-third on Sundays and on bank holidays. The only way he could keep our jobs, Ben explained, was to cut us all down to eight an hour, and to get rid of time-and-a-third until further notice.

He didn't want to fire anyone, he said, because we were like family. But he urged us to look for jobs. "I can be flexible if you guys have interviews," he said mournfully.

People took the hint. Sabrina, who I still quietly saw as a rival, handed in her notice the next day. She was moving to New York at the end of the summer. A few others started working for the big call centre out in Bishopstown. Carey, James and I were all terrified of the big call centre in Bishopstown. It made us feel like old horses, about to be turned into glue. Carey didn't help matters. He had a phone job when he worked at Apple.

"Apple is the best of the best, fruit baskets and all that, and I *still* wanted to kill myself." He grimaced. "Can't imagine what that other place must be like."

James and I were like those old broke ladies you meet in London, who say "of course, I could never live south of the river" and would rather starve in their pre-war Kensington flats. We had standards. We were *town* people. We would rather be on our feet all day, working at GAP, than tied to some desk phone.

People left O'Connor's, which meant there were more hours for me and James, but now that our wages had been cut we were still taking home the same money. We became very bratty, and absolutely awful at our jobs. We closed progressively earlier every day, blared our own music during work hours, failed to update the bestseller charts every Thursday night. We developed a deep hatred of women who bought *The Help* to read on holiday.

"They should *The Help* us," James sniped. "Their husbands should have *The Help*-ed the country by not *The Help*-ing themselves."

We didn't understand what was going on with the economy. Just that it was bad, not just regular bad, but corrupt bad. There were a few buzz phrases that we picked up from the customers, who would recycle information that they had heard on the radio. "The bloody banks," we would say. "Bertie Ahern and his *fucking* brown envelopes."

I missed Fred Byrne. I felt like he could have explained to us what was going on.

I never got to hear what went down in Dingle. James disappeared behind a cloak of shame and ironing starch spray on the matter. The only clues I was ever given were through his TV script, which was in full flow again, and even had a title: *Discs*.

James decided that if he was going to work more hours for the same money, he might as well get something out of it. He spent every spare minute in the Film & TV section, analysing screenplay writing formats and reading Robert McKee. He also took full advantage of the work printer, which he used to print off sheets of his script.

"I think I know what the big event is, at the end of the pilot," he said one day, while we were cleaning up. "I think Michael leaves his boyfriend, and has to move in with Alice."

"Michael has a boyfriend now?"

"Yes," he answered quickly. "We never see him."

"Like Maris? In *Frasier*?"

"Like Maris."

"So the set-up for the show is that Michael and Alice have to live *and* work together?"

"Yes! And like, how do they negotiate work and life balance?"

"How *do* we?"

"They're not like us," he said defensively. He was nervous of me interpreting Alice's actions as being too much of a parody. "We're very evolved."

INT: THE STORE

MICHAEL bursts through the doors, looking upset.
ALICE is already behind the counter.

ALICE

Michael, what kind of time do you call this?!

MICHAEL

Sorry, sorry!

ALICE

You missed the Horror shipment! Do you
know how sad it is to unload a truck-load of
perverted violence at 9 a.m. on a Tuesday?

MICHAEL

I broke up with Craig.

ALICE

Oh . . . So . . . I guess you do know!

MICHAEL

Alice!

ALICE

Look, I'm sorry, okay! I'm in shock here! But
you have to admit, your relationship with Craig
wasn't exactly . . . healthy.

I still have pages of that first draft in a shoebox. Every time I
move house, I dedicate another day to sitting on the floor, reading
all the voices James tried on before he found his own. I photograph
every page, send them to him, and he replies either immediately or
seven hours later with the vomit emoji.

One night we were having dinner at home. We were down to
the last bottle of Fred Byrne's wine and we decided to cook a spaghetti bolognese from scratch to honour it. The meal was horrible:
the mince simmered so long that it was grainy, the tomato sauce
splashy and slightly too cool. "I like it this way," I said, several
times. "I like the meat when it's crunchy."

"I think we should talk about our plan," he said, dripping the
last bit of the wine into my glass. "I think we should move to
London."

"Oh," I said, chewing my chewy meat. It had the consistency of
scabs. "Really?"

"We can't hang around here. Cork is dying."

I nodded. "Cork is *dead*."

"I've almost finished *Discs*. When I'm done I'm going to send it
over to production companies in London. And agencies, too. So I
can get an agent."

"Jesus." I swallowed. "You've thought about this."

"I haven't thought about anything else. I've been looking online.
I think we could get a flat in London. Not, like, near the centre of
the city or anything, but somewhere further out."

I had heard tales of people in the suburbs who commuted to the centre of London every day in the time it took to get a Ryanair flight. It sounded awful.

"I don't know," I said, thinking of Carey, of Deenie, of the tendrils of life I had in Cork that were fragile but would also mean nothing without James.

"She would write you a recommendation for one of the English publishing houses," he said; "she" meaning Deenie. "And you could ask Carey."

I rubbed my ear. "Ask Carey what?"

"To come with us."

I dropped my fork. "What?"

"Why not?"

"You would want to live with him?"

He shrugged. "I basically live with him already."

"He's not here that much."

"No." He looked at me with sly eyes. "I mean I basically *live with him* already."

"Oh, come on. I'm not as bad as him. I'm housebroken!" I was washing my sheets now. Had he not noticed?

"Sure."

"James!"

"The point still stands. Ask him to come with us. If we get a two-bedroom and the three of us are splitting rent, we're quids in."

MICHAEL

What do you mean? We were very healthy.

ALICE

Well, for starters, you never stayed at his place.

MICHAEL

He lives with his wife!

ALICE

And he lives with his wife!

MICHAEL

He's saving on rent!

I had no idea when James became so business-minded. If I were to guess, I would have said that it came from the crisp, cut-and-dried Hollywood screenwriter language he was reading in all those books. The ones that were always saying things like: *One page per one minute of screen time. Figure out what they want and don't give it to them. Show, don't tell. No character should have five lines of uninterrupted dialogue at any time.*

"I don't know. I don't know if me and Carey are . . . there. It's a big deal, to emigrate with someone."

"Christ, I'm not asking you to get on a coffin ship with him. If it doesn't work out, you'll break up with him and he'll fuck off back to Cork. What do you have to lose? You're mad about him, aren't you?"

"Yes," I said. "Of course."

He was mad about me, too, in the moments he remembered I existed. And wasn't this the whole point of our joint effort to be adults? Wasn't this where it was all going? I began to imagine him, imagining himself. How much he'd like to tell his parents that he was moving to London with his girlfriend. How pleased everyone would be. I imagined his sister Cate calling me in our shared flat, asking me to put him on. I imagined meeting Cate.

We knew people who had moved to London, of course. All of them talked about how hard it was, how tiring, how competitive. How diffuse it was, with everyone miles away from everyone else. How cold the British could be, full of mixed signals towards friendship that could leave you years before you got an invite to anyone's house. But moving to London with my best friend and my boyfriend. It wouldn't matter how cold anyone was then, would it?

I thought of me and Carey on the tube together, him filling out the crosswords in the free newspapers.

James and I talked until late about how a move to London might work. We would need to save money. How to do that was a mystery, considering we were barely supporting ourselves as it was.

"Could Deenie give you a raise?" he asked.

She was still giving me fifty euro for three mornings a week, but she had also mentioned some extra work coming in, a poetry anthology she might need help with. I wondered if that counted as outside the remit of my internship, and was just labour.

"Maybe," I said. "And I could always look at bar work."

"Don't bother," he said. "There's none going, and they're giving all the glass collecting jobs to hot Polish girls."

I tried not to look too offended. "Because they do it for cheaper," he clarified. "Not because—"

I put my hand up, a silent request not to be patronised.

"We'll figure out money," he said. "You think of stuff, and I'll think of stuff."

MICHAEL

Look, I know Craig wasn't perfect, but it's still
tough to end things!

ALICE

Of course it is! So what did you say?

Michael takes a moment

MICHAEL

I said . . . that things can't go on like this, you
know? I said that I keep trying, and he keeps
not-trying, and at some point, we both have
to agree on one or the other. And . . . he won't
try. And I know he won't. And it breaks my

heart, because . . . I love him. I love him, and I
really wanted this to work, but I can't try if I'm
out there just trying and trying and trying on
my own.

It was over five lines of uninterrupted dialogue, but I still think
it works.

15

W E DECIDED THAT, in order to move to London, we would need at least £4,000. That would cover us on a deposit and first month's rent, and give us about ten days' leeway to each get new jobs.

"We can put away that much by the New Year," he said, with great certainty. "And we'll be getting our deposit back for this place, once the lease is up."

"We need to fix the shower," I said, which still had a black bin liner over the place I had kicked a hole in the tiles.

"That's just a hundred quid a week, really. Each. Ask Deenie to give you a raise."

"You think Deenie is going to suddenly *double* my salary?" I replied. "If you can even *call* fifty quid a salary?"

"Well," he continued, undeterred, "once Carey gets involved, he can start chipping in on the fund, too, can't he?"

"Let's not complicate things," I said. I had not asked Carey yet. I was terrified of how he might react. There was a lot of talk around then about "commitment," not just in my head, but in the culture. The context for commitment was that it was something that women wanted but that killed men. The words "commitment," "commitment issues" and the decidedly medical "commitment-phobe" were thrown around constantly, so much that I forgot what the word meant, which was usually just about having someone sleep over a lot and occasionally go to weddings with you.

So I continued not to mention London to Carey. The longer I put off asking Carey, the more I could live in a fantasy where he said yes, and we could all begin planning our new lives together. If he said no, it would be the first in a long series of conversations that would inevitably lead to our break-up. I had gone through that kind of heartbreak once that year already. I didn't have the stomach for it twice.

He brought me toast in bed one morning. It felt very romantic, even though it was my bread. He was so rarely up before me.

"Sit up, now; don't be covering yourself in crumbs."

I did as he said, loving the fuss. He kissed a spot of peanut butter off my chin.

"Are you all right, Rache?" he asked, sounding suddenly very shy.

"Of course! Why?"

"I just . . ." He grabbed at words with a kind of lucky-dip energy when he was nervous. "You've been very *lugubrious*, of late."

"Lugubrious!" I barked with joy. "I don't even know what 'lugubrious' means. There's my English degree for you."

"Sad, sort of morbid," he answered. "And you never want to go out. You're a bit stuck to the house. When you're not working, I mean."

"Ah, well. That's money."

"You do all right. You still have the shop, and Deenie. We can afford to go to The Bróg for one."

This was the time to tell him. He was curious, concerned, alert, focused. My boobs were out. It would have been so easy. *Me and James are planning to move to London. Come with us.*

"It's just, we're trying to save money," I said honestly.

"We?"

"Me and James," I said.

"For what?"

I didn't want to lie to him, so I didn't. Not technically.

"We want to move to a better place," I said, and I waved my hand around, motioning to the damp line crawling up my wall, and to the street outside my window. I implied better places might be up the road, and not in a different country.

"Oh," he said. "Right."

I felt a jolt of fear, like I was hiding an affair and moments from being caught out. I thought about telling him. I imagined him pulling away, feeling the pressure of my request, the expiration date of my immigration. The panic at losing him took over, and I put the plate on the floor and pulled him close to me. It was the first time we had sex where I felt aware of wanting to impress him, keep him. Of wanting to put on a show. I felt myself becoming louder, more performative. I remember looking down during it and thinking he looked confused.

Afterwards he petted me on the head, like a horse. "That was a treat for a Tuesday morning," he said, and I didn't see him for two days.

In my heart, I didn't believe I would be moving to London. Some plans get made and they drop right into your hand like a warm egg. Dr. Byrne's book launch, for example. Others feel vague from conception, and carry on feeling vague no matter how many details you hammer onto them.

This was not how the plan worked for James. He saw himself in London, and spent hours researching different neighbourhoods he thought we could live in.

"Look at this flat I found in Mile End," he said. "Two bedrooms. A thousand a month."

I looked at the pictures. It looked dismal, and like it was high off the ground. From the sliding door I could see the tops of buildings.

"A thousand *pounds*?"

"Split three ways. That's not much more than we pay now. Of course, there's council tax and all that in the UK."

"We still don't know if Carey is coming."

"And we won't know if you don't *ask* him."

"I *will* ask him."

I did not ask him.

A week later, James came tearing down the stairs, holding his laptop. "RACHEL!" he yelled. "RACHEL!"

I was reading a week-old magazine and feeling depressed about money.

"I've got an email! An email about *Discs*!"

> Hi James,
>
> Thank you so much for submitting your script *Discs* to us. Unfortunately we are not able to take this any further as we are unable to produce unrepresented writers. However, I wanted to reach out personally and say that I thoroughly enjoyed your writing, and find myself very curious about what happens next with Michael and Alice.
>
> I expect you will run into many of the same issues with other production companies. Can I recommend you try submitting it to the BBC Writersroom, or perhaps Sky?
>
> Many thanks,
> Jennifer Romley
> Development Executive
> Elephant Feet Productions

It was a rejection email, but it was all he needed. The facts of this email warped rapidly to suit a new mythology, one where James *almost* had a TV deal, and the only reason he didn't was because of not having some poxy agent. He followed Jennifer Romley's advice, submitting to Sky and the BBC, and including the line "I've had serious interest from Jennifer Romley, at Elephant Feet" in every cover letter.

"It's all about who you know," he repeated. Jennifer Romley was probably someone not much older than us, and tasked with going through the slush pile just like I had to go through Deenie's. In the 2010 fantasy, though, she was a huge person in the industry, someone whose name would be recognised anywhere. We imagined her in the Groucho Club, talking about "this fabulous new Irish writer," and being overheard by someone from the BBC. Someone who had coincidentally received *Discs* that afternoon.

The agent thing was proving more troubling. No one was returning his emails. He called and called, and eventually received some curt advice from a receptionist. "Listen, mate," she said, "no one knows who the fack you are."

She became more English every time we told the story. It became a thing we shouted at each other, up the stairs, across the street. "No one knows who the FACK you are!"

"Why are ye always saying that?" Carey asked once, when he was round. "Doing the English voice?"

"For the craic," I answered brightly. It was a good enough excuse. It was why we did everything.

"This is why I'd never live in England," he said, rolling a cigarette. "That voice. Nails on a chalkboard."

"Never?" I said, my guts trembling.

"God, could you imagine me?" He chuckled. "I'd be singing 'Come Out, Ye Black and Tans' on the tube."

He was joking. Or he wasn't. It's hard to know. His wider family had seen a fair amount of persecution during the Troubles, as many Catholic families in Derry had. It was difficult to parse how serious his grudge against England actually was. Should it matter? Plenty of people moved to England who hated it.

In any case, I took it seriously. Which is all that really mattered, in the end.

"I need you to come to Fermoy with me on Sunday," James said. "I'm going to come out to my mum."

I was in the shower when he said this. I was sure that I heard him wrong. "What?"

He raised his voice. "I said, you need to come to Fermoy with me on Sunday, because I need to come out to my mum."

I turned the water off and put on my towel. Out in the kitchen, the door was open, and James was smoking a cigarette in the beam of sunlight coming in from the yard.

"What are you coming out to Nicola for?"

There is a friend of a certain vintage who will take too much comfort in a mother's name. James and I were of that vintage. We were best friends, despite not knowing one another very long, and we were determined to make up the time lag in our friendship with family intimacies. I was always asking after Nicola and Frank; he wanted to know about Bridget and Paul.

"She needs to know, doesn't she?"

He had received an additional email, identical to the one he got from Jennifer Romley at Elephant Feet. It was from another bizarrely named production company, another probably quite junior person. They said his writing was "lively" and that it was refreshing to see "rounded gay characters" in a script. They also suggested the BBC Writersroom.

One thoughtful rejection letter was good. Two was even better. Two was "buzz."

"If I'm going to become known for my rounded gay characters," he said, "I better have a rounded gay life."

We took the bus out and walked a mile from the village. I asked him why we couldn't just ask his mum or stepfather to collect us, and he said he needed the walk to figure out what he was going to say.

I thought that he wanted to try out his different coming-out lines on me. He didn't. We were silent the whole time, James walking a little ahead.

There were plenty of distractions, when we finally arrived. Nicola had a Burmese cat that had just given birth to kittens, and we cuddled them over a box in the garage while she talked us through the breeding process. She was a sweet woman, all blonde hair and gold jewellery, and constantly surprised at having ended up on a farm in Ireland. James's stepfather was always off doing something, somewhere. I never knew enough about farming to understand what.

She touched her son a lot. Her hand on the nape of his skinny neck, her thumb rubbing along his hairline. I held the kittens, one in each hand, their claws hooking my dress.

"We're hoping to get four hundred for the boys," Nicola said. "Five for the girls."

"Mum, I'm gay."

Nicola looked at her son, then at me. I had presumed the gay conversation would happen while I was in the bathroom. I turned my attention to the cats.

"Okay," she said, at last. Then she reached her hand higher under James's hairline, and drew her son close to her. She hugged him for a long minute. Then she started to cry.

I've had enough queer friends in the years since to know this: the mothers always cry. No matter how much they knew already. No matter how obvious it was. It is the kind of crying you do while watching a movie on an airplane. Intense and unreal, high on silent terror and recycled air.

Nicola kept crying, and I put the kittens down and slowly moved out of the garage.

There was nowhere to go, so I sat on a wall and looked at an empty field. Someone, possibly James's stepfather, was riding a lawnmower.

It was some time before James and his mother came out of the garage. "It's nothing to do with that," I heard him say to her. "It was always there."

I didn't turn around. I didn't want to make them self-conscious with my presence.

"Rachel!" Nicola called, her throat sounding dry. "Will you come in for a sandwich?"

We ate ham sandwiches at her kitchen table, and then she drove us to the bus. We moved through the motions like people after a funeral, with a sense that, even in the worst situations, people still need to be fed and get places. I knew that there was something else going on here, and that the mysterious *solve for x* that surrounded James and his sexuality was being revealed to me. I was being given evidence, but of what, I didn't know.

We didn't speak much on the bus, or at all until we were safely back at the house in Shandon Street. We got into his bed without saying a word.

"Has nothing to do with what?" I asked.

He sighed. "I was abused."

It reads strangely, but that was how he said it. He didn't want to give me lots of editorial detail, lots of camera angles, and then let me come to my own conclusion. He had a lot of charisma, but he didn't want to use it for this.

I got those camera angles, eventually. In dribs and drabs, and over the years. The sister's friend from college. The guest room with the small TV, where James went to watch cartoons, and where the friend was staying. The soft, funny discussions that turned into harsh reality and finally a dull, oily feeling of distance.

"Oh my God. I'm so sorry."

"It's okay." He looked at me for the first time since we left earlier that morning. "It was after we moved to Ireland. It only happened once. I told them straight away."

He said it all like he was reading from a telegram.

"She spent so long trying to keep us safe from my dad. I think it broke her that she had forgotten to keep us safe from other people."

"Oh, James." I had nothing else. Just, *Oh, James.*

"You know, bad things used to happen so often, back in England, to people we knew, to people in our family. I always just thought: *Something is coming for me eventually.* So when it happened, I almost thought, *Oh, here it is.*"

I laid my head on his shoulder.

"But she . . . she was sure it would screw me up. It ruined her. I didn't want her to be right."

"You're not screwed up."

"Yeah." He didn't sound like he believed it. "I don't know, I was giving off gay kid vibes before I could stand. Which doesn't help. I think men notice that kind of thing." He paused. "Thank you for coming."

"Thank you for taking me," I replied. "And for telling me that."

He put his arm around me, and I moved my head to his chest. We lay like that for a while. James and I slept in the same bed a lot, but we never cuddled except for that night. We fell asleep like lovers.

I woke up a few hours later, bra still on, my ribcage straining at the band. His eyes opened, and we looked at one another, conscious that we had woken up in a new world. He stroked my face, whispered my name, and softly kissed me on the mouth.

The kiss lasted ten seconds. Fifteen, tops. I don't remember how it stopped, or why, but we went back to sleep, untroubled as babies.

We've never talked about the kiss. I've thought about it, of course. Now that he was out, was kissing a woman the last taboo left? Was he saying goodbye to women, and to the notion of straightness altogether? Was it a strange way of saying thank you for coming with him to Fermoy? The most boring answer is probably the most true one: that he simply wanted to mark the last day where he lived with secrets.

AUGUST WAS A MONTH so wild that now we only refer to it as one thing: The Gaynaissance.

If you were a gay or bisexual man and you lived in Cork in August 2010, then trust me, my friend James fucked you.

Unsurprisingly, James's coming-out changed very little. Most people were very gracious about it, and just nodded and congratulated him. Others did not behave so well, and ended up on our shit list because of it.

There is a certain personality type that is addicted to the concept of its own intellect. They are the people who insist they saw the twist in the movie coming, who always thought that the divorced couple were unhappy, that the female celebrity seemed crazy. They are also the people who always knew you were gay, and they can't resist talking about it.

"I *knew* that," Ben said.

"Well, now it's official." James was unfussed.

"I *always* knew," Ben repeated, suggesting that he knew before James did.

"Checked the store cameras, did you?" James said smoothly, and Ben's smug face turned shocked.

"You haven't?" he said, his face white. "In the shop?"

"Oh sorry," James answered. "I thought you *knew*."

James was no longer contained to the few queer nights that the city had on offer. He was free range now, pressing bodies up against every smoking area in Cork, and taking some of them home. I slept in my own room much more, which wasn't quite the death sentence it used to be. Having a boyfriend had been a domesticating influence. I now had clean sheets, flowers in a jam jar, pictures on the wall. I felt I was doing very well, for twenty-one.

We never fought, officially, about the boys he brought home. They were mostly earnest and sweet, made polite chit-chat with me in the morning, asked me about my bookshelves. But there were a few, and one in particular, who radiated a certain distaste for me, and for women generally. They thought of James as Juliet, and me as his flustered loyal nurse, calling him in from the balcony.

They tried, sometimes, to bully me a little bit. Jokes about fag hags, and the stupid things straight girls did. Veiled comments about my size, about how it must be nice that James and I were able to share clothes.

James never really came to my defence, but he didn't entertain these comments either. He didn't need to. Invariably, Lady Gaga would come on the iPod speaker and the two of us would dissolve into our own world, leaving whoever was with us on the fringes. We sang "bedroom ants" instead of "bad romance," because it was summer and the whole house was riddled with them.

The poetry anthology that Deenie was putting together proved to be more work than she had expected, so I was over at the Harrington-Byrnes' a lot. The anthology was separate from her day job, and to do with her father's literary estate. It was the twentieth anniversary of his most famous collection, and she had commissioned "Ireland's most exciting poets" to write a poem in response to his work.

"Ireland's most exciting poets," she said, "who will accept two hundred quid."

It was a lot of busy work. Emailing agents, setting deadlines, chasing them, sending updates back to the publisher. She was glad to have me, and said so often.

"I don't think I would have ever accepted if I didn't have you," she said. "Organising poets is like herding cats."

She was grateful for me, bought pastries for my coming over, but didn't appear to have any inclination to pay me more. I felt awkward about it. Surely, the internship was now over? I looked up what a publishing assistant did, and I ticked every box. I managed correspondence. I forwarded invoices to accountants. I wrangled spreadsheets. I had taught myself all kinds of Microsoft Excel tricks to keep up with the various deadlines, and surely that was worth more than fifty a week.

It was the summer of un-aired grievances. I was too anxious to tell Carey about London, too frightened to ask Deenie for a pay rise. James wasn't the only one writing scripts. I wrote countless long ones in my head, all conversations that revealed me to be righteous and long suffering, and other people to be insensitive and cruel.

RACHEL

You sit here in your big house, with your lovely
husband, and your glass kitchen, but you don't
see what's in front of you! Me, the person who
walks here, because she can't afford to take the
bus every day!

DEENIE

(Appalled) Rachel . . . I had no idea. Please.
(Opens purse) Take my money.

I was terrified of appearing ungrateful, so instead I said nothing, and just became resentful. The first time she left me alone in her house I thought it was a magnanimous and very trusting gesture. She was meeting an author for lunch and didn't have any qualms about leaving me alone with her things.

She should have had qualms. I sat still for twenty minutes to make sure she was really gone, and then I went nosing around. First, I just wanted to examine things. To turn over the trinkets of her life, and wonder how one could own both a George Foreman grill and a handwoven Nepalese rug. It was a life I wanted for myself, and still the standard by which I judge my own aesthetic choices: *Would Deenie have this in her house?*

I found small, stupid ways to act out. I went into her bedroom to use her hand cream. I looked in her knicker drawers. I fed her cat Honey Nut Cheerios from my hand, even though he was very fat and supposed to be on a diet.

I was angry at her for not recognising that I was no longer a simple intern, but I know that wasn't everything. There was something spikier, crueller, underneath it. I was fond of Deenie Harrington, but in my head I had normalised that it was okay to do bad things to her. Relationships grow in the cradle they are born in. The cradle of me and Deenie would always be that she was the clueless wife of my best friend's lover. There was a slice of me that would always condescend to her, no matter how sweet or clever or kind she was.

I found ovulation strips in her bathroom. I used one, out of interest. I was not ovulating. I was on the pill. The tests were interesting regardless.

The next time I checked the bathroom cabinet, the ovulation strips were gone. Deenie had either noticed that I had used one or run out from using them so much herself. She talked, sometimes, about her friends who all had babies, but never said a word about starting a family herself.

"Do Fred Byrne and Deenie have sex?" I asked James that night.

He shrugged. "Must do. They *are* married."

"I thought maybe . . ."

"That they were two people in the nineteen fifties with 'an arrangement'? And they sleep in separate twin beds?"

"Well, yes, sort of. You never talked about it? Their sex life?"

"No," he said, eyes still on the TV. "Oddly enough, married men don't tend to want to talk about their wives."

It was the first conversation we'd had about Dr. Byrne in weeks, but the uttering of his name seemed to summon him to us. He rang James the following week, and asked him to go for coffee.

"Coffee?" I said. "In the . . . world? In public?"

"Coffee in the world," James replied, equally dazed.

When he came back, he flung himself onto my bed, delighted with himself.

"Oh my God, Rachel. He's *weak* for me."

"Did he say that?"

"Basically. He went on and on about how much he missed me, how special it was, what we had, and then he asked if I missed him."

"He asked if *you* missed *him*?" I was so bad at asking people direct questions that it amazed me when others managed it. "What did you say?"

"I said that I did, sometimes, but now that I was out, my life is all about looking forward, not back." He looked proud of this, and rightfully so. I was proud of him, too.

Of all the people we expected to take James's coming-out badly, we had never considered Dr. Byrne. He may have been closeted, but he was still a queer person, too. We thought he would be delighted. In the moment, he was. But it planted a seed of something bad in him, and the seed sprouted wildly over the next few weeks. Dr. Byrne started ringing up James constantly, first telling him how wonderful he was, then confessing that he was "really very worried" about James, and that he needed to "rein it in."

"He said that he didn't want me to become one of those kinds of gays who lives for the party," James said, baffled. "He was acting so prudey. I said he was trying to slut-shame me."

"He *is* trying to slut-shame you," I said. "Tell him to fuck off."

"He's just jealous. And lonely. He's in the closet alone, now."

He was so full of empathy for Dr. Byrne that it made me realise, at last, what went on between them that first day at the bookshop. All that casual chat about Canada and Fermoy and DVD players, the small talk that somehow became the defining passion of my friend's young life. I realised it was loneliness. They saw it in each other instantly. Both were charismatic, both were well liked, and yet both were litter mates of solitude.

———

The Gaynaissance brought a welcome, summer atmosphere to our boiling and ant-filled home. It was also prohibitively expensive.

There was a patch of grass behind the Shandon Bells that got good sun. We started drinking earlier, going out later, and ending the night in the cold, blue dawn, perched on the flat roof of our cottage, overlooking our dying city.

"It's just the two of us, at the end of the day, Rache," he said. "No one is going to look out for me the way you look out for me."

"You, too," I said limply, my chin in my knees. I thought of Carey, who adored me, but who couldn't make a plan more than a week in advance without looking agonised by circumstance. "Sometimes I feel like I was in a coma or something, before we met."

"I know exactly what you mean," he said, and I didn't know if he meant that he had recognised my coma, or that he had been in one himself. I leaned my head on his shoulder, and he rolled me a cigarette from the dregs of his packet of Amber Leaf. The leftover tobacco was so fine it was almost like tea leaves.

17

W E SAVED AND SPENT like crash dieters. Whenever we managed to put a few hundred euros aside, we would declare that we deserved a celebration. James would run to the off-licence and get us a *nice* bottle of wine. "Nice" meant Rioja or Pinot Grigio, which usually cost somewhere close to a tenner and felt more like Europe. We would drink it on the roof and talk about how it was much healthier to enjoy a decadent treat once a week or so than to thin one's insides with paint stripper every other night.

Sometime around ten we would go looking for paint stripper.

Someone would find a fiver from somewhere, a fiver that had not yet been counted as part of our savings because it was loose in a coat pocket. Another trip to the offy. At midnight, we would decide to go pint-stealing at The Bróg, an easy job because everyone had to leave their drinks on the cigarette machine if they wanted to go out for a smoke. Eventually we would get paranoid that the bouncer was onto us and bought some vodka lemonades. Doubles, to save money. We would wake up the next morning to find that we had somehow spent forty euro.

It was on one of these nights, in the middle of the Gaynaissance, that I ran into my own boyfriend.

We were on the dance floor when I felt Carey's arms around my waist, his rough blond stubble on my neck. He was out with his housemates, who were used to seeing me in his boxer shorts and vest, slobbing around their house and eating their cereal.

"What are you doing out, Rache?" he said. "I thought you were broke?"

"Oh, I am," I said, wrapping myself around him. I was wearing a small dress, and I wanted his housemates to see that I was not a cretin, but a very sexy girl. "I'm saving money."

"*How?*"

"Oh, the gentlemen callers, the gentlemen callers," I replied. James and I had these characters we sometimes played, two Southern belles who were desperate for money but equally desperate for glamour. "We always rely on the kindness of strangers."

I picked up my stolen pint of Bulmers and winked at him, which must have looked more like an asymmetrical blink, somewhere between Scarlett O'Hara and Blanche DuBois. Carey turned away from me and started talking to his friends.

I wavered on my feet, waiting to be looked at again. I couldn't see James anywhere, and Carey's back was to me. Why was his back to me?

I tapped him on the shoulder, my finger rigid. "I'll allow you to buy me a drink," I said, which was supposed to be funny, but only sounded petulant and spoiled.

Carey made an odd face, like he was moving his teeth around in a new order. "I don't know, Rachel," he said, and then went back to talking to his friends. I was mortified. The friends looked awkward and sorry for me. Was this it, then? Was Carey done with me again?

I did the only thing available to a woman in a situation like this. I stormed out.

The cold air hit me immediately, and I realised that the further and faster I walked from The Bróg, the less chance there was of Carey having a sudden change of heart and rushing out to find me. It was still half an hour until closing time, so the footpath was scattered with groups of girls who were either crying or getting sick.

I refused to be either. I sat on my own, freezing without a coat, and bummed a cigarette off a man walking past. I shivered, looked glassily ahead, and waited for him to come.

He did, of course. Built like a terrier and every bit as common.

"Rache," he said. "What are you doing out here? You'll freeze."

It strikes me now that no one in Cork ever worried about each other's safety. Just our body temperature.

"What do *you* care?" I said dismally. I was extremely drunk, but I was never much of a shrieker. My version of being a bad drunk was suddenly becoming surly and immovable. "You're breaking up with me anyway, aren't you?"

"I could say the same to you," he said, genuine fury in his voice. "What's all this about? You were the one who wanted to be all official. Now you're out here dressed like this, not telling me, not wanting to get pints with me during the week. Going on about gentlemen callers."

Every so often a feminist argument makes it into the public consciousness that even the most self-hating of young women will adopt. There was a lot of chat around then about slut-shaming, around men policing how women dressed, around what the term "asking for it" actually meant. We had identified Fred Byrne's slut-shaming tendencies not two weeks prior. The idea was in my mind, and so I seized on this fragment of what Carey was saying—*dressed like this*—and ignored the context of what he was actually talking about. What he was talking about was secrecy, and the possibility that I was cheating on him. What I had heard was a critique of my outfit.

"Fuck you, Carey?" I said, my voice low and serious. "I can dress how I want."

That set us off. Suddenly we were in the kind of fight where both people act like they're in a film, mugging for a camera that didn't exist. We kept saying strident, passionate and broadly untrue things. I accused him of being jealous, which he wasn't. He accused me of being uncaring, when that couldn't have been further from the truth. I cared so deeply about preserving the status quo with Carey that I was always hiding the facts of myself from him. Not just London, but the stuff with James, too: his relationship with Dr. Byrne, the afternoon trysts at our house, how I had got the job with Deenie. I was hiding so much from Carey that sometimes I wonder what on earth we actually talked about.

"You can do whatever you fancy, Rachel, but you don't have to make me feel like a fucking *idiot* when you do it." He exhaled heavily, like he was trying to control himself from slapping me. "The lads were saying to me all evening, why not get Rachel over, we'll all go out, she's hardly over here any more. And I'm like, ah, she's broke, she's saving money, she's worried about her job. Then we get out and you're already here, three sheets to the wind."

My rage started to melt away. I saw his point of view perfectly, but rather than empathise, I was stricken with this romantic idea of a Rachel that existed when I wasn't around. Mysterious, desired, unable to be kept on a leash. Capable of driving a man crazy.

"I mean," he carried on, "what? Do you just not want to be seen with me, is that the issue?"

A sober woman would have explained what was going on. A sober woman would have explained about London and saving money, would have owned up about her inability to say no to James and the effervescence of his Gaynaissance. A sober woman would have asked Carey if he wanted to move with her.

But I wasn't a sober woman. I wasn't even a woman. I was a girl, a drunk girl, in a tiny dress. And I was cold.

So I kissed him. I grabbed him, and trusted that the might of our physical connection would say all the things that I wasn't presently capable of putting into words. He pulled away at first, his mouth tight, his jaw set.

"Come home with me," I said, my finger on his collar. "Come home and we'll talk."

He came home. We didn't talk.

The curtains in my room were thin. The street lamp outside

shone a perpetual white shaft of light across the bed, one that narrowly escaped the pillows but cut a strip diagonally across the mattress. His skin looked lunar that night, like something the sky had given birth to.

"I love you," I said, my thumbs on the famous stomach. "I love you like I've never loved anyone."

"Rachel," he said, sounding a little sad, "you love everyone."

That wasn't true. But it must have seemed true, to him. I loved him, and I loved James, and because that was the only sample group that Carey was working from, he had no idea how indifferently I felt about the rest of the planet. Everyone else could go to hell.

"No," I said, starting to get upset. "You have to believe me, Carey. It's never been this way with anyone else."

I wanted this conversation to be as full of meaning and love as the roof chat between me and James, but that only worked if both people played ball.

"I have to go to Derry tomorrow," he said. "Mam is sick."

"What? Why didn't you say? What's wrong?"

"She's got to go into hospital for a few days. I need to look after Dad. He's a bit defenceless, you know. He'll be making tomato sandwiches for every meal."

"But you're coming back? Aren't you?"

"Yes. Yes, of course."

He fell asleep soon after that, and I watched him. Not the affectionate gaze of a lover, but the frantic, anxious stare of someone trying to bend spoons with their mind.

He was going again. He wouldn't come back. The fear of heartbreak was almost worse than the reality of it. I felt as though I had swallowed a wet bath mat.

The worry and the vodka doubled on me, and I crawled on my knees to the bathroom. I vomited until I was too tired to stay awake.

18

WAS FULLY PREPARED for Carey's second exodus to be the worst thing that would happen to me that summer. I was ready to simmer in it, to make a feast of my devastation. James mourned Dr. Byrne at the start of the summer; now I would grieve Carey again at the close of it.

And then Ben fired me.

"It's not that you're a bad worker," he said sadly, although I was. "I hate to do this. It's just, I have to think of everyone here."

"Are you firing James?"

"No."

"What?" I screeched, all loyalty temporarily thrown out the window. "He's worse than me."

"I know. But, you know, you've got a degree, Rachel. You can get office work."

I couldn't believe it. Since when did Ben care about us, or anything other than the phantom "industry" he liked thinking he was a part of?

"I don't know if I can, Ben," I said. I sat, dejected, in his office chair, taking in every cracked ceiling tile. I had been working at the bookshop for three and a half years. Was this really the last time I'd see inside the back office, where I had bitterly counted out the morning float so many times before?

I couldn't look at him. He felt too sorry for me. I just looked past him, at the printer with the sign above it that said, WORK USE ONLY, JAMES.

"What's my redundancy pay?" I finally asked.

"Well, you've got ten days' holiday you haven't taken."

"That's it?"

"I'm afraid so."

"Fucking hell, Ben. Is that even legal?"

He blinked. "I'm afraid so," he said again.

I glared at him. It wasn't his fault. He didn't own the shop, after all. But the owner lived in Tipperary and we never saw him, so he might as well have.

"I think you're full of shit," I said.

"You can work out the rest of the day. Say goodbye to everyone, and all that."

"Am I getting paid anyway?"

"Yes."

"Well, then I think I'll fuck off. I think that will be best for everyone, won't it?"

I left quickly, my shoulder bag slapping furiously off my bare thigh, rage coming off me in a deep sweat. I regret it now. In the years since there have been many studies done on the nomadic work life of millennials, and sometimes I feel like my adulthood has just been a case study for a *Guardian Weekend* article. I have never been employed at a website, a magazine or a newspaper for longer than two years. After that I am usually made redundant, or the website goes bust. Now, on the cusp of maternity leave and still undecided about whether I'll return to the office full time, I'm starting to wonder whether I'll ever be a true member of anyone's staff ever again.

What if I had known, then, that O'Connor Books would be the longest I would ever work somewhere?

I called Carey as I walked down the street, his voice already more Northern, the good salt water of home buffeting away at him.

"Aye, Jesus, Rache, that's awful. What are you going to do?"

"I don't *know*."

"What do you *want* to do?"

"I want to see you," I said, feeling the tears rising in me. "Can I come see you?"

"With what money?" he said. "It'd cost you a bomb to get up here. And do you really want to spend the week with my eighty-year-old dad?"

It struck me as perverse that anyone I was sleeping with could have a dad that old. But his dad had started late, and Carey was the baby. We chatted for a while. His mum still needed more tests. She was being kept in another week. My phone beeped, thirsty for more credit.

"Just don't vanish again," I said, and I was unable to keep the hard-bitten plea out of my voice. "Keep your phone charged, okay? I love you."

And it cut out before he could say it back.

———

I walked all the way to the Harrington-Byrnes'. It was a Saturday, and they were both home. It never occurred to me what they might do when they were both at home together, but here was the answer: lunch.

Deenie answered the door. She was wearing a silky teal dress. She had the kind of white, pearlescent skin that worked beautifully with the colour palette of the early 2010s: emerald, raspberry, teal, sapphire. Colours that made her look like a little jewel and made me, with my dark blonde hair and invisibly fair eyebrows, look like mother of the bride.

"Rachel! What are you doing here? Oh, God, is something wrong?"

Deenie's cat, whose name I've just remembered—Jupiter!—came

out to the doorstep and curled himself around my legs, bumping his head off my calves.

"I've been *fired*," I erupted.

"From the bookshop?"

I nodded, and Jupiter started batting at a loose string dangling off the hem of my skirt.

"Oh, God, I'm so sorry. Come in, come in, come in."

In my head, I had come to the Harrington-Byrnes' to demand a raise from Deenie. In my heart, I went because I felt they were the only people I could fall on. Carey was away; James still had a job, and would feel guilty; my parents would worry and suggest I moved home.

And besides, I wasn't really close with my parents, at that time. Deenie and Dr. Byrne had replaced them, as the influential adults in my life. The parallels weren't perfect, but they were close. Deenie and my mother were delicate and loving, and diminutive enough in character that they allowed me to be self-obsessed. Like my father, Dr. Byrne was often remote, but would occasionally talk straight to me and reveal the truth of the brutal world. Plus, they were both doctors, but not the kind of doctor you want in an emergency.

The kitchen was warm from the reflecting sunlight, and there was a kind of high tea on the table. A little quiche the size of a fist. A plate of flaky custard tarts. Two sandwiches, one prosciutto and brie, one red pepper and goat cheese, each cut to be finger-sized. They had obviously been to the English Market that morning. Everything had a rough dusting of yellow semolina flour, and was slightly battered from brown bags.

"Sit down, Rachel, sit down. Have a glass of wine."

Dr. Byrne poured me a cold glass of Sauvignon Blanc that I recognised from his spring visits to Shandon Street. I gulped it down deeply, like a marathon runner reaching for water.

"I've been *fired*," I repeated, in case Dr. Byrne hadn't heard me screeching in the doorway. "I don't have a job."

The sentence hung there, a ball waiting to be caught. I wanted Deenie to tell me that I did have a job, I was her assistant, and she was going to start paying me three hundred a week tout suite. Or, she was going to introduce me to everyone at her publishing house, and get me an interview for a salaried job. She would repeat to her colleagues what she had often said to me: that I was indispensable, that I was a lifesaver, that she wouldn't be doing the poetry anthology for her father's estate if I wasn't helping her.

The ball dropped. No one suggested anything.

"You poor thing," Deenie said soothingly, instead. She smoothed her hand over my back. "God, it's so hard, isn't it?"

"Dreadful stuff," said Dr. Byrne, shaking his head. "And not a great sign for books."

"No," she responded sadly. "Not good for books at all."

A seed of rage sprouted in me. I had just lost my job, had been criminally underpaid by the Harrington-Byrnes for months, and here I was, a case study for the industry as a whole. I finished my wine, and then poured myself another.

"Publishing is a mess," Deenie said. "And everyone's still freaking out about the Kindle."

He touched her hand. "Now, every study says that people who buy e-books are still buying physical books, too."

He said this like he had said it a lot. Like it was a bedtime story he sometimes tucked her in with.

"Can I use your bathroom?" I asked, not waiting for an answer, just getting up and marching to the loo.

On reflection, I can see that Deenie and Dr. Byrne weren't trying to make my firing about them. What they were trying to do was send an adult signal to someone who didn't yet have the language to translate it. When Deenie said "publishing is a mess," what she meant was: *I would love to help you out here, Rachel, but the truth is I'm hardly holding on to a job myself.*

But I didn't have that hindsight yet. All I had was their bathroom, my rage, and the faint smudges of toothpaste on the mirrored cabinet over the sink.

I opened it. Deenie kept all her cosmetics in her bedroom, but she had some goodies in here, too. There were a few tiny perfume samples and a tube of something from L'Occitane. The ovulation strips were back. I stuffed some things in my handbag, not caring if she noticed or not.

I felt a rippling calm go through me. I didn't have to leave, or sit through their gracious hospitality while hating them. I could drink another glass of wine and feel easy about the fact that we had all wronged each other.

I went back out, and the Harrington-Byrnes were both louder, more fun, slightly less parental.

"Listen, Miss Murray," Dr. Byrne said, taking out a bottle of gin while his wife sliced cucumbers. "Sometimes, in life, people get fired."

"It's troubling," Deenie said. "And it sucks. But things always work out."

Dr. Byrne spun around, always nimble despite his bulky frame. He pulled a plastic bag of ice from the freezer, smashed it off the tile floor, and gathered lumps of it into his big hands. "And in the meantime," he sang, "there's booze."

He slammed the ice into tumblers, then covered them with gin.

Deenie moved from the cucumbers to the vinyl player. She reset the needle, and "Bad Moon Rising" by Creedence Clearwater Revival began to play.

I set my bag down, making sure the flap was closed. Fred Byrne handed me my gin. I banged it back, the big cubes of ice tickling the tip of my nose, bitter quinine coating my tongue.

I think they felt guilty that they couldn't help me in the way that I wanted to be helped. But we would get through it the way Irish people traditionally get through things. By getting shit-faced.

Any nervousness I should have felt about getting drunk with my employer and my ex-professor evaporated. The Harrington-Byrnes threw themselves into what must have been a frequent role for them: the charming, childless couple whose lack must be covered to prevent anyone from feeling sorry for them.

Dr. Byrne told stories about the head-cases who ran the English department, stories he could comfortably tell me now that life was over for me at UCC. The professor who wore women's used tights under his trousers. The Ph.D. student who wouldn't stop sending love letters to his supervisor, a married woman in her sixties. The *very* famous author who graduated UCC in 2003, but told the papers he went to Trinity. We laughed, got drunker and drunker, and every so often I found myself shooting glances at Dr. Byrne: *And the English professor who is still obsessed with his twenty-two-year-old ex-boyfriend.*

Deenie, for all her softness, was also capable of a good story. They came via her late father, who had rubbed shoulders with the likes of Patrick Kavanagh and John Berger.

"Kavanagh was just an old piss head, apparently," she giggled. "He used to go around eating baking soda from the packet."

I had my stories, of course. Stories of young passion and squalor that people in their thirties find so refreshing to hear about. Entertaining reminders that there is nothing much about youth to miss.

It was a beautifully hot day, and we moved out to the garden, drinking and squawking at each other.

"What's happening with your boyfriend?" Deenie asked. "Casey?"

"*Carey*," I stressed, mournfully. "Carey get out your cane." I took another gulp of my gin. "Carey, I'm *getting* caned."

"I don't like him for you, Rachel," Fred Byrne said. "You deserve better than an invisible man."

"What do you know about it?" Deenie asked, mystified.

A dart of panic. Dr. Byrne had forgotten that he wasn't supposed to know me very well at all, only as a student, only as a bookshop worker.

"Oh, God, I was always sitting in Dr. Byrne's office," I laughed, trying to smooth things, "telling him my tales of woe."

"Were you?" Deenie said. She wasn't uncomfortable exactly, but she was struggling to square the circle. "You were never like that back in my day, Fred. No patience for student woes."

"I've softened in my old age," Dr. Byrne said, a song in his voice.

Deenie closed her eyes to the sun. "I need suncream. I'm starting to burn, I think."

"I'll get it for you." Dr. Byrne jogged into the house, anxiety sticking to his footprints.

There was a brief silence between Deenie and me, but it felt cosy enough. We had spent so long being silent together, during our long afternoons at her kitchen table.

"Dad was a professor, too, you know," she said. "For a few years."

"Oh yeah? In Cork?"

"No. Dublin. UCD."

"But you grew up here?"

"Mmm," she said, the sunlight dancing on her eyelids. "He would live up there during term time."

"That must have been hard."

"Mmm," she said again. "I didn't notice, really. I was a teenager. But I think Mum felt it most of all. Lonely, you know. No idea what he was doing, what he was up to."

"Yes," I said, feeling uneasy about this line of conversation. "Yes, that must have been hard."

"She always said, 'Men must be allowed to have their private lives, Aideen.'" Deenie laughed softly at the memory. "I always wondered if she thought women were allowed to have private lives, too."

James rang me. He was on lunch break from his shift, which had started an hour after mine, and had been told the news about my firing.

"Rache, are you all right? Where are you? Why didn't you call?"

"I'm fine," I said breezily, stretching out the vowel sounds. "I'm at the Harrington-Byrnes'."

"What? *Why?*"

"To get drunk."

"What? With Fred?"

I wasn't sure how much of his side Deenie could hear. Her eyes were still closed.

"Rachel, you're being annoyingly elusive," James barked. "What's going *on?*"

"I'm fine! Let's talk later!" I hung up before he had time to argue.

Dr. Byrne was jogging back across the lawn with the SPF. Deenie opened her eyes.

"My housemate," I said. "Checking to see if I was okay."

"You call us the Harrington-Byrnes?" Deenie asked, sounding amused. She smeared the cream on her freckled arms. "*Why?*"

"What does your housemate do?" Fred asked. Too upbeat, too curious, too clearly for show.

"He works in the bookshop," I said, resenting the theatre of this. "How did you guys get together, anyway?"

It was an important life lesson to learn, and I've used it a lot since: if you're looking to distract a couple, just ask them how they met.

She had been his student, of course. That much I already knew. He was slightly young for a professor; she was slightly old to be doing a master's. They bonded over Thackeray. Their love affair had the thrill of being somewhat controversial but not exactly scandalous. It was a story littered with "somewhats" and "slightlys."

The evening grew cold, and we went back inside. That should have been the cue for me to go home, but I was too drunk to think about it. We danced on the kitchen tiles as it got dark, and I said a lot of things. About my parents, my brothers, and eventually, about Carey. I wept on top of Deenie, slouched on her arm while we sat on the squashy green couch.

"I just feel like I want to staple him to the ground, you know?

Like, nail his shoes down," I said, tears slipping off my chin and onto her. "I feel like we could really do love properly, if he let me."

I don't know why I was so upset. Carey and I were, technically, still together. But he couldn't be relied on, and I needed so badly to have one thing I could rely on. The uncertainty overwhelmed me.

"Oh, baby." She stroked my hair. "Men are awful. It's a cliché, but it's true. I'm sorry."

"He's not even awful. He's very nice."

"What's he like, exactly? You've never said."

"He's very kind," I explained, wiping my nose with my hand. "And very weird. Can I call him?"

"Off our phone?"

"Mine is out of credit."

"Sure."

I lay back on the green couch as she passed me the portable house phone. I rang Carey's mobile and he picked up, suspicious of the ROI number. He softened when he heard it was me, and sounded glad that I was drunk and being taken care of.

"I know you think I'm too young," I said. "But I think we could make a real go of love."

"Yeah," he said grimly. "Yeah, I know."

"What's wrong?"

"My mother has cancer."

"*What?*" I spluttered. "I thought she was having *tests?*"

"She was. Tests for cancer. She has cancer. Pancreas."

"Oh, Care. I'm so sorry. Are you all right?"

"I'm . . . I don't know. Dad is in bits."

"Of course, of course."

"The girls are all coming home tomorrow. But they all have families, Rache. Babies of their own. I'm the only one . . ." He trailed off. I remembered our conversation, back in the bread shop. James Carey was a dosser, a born dosser. His attempts at adult life had played out like Peter Pan trying to trap his shadow. In that one unfinished sentence, he was coming to the realisation that some people create their own adulthood, and some people have it thrust upon them. He, it turned out, would be the latter kind of person.

"I need to look after things here, Rachel. I . . . I don't know what I can say to you, really."

"I understand," I squeaked, the tears falling again.

"I *do* love you," he said. "And maybe, when things settle down, you could come up for a bit. Or I'll meet you in Dublin. But . . ."

"I get it," I said. "You need to be there for your family. For your mum."

"Yes." He sighed. "I don't know if I'll be much use."

"You will be. Can I call you, still?"

"Rachel, I'll go mad if you don't call me. Just once a week, with the news or something. Please. Please don't drop off."

I couldn't believe this reversal. Suddenly he was the one who wanted to nail my shoes to the ground.

"Of course," I said.

He sounded like he was going to cry. "I have to go now."

"You don't have to."

"I need to."

Deenie had gone to the kitchen, to give me privacy. There was a new record on, a jazz singer, Dinah Washington or someone like that. Deenie was in her bare feet, five foot nothing, and dancing with her husband. Looking so small that for once, I wasn't even jealous. She looked like she could smash to pieces.

I left at around one in the morning, my bag full of stolen goods. I remember thinking that, whatever happened next with Carey or with my employment situation, it wouldn't be so bad if I could have this little corner of adult fabulousness, this friendship with the Harrington-Byrnes.

When something good happens to you at that age, you can't settle with the notion that it's a one-off. You want it to be the beginning of a tradition. That's how I felt about that night: I wanted it already to be a memory, a foundational one, a first evening of many similar evenings. I wanted future nostalgia, a rear-view, years-old fondness for something that had literally just happened.

That was over ten years ago, which makes it a genuine memory, and not the pretend one I fantasised about in the cab ride home. The problem with genuine memories is that you know too much. It ruins everything. I can love that night for what it was, but I also know this: that I would only step inside that house two more times, and by winter I would never see Deenie Harrington again.

19

A CALL CENTRE had opened up in Monkstown, near where I grew up, and one of my father's contacts got me a job there. By that point, I was in no position to draw arbitrary lines between town work and any other kind. They were offering me thirteen euros an hour to call charity donors and convince them to increase their monthly donations. "One week you could be working with Irish Guide Dogs," my new manager told me, "and the next it could be cleft palate."

This was sold to me as being a perk of the job. "Variation," I was told. "You'll never be bored. There's always plenty to learn, if you want to learn it."

The call centre was a large prefab the size of the auditorium of my secondary school. It smelled new and cheap. There were two vending machines, one for snacks and one for energy drinks. The snacks machine cost money but the drink machine was free. On my first day I was shown around by a girl my own age who was already a manager, having started work there in May. It was now nearing the end of August.

"What's nice is that it's really flexible," she said. "Like, no one is going to call you into the office if you're not at your desk by ten past nine, or whatever. Just meet your targets and you can do what you want."

She looked like the girls I went to school with. Golden, highlighted and virtually eyebrow-less, dressed in baby blues and light pinks. She was probably very nice, but I felt myself resisting her. I had spent so much of the last year in a different world, one of gigs and septum piercings and page proofs, and I resented being pulled back into the world of girls I never truly liked.

I was shown to my new desk. There was a phone, a computer, and it had privacy partitions on each side. There was a stapled two-pager waiting on my chair, which I presumed would be an introduction to the company but was actually a script about blood cancer research.

"There's great opportunity for advancement," she said. "I'm on sixteen an hour, now."

"Six*teen*?"

"Well, I don't just do phones. I'm management."

"Sure, of course."

"The important thing is to just keep people on the phone. If they've talked to you long enough, they'll feel guilty. Ask them about their pets, their grandkids. Eventually they'll agree to donate."

"Right."

"But don't spend too long on, either. Some old grannies will chew your ear off. You have targets."

"Right."

As soon as I was on the phone, I felt myself becoming righteously angry with James. I was so obviously wrong for this job, and he was so obviously right for it. Who was better at convincing people than James? Meanwhile, he was continuing to work at O'Connor Books, despite the fact—and this last came in the bitchiest voice of all—that he didn't even read real books. Just screenwriting manuals.

I called Carey on my lunch break. There was nowhere to eat your lunch, so I found a bit of grass next to a road and leaned on a fence there.

"Is it awful?"

"Dreadful. No one wants to talk to me."

"I want to talk to you."

"Can you pay me thirteen quid an hour? Anyway. How's home?"

"Mam's in the hospital for the time being, and Dad's hip is bad again, so I'm driving him to physio every other day. Only, he won't do the stretches or anything, so I have to do them with him."

I had wished for Carey to be stapled to the ground, and now he was nailed there good and fast. His life was steeped in chemo appointments, pick-ups, drop-offs, nieces, nephews, getting lunch on, getting dinner on, managing his sisters' in-fighting, his mother's depressions, his father's stubborn refusal to move his leg clockwise and anti-clockwise in repeated, circular movements. My longing for Carey to become dependable had sprouted into him becoming absolutely reliable to everyone in the city of Derry, which was approximately three hundred miles away.

"You're an amazing son," I said to him. "And brother. And uncle." I was about to add "and boyfriend," but we were consciously avoiding titles. We knew we loved each other, but we didn't know what to do with it, given the current circumstances, or what it meant. Neither of us knew how long this would go on for, and neither wanted to hold the other down.

"I'm not, really," he replied. "Just paying back debts."

Monkstown is closer to Douglas than the city centre is, so on the nights I was too tired from cold-calling, I would get off the bus early and go back to my family home, where it was dull and warm and full of food. I was hungry all the time now, taking my mother's shepherd's pie from the oven and eating it in bed with my laptop. Chris was almost never in. We had an unspoken agreement to not talk about the night he fell over my garden wall, although he still wore the jeans with the hole Carey cut in them. I saw a little bit of Kevin, who had yet to hit the growth spurt that Chris and I had at his age. He was slender and small and quiet, and Dad seemed constantly annoyed at him. Dad and I, on the other hand, had found a strange new equilibrium. We were both incredibly sad, and we didn't want to be convinced out of that sadness, and so we sat together and silently watched films.

James rang me during one of me and Dad's maudlin movie nights, fretting about when I was coming home.

"Where *are* you?" he whined on the phone. "This is the second night in a row you've been at your parents'."

"It's just easier. I'm so tired."

"You're always *tired* now," he said grumpily. "I'm the one on my feet all day."

I felt my eyes droop as we spoke. "It's different on the phone. It's tiring in a different way. It's tiring on the *soul*."

My dad nodded on the couch next to me, as if he agreed. He was soul-tired, too.

I finished one Friday at six o'clock, having somehow completed my impossible targets for the week, and found myself excited for the weekend in a way I hadn't been in years. I left the office saying, "Thank *God* it's *Friday*," with an enthusiasm that felt so oddly overblown that it was camp. I caught myself: Who actually says that in *real life*? I got the bus to Shandon Street, clutching to the golden orb of the weekend, choking on the joy that I wouldn't have to be back in Monkstown until noon on Monday.

I opened the front door and heard bodies. My first thought was that we were being robbed. I heard a falling against the table, the sound of something being shoved.

I didn't know whether I had the energy for a robbery. *What if I just turn around and leave?*

"Rachel?" I heard James say. "Is that you?"

"Who else would it be?" I called.

"Give us a second."

It was unusual for James to have a guest so early in the evening, but also fair enough. He probably wasn't expecting me home for a few hours.

"Okay," he said. "You can come in."

James was scarlet in the face, still doing his belt buckle up. A plume of cigarette smoke came from the back kitchen door.

"How'ya, Rachel," said Dr. Byrne.

"Hi . . . Dr. Byrne."

I turned to James, aghast. "Were you guys just fucking on the table?"

James rubbed his chin. "Yes."

"How long has this been going on again?"

"Um. A few weeks?"

Dr. Byrne came in from the yard, red-faced and smelling of smoke. I was too tired to put up with this shit any more. Too tired, too hungry, too sad.

"She's going to find out eventually," I snapped. "Why the fuck do you do this? Why can't you just have respect for your wife, who loves you?"

"I love her," he replied.

"And you think this is good enough?"

"Why are you so *annoyed*?" James asked. "You were fine with all this when it was getting you jobs."

"Jobs!" I screeched. "*Jobs! I had an internship!* And I worked my ass off at it. For very few results."

"Rachel . . ." Fred Byrne put his big hand on my shoulder.

"I was in your house *less than three weeks ago*. I saw you dance with Deenie in the kitchen. I'm her friend, now. And I care about her. It's not fair."

"No," he reasoned. He sat down on the couch. "It's not."

A wave of sleepiness came over me again. He looked so comfortable, sitting on our couch. I sat next to him. "Sorry," I said, though I wasn't sure if I was sorry, just not in the mood for a confrontation, despite having started one. "I'm just tired."

Dr. Byrne and I looked at each other. It was impossible to believe that he had once been my mysterious and beloved professor. Equally strange to think that he was the benevolent god who plied me with gin when I got fired. I felt now like we were two sad clowns in a nursery painting.

"Well, you two are gas craic," James said witheringly. "Shall we open a bottle of wine, or something?"

He rummaged in the kitchen.

"You're trying for a baby together, aren't you?" I said to Fred Byrne. "You and Deenie. Why, when you're trying to start a . . ."

He rubbed at his temples.

"What are you *doing*?" I said it like it was my only chance to find out how, exactly, the grown-up world worked.

"Rachel," James snapped from the kitchen doorway, "that's not your business."

"It is, I think, when I have to—"

Dr. Byrne put his hand up. "She's right, James. Rachel is part of this, in her own way, and it's not fair.

"Me and Deenie . . . we've been trying for a few years. It's never worked. She wants one, very badly, but it doesn't work."

"What? Sex? Can you not . . . ?"

He looked offended. "No, of course we have sex, Rachel, Jesus. She's gorgeous. I'm very attracted to her. I love men and women. It's fine. I've always been quite ambidextrous."

"Just *say* bisexual," James said, rolling his eyes. It sounded as if they'd had this discussion before. "Like a *normal* person."

Dr. Byrne pulled a face. "But I . . . never thought of men as . . . as *viable* for a relationship. You'll find that very old fashioned I'm sure, but you know, I'm almost forty."

I've noticed, in the years since, that queer men of a certain vintage sometimes do this. They state their age, and they wait. They let you do the math. They look at you with an expression that says: *I was born in 1972. I was a teenager in the eighties. Think about the things I've seen, the news stories I was terrorised with, the deadly body I was told that I might become.* I later wondered whether Dr. Byrne's famine obsession wasn't just about being thin, but about AIDS, and the freedom to think about wasting.

"I never saw any men for the first years of our relationship. I swear. That was all over for me. A young thing, you know. I loved her. Love her."

James sat down on the armrest, his face softer now. He kissed Dr. Byrne on the top of the head, then passed him his cigarette. It was amazing to me, how tender he could be despite the sentiment: the idea that men were a youthful treat, but not for real loving.

"But the more . . . the more the baby thing didn't work, the more we tried, the more I felt like I was . . . disappointing her, I suppose, the more I needed . . . It's hard to explain. Sex with her, sex with women, became a bit . . ."

"Heavy," James finished.

"Yes," Fred Byrne agreed. "Heavy."

I looked at James. I couldn't believe how little I had heard of all this, and how much James knew but hadn't shared.

"James wasn't my first slip," Dr. Byrne said carefully. "But he was—is—my first lover."

"Oh, God," James said. "Just say *boyfriend*, like a normal person."

"So when you ask me what I'm doing, Rachel, the answer is . . ." He looked at his hands. "I don't know. I know that I've been miserable for months. That I love my wife. But I also . . ."

He took James's hand.

"I love this young man, here."

For once, James had nothing to say. His eyes looked enormous. "Christ," he said at last. "I didn't think you'd ever say it in front of . . . well, anyone."

"Should I leave?" I said, feeling uncomfortable.

I was once again the third wheel in an evening that hinged on Dr. Byrne. It was like the night at their house, but in a parallel universe where the budget was much lower. We drank all the English Market wine and then went to the off-licence for beer and Monster Munch. We talked and smoked a lot, even though there was a dull, snapping tiredness under everything I did. I started to fantasise about bed, and eventually I went there.

Hours later, James climbed in next to me, his cold feet zapping me awake.

"*Fuck,*" I squealed. "What are you doing? Have you been outside? *Why are you so cold?*"

He snuggled down, the duvet up to his nose. "Fred just left. I walked him out. How did we seem?"

"He just left? What time is it?"

"Two," he said. "So? How did we seem? Compared to them?"

I was awake now, and resentful of it. "I don't know. He obviously adores you."

"It feels really different now, Rachel," he said, excited. "He used to be so withholding. But now he wants to talk about things. About how he feels about me."

I put my head under the covers. "He's not going to leave her."

"You never know. Maybe after we move to London, he'll miss me so much that he'll want to start a new life."

"You're insane."

"It could happen! He's got nothing tying him down. No kids."

"You're forgetting that he loves her," I said. "And that she's very nice."

"Oh, what do you know?"

But things did change, after that. Dr. Byrne finally understood that James could not live on wine and fancy cheese alone, and periodically we would get a knock on the door from the Tesco delivery man.

"Rache," James hollered up the stairs, "Fred has done us a BIG SHOP!"

The big shop was an embarrassment of riches. Tinned beans, peas and spaghetti hoops. Bacon. Chicken breasts. Brown bread, packets of smoked salmon. Real coffee. Receipts were always in the delivery, and he never spent less than 150 euro. I thought of these as not just deliveries for James, but for us, for the household. He would sometimes tell me that I looked tired, or too skinny, and I would roll my eyes and say I was fatter than ever.

At last, putting away money was possible. I was making more money, but I was too exhausted to spend any of it. James was focusing his faith on Dr. Byrne, so wasn't going out as much either. Our saving got so good that we opened up a joint account. We each had a card for it, and would sometimes walk to the ATM together to see how much was in there. Before my call centre job, our savings never got above 200 euro. Now we were almost triple that. A January emigration seemed feasible.

In our fantasy, it went like this: in January, we would move to London. James would get an agent immediately, and I would get a job at Penguin Books. We would spend three to six months being wild and discovering the city, and then Carey's mother would die, and Dr. Byrne would leave Deenie. They would both move to London, and we would live in a fabulously modern house, all of us artistes and writers (Carey would discover a great talent, we decided), and when we died our biographers would talk about us like we were a great collective of twenty-first-century geniuses. Our letters would be anthologised, just as soon as we got around to writing one another letters.

It was a nice fantasy, and perhaps it might have happened—a little of it, anyway—if I hadn't been pregnant.

20

DIDN'T SEE DEENIE for a while after getting my new job, and so when she called me one Thursday in early October I left my desk immediately, walking out into the car park to speak to her.

"Rachel," she said, her voice sounding cheerful, and like she had missed me. "How are you? Listen, I'm having a dinner next Friday for dad's book. The fifteenth. Will you come?"

"Seriously?" I asked. "You want me there?"

"Of course," she cried. "You worked hard on this. You're part of the team."

I didn't know I was pregnant yet. My seven-day pill breaks were decorated by brown spotting and nothing else. I thought that was fine.

Truthfully, I thought if anything was wrong with me it was that I was depressed. I even looked it up a few times online. I was tired, sluggish, snappy. I hated my new job, hated phoning people up to guilt them into charitable donations when many of them were on the verge of poverty themselves. I heard this a lot. The businessman suicides started up again, and I ended up talking to quite a few middle-aged women whose healthy husbands had suddenly died. This all struck me as good reasons to be depressed.

"I'd love to," I said. "And I can't wait to read the book!"

"Why don't you come round on Saturday? As in, the day after

tomorrow. I have a big box of advance copies. I'll give you one, and we can have a glass of something."

It sounded like heaven. I agreed immediately.

I came to the house on Saturday to find a journalist from *The Irish Times* talking to Deenie and a photographer snapping away at her next to a stack of her father's old editions. Being the young, photogenic daughter of the dead poet, the PR people had put her forward for all kinds of interviews in the Irish press.

She was sunny for the hour they were there, but as soon as *The Irish Times* left, she went to the bathroom to wash her face.

"So sorry about that. I totally forgot they were coming. This isn't really my scene at all," she said grimly. "But I suppose it has to be done."

I thought she was being falsely modest. "Oh, come on. Getting your photo in the paper, hair and make-up."

She gave me a look. "Christ, don't remind me. Seriously, I wish I didn't have to, but we're really hoping this makes a bit of money. Dad's poetry brings in fuck all. I honestly have no idea what Mum is going to do. The cash won't last another five years. Never marry a poet, Rachel."

I couldn't tell how much of it was an exaggeration. In my head, Deenie was rich. She was in her thirties and she had nice clothes and a nice house. Surely if her mother was broke, Deenie wouldn't live so well. I didn't understand, then, that having extra at the end of the month to spend on pastries and wine is not the same as having a mother who can retire. One was a matter of hundreds, and the other was thousands.

"How's Carey?" she asked.

"Oh . . . I don't know," I replied, not wanting to talk about it. "If I'm honest, I think it's over for good. Our lives are just in very different places."

"That's awful," she said, and she sounded genuinely sympathetic. "I know you were mad about him. Are you okay? You look a bit . . . is heartbroken too presumptuous?"

"It's not *not* accurate."

There was a box of books on the kitchen table. *Little Fire: A Response to the Poetry of Alistair Harrington.*

(Years later, when *Little Fires Everywhere* came out, I wondered whether the sales of the poetry anthology went up. I checked Amazon; it is no longer in print.)

The book was beautifully made, olive green with reflective red foil flames. It was classy. Something you'd buy as a gift. There was a foreword written by Deenie, a dedication to her mother, and then thirty or so poems.

"It's gorgeous," I said admiringly.

"Look in the acknowledgements."

There was effusive praise to the poets, the people who managed the estate, the publishing house, the Harrington family. And then, a few lines from the end:

To Rachel Murray, who helped police the vibe.

I smiled at her. "Thank you. I *did* police the vibe, didn't I?"

She nodded. "You're going to have a huge career in publishing, babe. I can tell."

The final line of the acknowledgements was apart from all the others.

To Fred, the Bill to my Grover: thank you. For everything.

"Who are Bill and Grover?"

"Oh, God." Deenie looked embarrassed. "Bill Withers and Grover Washington?"

"Okay."

"It's a silly thing. They sang 'Just the Two of Us' together. It's a bit of a lame private joke."

My heart thudded and my armpits began to sweat. Fred Byrne's stricken face came back to me, his soft voice telling me that he was always disappointing his wife. The psychological heaviness of sex with her that followed their many pregnancy attempts.

I became extremely nauseous, a symptom of both my nerves and the fact that I was—unbeknownst to myself—eight weeks pregnant. I sat down on her kitchen chair.

"Can I have a glass of water, please?"

"Sure." She looked worried, and fetched a jug of filtered water from the fridge. She put a heavy-bottomed glass in front of me. It felt expensive. "Is something else wrong, Rachel?"

I took a long glug of water. "I'm just not feeling so well lately. Ever since the new job."

"Is it that bad?"

"It's a call centre," I said. "I need to find a way out."

"I really wish there was something I could do for you, but absolutely nowhere is hiring. I heard my company is taking on unpaid interns who actually have master's degrees. It's a terrible time to start a career."

Deenie said this like I had chosen 2010 to start looking for a job, against all better business advice from my accountants.

"What about . . . other editors like you? Slush pile reading?"

"I don't know. No one likes to admit they need help, and it's not . . . it's not a very well-paid industry as it is. I don't think people can afford to employ someone in the way I did for you."

I smarted at this, this note of charity in her voice. *The way I did for you.* Deenie had underpaid me hugely. Exploited me, really.

"Maybe at the dinner next week you could make a few contacts. Get your face seen. It will be a lot of publishing people."

"How's Fred?" I asked, feeling vomity already, and even more so at the thought of pecking away at Deenie's contacts like a crow over a dead body.

"Oh, fine." She furrowed her brow briefly. "I don't know. He's a bit international man of mystery sometimes. I think he's a bit disappointed about *Kensington*. There was a piece in the paper about Dad's book and . . . Oh, I don't know."

"What did it say?"

"Oh"—she waved her hand—"about how I'm the daughter of a poet and I married an author."

"Okay?"

"And, well"—she rolled her eyes, to let me know that the article was definitely full of shit—"the kind of author Fred is. It was some nothingy aside about him being . . . ah. Middlebrow, I think was the word."

She looked at me, slightly desperate, hoping for a contradiction.

"That's bollocks," I said dutifully.

Even through my nausea, it was curious that James had never brought this up. Maybe he didn't even know. Was Dr. Byrne really so in love with James, or was he just a balm for his ego? Did having a young lover and the hatred of the press make him feel like Oscar Wilde, or something?

"The sales have been a bit . . . well, book sales overall have been down. As you know."

Another wave of sickness passed over me. I felt like I had been riding in a too-hot car for too long, over bumpy concrete and twisting roads. "Can you open the window or something?" I said, putting my hands over my eyes. "Sorry, this is embarrassing. I just feel . . ."

Deenie opened the sliding door of the kitchen. The air was dead and didn't offer much relief.

"I think I'm going to be sick," I said at last, and the words were a surprise to me. I was not a vomiting person. I was a headaches and diarrhoea sort of person. The last time I had vomited was the night before Carey left, and the time before that was at a birthday party when I was twelve.

I went into the bathroom and kneeled in front of the toilet. But I got terrible stage fright. I couldn't stop thinking about Deenie in the kitchen, listening to me abuse her lovely bathroom. I stayed on the floor for ten minutes then heard Deenie go out into the garden, obviously trying to give me privacy.

At this point, it was habit to go through Deenie's bathroom cabinet. It was as instinctive as washing my hands. Sudocrem, more ovulation strips, a box of hair dye for covering greys. That was quite exciting. I had seen it before, but never inspected it properly. I was quite fair, so hadn't ever considered the drawbacks of Deenie's dramatic dark brown locks. I took it down and revealed another rectangular box hiding behind it.

There, with a thin film of dust coating the cardboard, was a Clearblue pregnancy test.

It had obviously been there a long time. When I took it down, the dust around it left a fine imprint, like the chalk outline of a body.

Digital results—five days early!

It was the first pregnancy test I had ever seen outside of a pharmacy shelf. I had never taken one, never had a friend who asked me to buy one for her, never held a hand while she waited for the results. I knew you pissed on them, and that was all I knew. You always rush past these things in Boots, never wanting to appear too interested in the sexual health section.

I don't know when the realisation dawned on me, except that I felt a cold trickle of sweat slide from the hair underneath my ponytail and down my neck. My heart started to beat, hard and heavy in my ears. It was like my body knew before I did. I started counting weeks. The sickly wave came over me again.

"Rachel! Are you okay? Do you want some water?"

"Fine!" I called. "Two minutes!"

I opened the box and slid out the packet and the instructions. I stuffed them in my bag, then replaced the box and the hair dye in front of it, closing the mirrored cabinet as gently as I could.

I came out of the bathroom, my face red.

"You poor thing," Deenie said. "You know, I think there is a bug going around. Do you want to lie down?"

"No, I don't think so," I stumbled. "Deenie, would you mind driving me home?"

"Of course, of course."

Dr. Byrne and Deenie shared a car, a silver Golf, and I was surprised by how messy it was. There were crumbs in the creases of the seats. She seemed to clock this, despite all of her concern. "He always eats in the car," she said, sounding fed up. "One time I found a Wagon Wheel in here."

I rested my head against the open window and feigned sleep. My brain could not have been more awake, groping at my last period memory. I was coming up with nothing. My memories don't tend to work unless they involve other people: people I talked to, people I drank with, people I complained at. Not only could I not remember my period, I could not remember talking about it to anyone either. Back in secondary school, we were constantly talking about our cramps and our cravings, and even at the bookshop I could nudge Sabrina and ask her for a tampon. But my life was filled with men now, and I never mentioned my period to any of them.

I finally unearthed a memory. One of sunbathing in the church-yard by the Shandon Bells, and feeling the unmistakable dampness of a tampon deciding it had seen enough. "I have to go," I remember groaning to James. I stumbled to my feet, resentful of having to walk the five minutes home just to get a fresh Tampax.

That was early August, or perhaps even the end of July. It was October now.

I was on the pill, and while I was usually good at taking it, I wasn't exactly Old Faithful. I could take it at 9 a.m. one morning, and then not remember until midnight the following day. Did that kind of thing really matter? Then I remembered the night with Carey. The night where I was so drunk and anxious that I must have vomited up the pill that I had probably only taken a few hours before.

Calm down, Rachel. You're diagnosing a problem that might not exist.

"Where do you live, Rache? I know you're on the north side, but . . ."

"Just off Shandon Street," I murmured. "By the old Butter Exchange."

I didn't register her silence as anything particularly strange.

"Which house is it?" she said, five minutes later. Her voice was peculiar, but far away. Distant and interrogating, like a policeman in the next room.

"Oh, never mind," I said drearily. "I'll just get out here."

I thanked her and got out of the car. I walked slowly, dragging my feet. Sick and full of dread, knowing that the second I got home I would have to take the pregnancy test, and that it would confirm something that was so extremely obvious.

I didn't look back, but if I had, I'm certain about what I would have seen: Deenie Harrington's world coming apart as I put my key in the door.

21

LONDON IS FIVE HOURS AHEAD of New York. James has started texting me when the show finishes, the last few months, knowing that my sleep has been all over the place.

The morning after the *Toy Show* at 6 a.m., James is getting off work. He messages me:

> How's my best girl?

I look at the message, blinking at it. How do you just tell someone that their ex-lover is in a coma?

> How's the baba? James Jnr?? xx

I write back. I'm not calling him James.

> You should.

> How was the show?

> Grand. Except the second guest didn't show up and we had to put on some random woman and her pug.

Her pug?????

The pug is a big deal!

I start to type. I was out tonight and met someone who heard Dr. Byrne was sick and is in a coma.

I delete it quickly. Go on, I send instead. What's the pug's Instagram?

It's an exaggeration to say that James and I never talk about Dr. Byrne. But the talk is limited to a certain time and place. That time and place is my living room, at about 3 a.m., on the second night of a three-night visit. When we've chewed through all the old nostalgia, updated each other on everything we can be updated on, piled on a few fresh memories so the old ones don't get stale. When we have tended to our friendship like the rare orchid that it is, he will nudge me with his foot, top up my drink, and say: "What do you think is going on with Fred Byrne? Where do you think he is now?"

We mull over hypotheticals, and eventually, we crack out the laptop. Aideen Harrington, Deenie Harrington, Deenie Harrington-Byrne, Fred Byrne, Frederick Byrne, Dr. Frederick Harrington-Byrne.

The only social media that either of them has is Deenie's locked Facebook page. The only photo we can see is her, in sunglasses, in front of a white wall in a hot country. The photograph has not changed in four years.

Dr. Byrne still teaches at UCC. He hasn't published a book since *The Kensington Diet,* and when we're feeling egotistical, James and I wonder if that is because of us.

———

I took the test as soon as I got home and climbed into bed with it. The result turned positive and I phoned James.

"Where are you?"

"At work," he said sternly. He was resentful that I no longer had to work weekends.

"I'm pregnant."

"Fuck."

"I know."

"Hold on. I'm coming home."

I don't know what he said to Ben, but he was home in five minutes, and then stayed with me for the rest of the day.

"What are you going to tell Carey?" he asked. "It *is* Carey's, isn't it?"

"Of course! Who else's would it be?"

"Well, I don't know! I didn't even know you were late. Who knows what secrets you've been hiding."

He didn't know what to do with me. I didn't know what to do with myself. I've never been good at melting down at the right time. A few years ago, when my mother was ill, I was glacially calm. I effortlessly went through the movements of good daughterhood. I looked as though I was coping magnificently, and so my friends stopped checking in as much, and then when the real breakdown happened a month later I found myself not just in tears but curiously alone.

That reserve, which James describes as my "ancestral middle-classness," had taken over management of my psyche. I was completely still, not able to compute the idea of a child growing inside me.

"What do you want to do, Rache?" he said, his arms around me.

"Do you still have your mum's car?"

Nicola was on holidays, and had let James keep the car for two weeks.

"Yes."

"Can we go to a drive-thru?"

"Sure," he said. "Which one?"

"I don't mind. I just . . . want to . . ." I didn't know what I was asking for, or why I wanted it. There was a McDonald's drive-thru near my parents' house, and it was where my mum would take us if we'd had a bad day at school.

We got in the car.

"Is there a chance it's a false positive?" James asked, trying to politely break my silence on this issue. "Should we buy another test?"

"No, there would be no point," I said. "The way I've been feeling . . . it makes sense."

We joined the queue at McDonald's. The car in front of us had two children in it, twin boys, and they were gurning their faces at us from the back window, pretending to be puffer fish. They flapped their hands next to their cheeks, miming the gills.

"How old do you think they are?" I asked.

"Six?" James ventured. "Seven?"

"I need an abortion," I said. "I don't . . . How do you get one, again?"

"Um . . . England."

"Well, obviously England," I said. "I mean . . . who do you call?"

I couldn't believe how little I actually knew about this process, despite the fact that I had been steeped in the abortion debate since I was a teenager. There was a defeated referendum to allow abortion for women whose health was seriously at risk in 2002, which was the year I first got my period. It was the earliest news story I remember paying attention to. It's impossible to think about your period without thinking about sex, and the long shadow of a potential abortion hung over every thought about it. I thought a lot about rape, and having a rapist's baby, and whether or not I would be suicidal enough to convince the state that I needed an abortion. I created huge soap opera narratives for myself, terrifying simulations that opened up like a flow-chart quiz at the back of *Mizz* magazine.

I read fitfully, discussed endlessly, got into huge fights with my dad about it. My dad, although he voted in favour of repealing the Eighth Amendment in 2018, was not so convinced in the early noughties. He talked about slippery slopes, abortion as "the new morning-after pill," and about women who regretted their decision to travel to England, of which he claimed to know many. He was a doctor and I was supposed to take what he said seriously; but he was a dentist and my dad so I didn't.

But in all those dinner-table debates, some of which ended in us not speaking for days, I never once looked into the practicalities of getting a termination. Who you phoned, how much it cost, all that.

"There are pills," James said. "You can order pills in the post. They're illegal, but you can get them."

I had read about the pills, mostly in situations where the pill-taker had either haemorrhaged or died.

We were at the drive-thru window now. I ordered fries and a milkshake. James got some nuggets. We sat in the car park and ate them so slowly that everything was cold.

"I really don't want to go to England," I said. "I really don't want to do this."

James's eyes went wide. He looked like one of his mother's cats. "You want to *keep* it?"

"No," I snapped.

"You want to . . . give it up for adoption?"

"God, no. I'm not in the nineteen fifties."

Adoption was somehow the most terrifying option of all. The idea of having Carey's child and giving it away, yet another part of him that was in the wind, and always a mystery to me.

Then it hit me. Properly. *Carey's child*. The first man I had ever really loved, who had ever really excited me, and now he was stuck in Derry indefinitely and I was carrying his baby.

I imagined a world where I kept it. There was a romance to this, and it was worth entertaining. There were no jobs in Ireland, anyway. I could bed down in motherhood and treat it like hibernation, poking my head back out in five years when the kid started school and I could take a real lash at the job market. I could tell Carey. I pictured myself, six months pregnant and looking like Tess of the d'Urbervilles, waiting at the train station in Derry. He would be shocked, and then once the shock wore off, he'd say something delicious and unexpected, the way he always did. He, who had always loved the bigness of my body, would fancy me even more when I was pregnant. Cradling my curves, my new puffy breasts, the big firm stomach.

There would be something beautiful about it. His mother failing, our pregnancy thriving. She would meet her grandchild, and she would love me. There were already so many young children in Carey's family that another strawberry-blonde kid running around would make next to no difference. We could live in the house with his parents for a while. It was a big place, or so he told me, and it was almost empty now.

I could see it. I could see it in the same way I could see London, a parallel universe that was accessible with just one definite step from me.

"What do you think?" I asked James.

He put both his hands up. "I'm not saying a thing."

"Why not?"

"Because this has to be your decision. I don't want to accidentally persuade you one way or another. But . . . whatever you do, Rache, I'm here. I'll go to England with you, or I'll help you with the baby, or whatever. We'll make it work."

A third world opened up. One where me and James Devlin raised a baby together in Cork, and that world, despite its sitcom value, was the most horrifying of all. I had ideas and an imagination, but James had an actual dream. James had to be a TV writer, and that fantasy was far-fetched enough when he was a gay Irish man with no connections. It would be impossible if he was helping to raise a baby.

I realised that the world where I moved to Derry, which was the one most attractive to me in this buffet of bad keeping-it options, was also the world where I didn't live with James any more. Would hardly see him. And while that sounds childish and clingy, I was, at that time, very childish and clingy. I couldn't bear the thought of not seeing him, not living with him.

"I guess we should start ringing places in England."

It was gone six o'clock, and a weekend, so calling England was out of the question until Monday.

"Will you phone in sick?" he asked. "At the call centre?"

I had just spent twenty minutes living in several related fantasy universes, and the fact that the call centre still existed despite all of them was shocking to me.

"No," I said. "It will cost money, won't it? Flights and all that. I'll need money."

I don't know how we got through that weekend. Despite the fact that I had decided to get an abortion, my inherited middle-classness told me that I should not drink. I did not want to harm the baby that I was planning to kill.

James did not drink either. We went back to our January routine of living in his bedroom. It felt like the days following a death, where the air stands still and cloaks you in a protective blanket. The stillness that says: *A big thing has just happened,* and the atmosphere will stall until there is space in the universe for more things to happen. We watched every movie that Cher had ever been in that we could find on DVD. *Mermaids, The Witches of Eastwick, Moonstruck.* We ordered two large pizzas and ate them slowly over the weekend, heating up slices in the frying pan.

Carey phoned me twice on Saturday. I didn't pick up either time. He called me for light relief, for a distraction from sickness, and I couldn't offer it to him. I knew that if I answered the phone I would want to keep the baby, and I would want to tell him about it.

It was the only time that James offered me any kind of directive. "Don't punish him," he said. "Tell him or don't tell him, but don't freeze him out. He's going through a rough enough time as it is."

We spoke on Sunday night.

"How'ya, my gorgeous girl," he said, sounding like he'd been in sunshine. "Listen, I've been thinking."

"About what?"

"Phone sex."

It was the first time I had laughed all weekend. He was such a deeply silly person, and he had no idea I was pregnant, and I suddenly wanted to do nothing more than to take a holiday within this phone conversation.

"Why are you laughing? I think we'd be good! We're both verbal enough, aren't we?"

"Oh, I don't know if I could take it seriously."

"Go on, give it a lash."

"Now?"

"No, let's talk for a few minutes, and then you can spring it on me, like a surprise. Just announce your clothes have fallen off, or something."

I laughed again, and we talked about what was going on in Derry. His eldest niece had started secondary school. He wanted to know when my graduation was going to be.

"I don't know, middle of this month sometime."

"You don't sound bothered."

"It feels so long ago now," I said, and I meant it. "College. It seems pointless. I don't know what I was thinking, an English degree."

"I really regret never coming to see you at college."

"To see me? Why?"

"Oh, I don't know. Seeing you write your little essays. Following you into the stacks. I've always had a library fantasy, since I was small."

I wondered whether this was the window opening for phone sex. "What was the fantasy?"

"Oh, you know." I heard a slight creaking of the mattress, and I could tell he had transitioned from sitting up to lying down. "Gorgeous big-titted librarian, trying to find me a rare book."

I had spent so much of the previous two days in my own interconnected fantasy worlds that it felt incredible to visit someone else's. "Go on."

"You know, you might get up on one of those stepladder things," he said, his tone still breezy. "And I'd . . ."

It was clear he had done this before. I've never been someone who asks about ex-girlfriends, preferring to presume that men were simply asleep before I met them. He talked about looking up my tight skirt ("Pencil skirt?" I asked, ruining the mood for a second), of running his hand up my legs, of feeling that I was damp down to my thighs. I sensed it was my time to take over, and I closed my eyes and talked about his body. It was easy. I had done so much thinking about his body already.

Despite everything, I was able to lose myself in it. Being pregnant almost added to the experience. I wasn't just a librarian. I was a librarian . . . *with a secret*. We touched ourselves and talked to each other, and it was magnificent until he started talking about coming.

"Jesus, I want to come in you," he started saying, all narrative now thrown out the window. He kept on saying it. I could hear him getting closer. I went cold. He had come in me, after all. That's why I was in this situation. I went silent. At this point, he was entirely on his own steam anyway.

When he finished, it was with a barrage of my name.

Fuck, fuck, Rachel, Rachel, fuck.

I wondered whether it was normal now to say goodbye and hang up the phone, but his voice returned fairly quickly.

"Sorry, I couldn't wait," he said.

"For what?"

"Well, for you."

"Oh, it's fine."

I knew I sounded strange, and that he could tell.

"Are you okay?"

"Yeah. That was fun."

"Do we have a new long-distance hobby, d'you think?"

"I should think so," I replied, and tried to keep my voice sexy. "I miss you."

We hung up the phone soon after. When I left my bedroom, I found a Post-it on the door, and on it was the phone number for Marie Stopes International.

It was a week for unusual phone conversations.

I called Marie Stopes on Monday morning. They told me that I needed to have a consultation first, then they gave me a list of clinics I could see in Ireland. There were two in Cork. After a doctor had seen me, they would refer me to a private clinic in the UK.

In the years since, I've spent so much time interviewing, reporting, and editing various Irish women's experiences with abortion that my mind has fused my own experience with theirs. Our road maps are too similar. It always starts with a phone call, and then a consultation, and after, you select a clinic based not so much on safety or medical prowess but on where Ryanair is doing a deal with that month. Sometimes Manchester is cheaper, and sometimes London is.

There's a limited field of options, and a limited field of emotions to go with them. Frightened, sad. Angry at having to travel. Angry at yourself for being irresponsible. Angry at the doctor for asking if I was absolutely sure that I wanted a termination, which I suppose is sensible to ask, but pissed me off anyway. Or did it piss me off? Have I just read so much about this particular experience that my feelings have attached on to a global nerve centre of Irish female thought on abortion?

It's impossible to say.

The only memories that are clear are the ones with James in them.

We went to the clinic in Cork together on Wednesday, where I took another test, and where the doctor confirmed that I was nine weeks pregnant. I counted that it was only six weeks since Carey and I had unprotected sex, but apparently that didn't matter. Pregnancy was, bafflingly, counted from the date of your last period. Then he left the room and said that a nurse would be back to discuss "our options."

"Oh my God," James said. "I bet he thinks I'm the father."

"Well, good. I hope he does," I replied. "I don't want him to think I got pregnant by being a slapper. I want him to know people love me."

It was the first time that James ever looked shocked by something I said. If we hadn't been there to schedule my abortion, he would have taken me to task over it.

He looked at the brochures for clinics in England. "You don't have to feel ashamed of any of this," he murmured.

I scoffed. Made a little disgusted throat-clearing sound, like it would be insane for me to feel that way.

But my Irishness got the better of me. "It's illegal, though."

"Yeah." He raised his eyebrow. "And so was sodomy, until like, nineteen ninety-three or something, so we're both basically criminals."

I raised my eyebrows. "Yeah, like Bonnie and Clyde."

We smiled at each other, because we had seen the Faye Dunaway film not long before. James took my hand, putting on his warbling Southern-belle voice.

"They call them cold-blooded killers, they say they are heartless and mean. But I say this with pride, that I once knew Clyde . . ."

My friend put his lips to my knuckles and pressed hard, then met my eyes to finish the verse.

". . . and she was honest, and upright, and clean."

The nurse entered the room with James still holding my hand, and he didn't let go while she talked to us. She told me that she could schedule a termination in the UK for two weeks' time, which would bring me to eleven weeks, and that I had a choice between medical and surgical. Medical was just taking a pill, but it was painful, and you did it over two days, which meant booking two nights in England. Surgical was more common for Irish women travelling. I nodded. If surgical was what most Irish women did, then that is what I would do.

I drifted out of the room then as the nurse was still speaking. I imagined my return to Ireland, all empty and scraped out.

"Excuse me," James said, jolting me back in the room. "Did you say five *hundred* euros?"

"Five hundred?" I squeaked. "Are you fucking serious?"

"We don't have that," he said.

"Yes, we don't have that," I echoed.

The nurse nodded with a practised sympathy. She probably had this conversation a dozen times a day. "Part of that is the consultation fee you'll pay today," she said unhelpfully. "Which is sixty-five. The rest you'll pay when you're there."

I was to phone later that day when I had decided what I wanted to do. I paid the sixty-five and we left the clinic. I leaned my body over the railings of the River Lee, trying to breathe in the wet air.

"Don't throw yourself in, for the love of God."

"How am I going to pay that, James?" I said. "And then there's the flights."

"And the hotel," he said gently.

"And the fucking hotel," I echoed.

He sat down by the railings. "And realistically, there's public transport, cabs, lunch, dinner for the two of us. We can bring sandwiches but not for every meal."

"The two of us?"

"I'm not letting you go *alone*." He looked into the river. "There's five hundred and fifty-seven euro in our fund."

"That's half your money."

"It's *our* money. We'll make it back. We'll just have to emigrate later."

I hugged him, my arms around his waist, his around my shoulders. We really did look like a couple. I felt his slim body tense, and

I loved him, not because it was easy for him to say goodbye to that money but because it was unbelievably hard.

"We need another two hundred, at least, for flights and all that," I said. "And we have to book it soon, too, so it'll be even more expensive."

"Two hundred!" he scoffed. "Three, at least."

When we got home we looked at flights. London flights were all in the high hundreds; we found a few Manchester ones for sixty-five euro each, provided we didn't book luggage.

"Do you think Ryanair makes all their money from abortions?" I said limply. "It's a pretty amazing business model, when you think about it."

I called the clinic back to confirm that I had decided on Manchester. We booked the flights using the card from our savings account.

"We need to go begging," he sighed. "Let's make a list."

Here was his list.

Rachel parents
Carey
James parents
Ben?
Call centre
Harrington-Byrnes

"My parents don't have it," I said. "And I'm not telling them, anyway. My dad is pro-life."

"And Carey?"

"Definitely doesn't have it. He's got no job, and he's looking after his parents." I looked at his list. "And I can't ask *your* parents, I don't know them."

I crossed out the first three, along with Ben, who was a stupid idea.

"I could ask the call centre for an advance," I said, and then felt a wave of depression settle over me. I didn't want to owe the call centre a favour. I already spent every bus journey hoping that it had caught fire the night before. "Maybe just a hundred, out of my next pay slip."

"And you could tap up Fred and Deenie for another hundred," James suggested. "Or maybe two. They love you. They'll give it to you gladly."

I squirmed. "I don't know. I don't want them to . . . to know this about me."

I pictured myself telling Deenie and Dr. Byrne about my situation. Particularly given what I now knew about their own luck with pregnancy. She would hate me for this. I had drunkenly stumbled into a state that she had been trying to get into for years.

"You could ask Fred," I said. "So Deenie wouldn't know."

He bit his lip. "I don't know. I think he's finished with me, again."

I sat up. "Why?"

James was always so thorough about Dr. Byrne's comings and goings. It was an act of remarkable grace that he hadn't shared these new woes with me while I was dealing with abortion planning.

"He's not answering my calls. I don't know. Maybe Deenie looked at his phone or something. Although I'm in his phone as 'dentist.' Maybe she cracked the code."

"No! You don't think?"

He nodded sadly. "I do think."

"Well, she hasn't said a thing to me."

"Yes, but why *would* she?"

I went to work the next day and asked to speak to my manager alone.

"I know I haven't been working here very long," I said, "but I was wondering if I could arrange an advance on this month's salary. It's an emergency. I swear I wouldn't be asking otherwise."

She laughed. "Nice try."

Later that day I was visited by the payroll assistant, and I assumed that my manager had had a change of heart. "Rachel Murray?" she said, while I was still on the phone. "We still haven't had your P45 through."

"Oh." I didn't know what to do. I had never had a new job before. O'Connor's had been my first. "How do I . . . ?"

"You need to call your old company, and get them to send it."

"Okay, I'll do that today."

She started to walk away. "I'll still get paid on the right day, though, right?"

"Hmm?"

"If I get my P45 tomorrow. I'll still get paid? On the last working day of the month?"

"No, it's likely you'll be put on emergency tax."

"Likely?"

"I don't know for certain," she said. "But probably."

I walked outside and sat on the grass next to the road, my head on my knees.

———

I received email confirmation of my appointment in Manchester, and realised that the day of my abortion was 26 October, the same as my graduation from UCC. That afternoon, I got a phone call from my father, asking when graduation was.

"Oh, I'm not going," I said, as breezily as I could manage. "Me and James are going to take a trip to Manchester; go on a jolly."

"Why aren't you going?"

"It's expensive for what it is," I replied. "You know, gown rental and all that. It's kind of a scam. And I never felt very connected to the course anyway. I think it would be awkward. I didn't really have any friends there."

"I think you should go, Rachel," he said. He sounded disappointed. I was his eldest child, after all, and I'm sure graduation is a thing a parent looks forward to. They had so few days out any more. "I think you might regret it, in time."

I closed my eyes and gulped like I was swallowing a pill. "I just had to *work* so much during college," I said. "I'm not really sure I'd get much out of it."

That did it. I knew it would. My poor father was now stricken with guilt at the university experience I did not have, because of the fees he could not pay.

"Well, if you're sure."

"I'm sure."

I didn't want to get off the phone right away. Not so soon after disappointing him.

"Dad," I said limply, "how are you, anyway?"

"I think your mother wants to say something," he said, and passed the phone on to her.

Somehow it became the weekend again, and I had the dinner party at the Harrington-Byrnes'. It was too early in my pregnancy for my body to show it, but I was paranoid nonetheless. Every outfit I tried on I looked swollen in, and my boobs were just getting to the tender stage, so my bras felt dreadful.

James sat on my bed and watched me try things on.

"I feel quite weird about you going over there," he said. "To their bougie little dinner party, while I stay at home, Cinderella with the mice."

"Sorry," I said, wrestling another dress over my head.

"Couldn't you bring me? As your date?"

"First of all, it's too late to bring a date into the equation. They've cooked already. Second of all, *no.* You and Dr. Byrne would be making eyes at each other all night."

I settled on a floral tea dress in mint green. My mother and I had bought it years ago for a cousin's christening party, and I had not worn it since.

"How do I look?"

"Like you've never had a finger in your ass."

"*James.*"

He lay down and looked at the ceiling.

"It's weird you're having dinner with my boyfriend when I haven't seen him in a week."

I walked to their house, clutching a nine-euro bottle of wine and practising conversation starters for adults. I had to treat this dinner party for the opportunity that it was. I had to get my face in front of people. Now that I was definitely not going to be a young mother, I needed to sort this career thing out, recession or no.

I knocked on the door, and could hear loud chatter and music from the other side. It felt like I was waiting for a portal to an adult world to suck me in.

A woman I had never seen before opened the door. She was about thirty with a sleek ash-blonde ponytail and a backless black jumpsuit. "Oh hello!" she said, waiting expectantly for me to say my name.

"Hi," I said shyly. "I'm Rachel? I work with Deenie?"

"Okay!" she said. "Come in, come in, sorry, Deenie is frying the scallops, I'm on door duty. I'm Ciara, by the way. I copy-edited the manuscript."

I hung my coat up, thinking: *I thought I copy-edited the manuscript.*

There were ten people in the kitchen, and four bundled up on the couch in the small living room. Deenie was looking anxiously at the scallops, and didn't seem to hear me come in. I couldn't see Dr. Byrne anywhere. Ciara introduced me to everyone, a flurry of book people who all nodded politely when I explained my role.

"I'm sort of an assistant," I said. "I helped with the permissions, and that kind of thing."

"Sort of like an internship?" asked a man with sandy hair, cut to his ears. He was another editor at Deenie's publishing house, and he looked like the sort of man who surfed in the winter. He had clearly never heard about me.

"Yeah, sort of."

"Christ, did you hear that they have people with actual master's degrees doing internships up in Dublin now?" someone else chipped in. "Do you have a master's degree?"

"No," I said, feeling deeply inadequate. "I've actually just finished my undergrad. I'm graduating soon."

"Oh wow!" the sandy-headed man said. "God, imagine getting all that experience before you even graduate. You'll be such a good candidate for the next internship you interview for."

I couldn't tell if he was being dry or just truthful. It was my understanding that you did one internship and then you got a job. And I had done one internship.

"Where's Dr. Byrne?" I asked. I corrected myself. "Where's Fred?"

"Oh, out picking up more wine, I think," Ciara said. "Come into the living room. It's so packed and hot in here."

I still hadn't said hello to Deenie, but I was steered into the living room anyway. There were three people from the university who I recognised from the English department. Only one of them recognised me. She was a lecturer called Dr. Anne Sheehan, and she had taught me in several film modules. She was around the same age as Dr. Byrne, but I had never considered that they might be friends, or that professors socialised together.

"Oh hello!" she said cheerfully. "I know you. Rachel, isn't it?"

"Yes," I said. I felt the size of a thimble. "Rachel Murray, I did your noir seminar."

A man, her boyfriend or husband, looked very excited about this. "Oh my God," he said, his arm around her. "We're having dinner with one of your students?"

"Ex-student," I said. "I'm actually graduating soon."

"This is a dream come true," the boyfriend or husband said. "I'm always desperate to sit in on one of Anne's classes, but she never lets me, says she'd get performance anxiety. I've always wanted to know just *how* good a teacher she is."

"Oh, well," I said, not sure what exactly he wanted from me. "She's very good."

"Let me quiz you," he said. "Let me see how good Anne *actually* is."

Dr. Sheehan squirmed a little. "Don't do that to her, Con. She doesn't want to be quizzed on her night off." She looked at me apologetically. "Don't mind him, Rachel."

Con was a bit drunk. It seemed he was that kind of man, the man who showed up too early to a party and drank everything in sight. I knew this character from my own house parties and was surprised to see that they didn't change in later life.

"All right, I won't quiz her; just tell me what you know."

"Know about what?" I answered uncertainly.

"Noir. Film noir."

I felt like a child who was being asked to sing their party piece. I was desperate for Dr. Byrne to come and rescue me.

"Well, ah," I began. "The visuals of film noir were based heavily on German expressionist painting, on the use of light to convey mood."

"Oh, Annie, you *are* good!" Con said. "German expressionist painting!"

I wanted to die. I looked at Dr. Sheehan. It seemed like she wanted to die also. For the first time in a week I wasn't thinking about being pregnant.

"That's enough, now. How are you, Rachel? Sit down."

I heard the front door slam, then the heavy footsteps of Dr. Byrne.

"I've got the booze," came his call. "Everyone can relax. We have enough to take out a baby elephant."

Ciara shouted, "That's no way to talk about yourself, Fred."

Then Deenie's voice. "Just in time. The starters are ready."

"Should we all sit down?"

"Let's all sit down."

The UCC gang, terrible Con and I filed into the kitchen. The table near the window had been folded out and dressed with white cloths. Some people came in from the back garden, where they had been smoking. Everyone had to pinch around the wall to find their seat. There were place cards at each setting, and some of the cards had nicknames on them, like "Boots" and "Woofter" and "The Nose." Some of them were normal, and just said "Anne."

I wondered if Deenie had a nickname for me that I wasn't aware of, because I could not find my name. I was the last person standing in a room full of seated people. It was then that the Harrington-Byrnes finally saw me. Ten weeks pregnant in a mint-green tea dress that, on reflection, was not as dressy as it should have been.

"Rachel," Dr. Byrne said. He was opening a bottle of wine, his face frozen in shock.

Deenie was plating the scallops, and looked up. Her white face became scarlet, her expression dead, her hands still.

"Rachel," she said.

"Hello."

I had only been in the house ten minutes, and had suffered so much humiliation already. I wanted to cry.

Then, with as much joviality as I could muster, I said: "Have I got the wrong night?"

Everyone at the table was peering at me in confusion. There were fourteen other guests, and two chairs for the hosts. There was no chair for me.

The fair-haired editor spoke up. "Were you going to make your intern eat in the garden, lads?"

"No," Fred said robotically. "Rachel. Lovely to see you. Aideen . . . forgot to tell me she invited you."

"Well," I said awkwardly. "Here I am."

He disappeared to his study and dragged an office chair to the top of the table. Deenie started passing out plates of scallops with black pudding.

I tried hard to disguise my horror. The office chair loomed over the other chairs, and if I sat on it I would be on display for the whole meal.

"Rachel, you take my seat," he said, with false cheer. "I'll take the throne."

At least half of the guests were dying of second-hand embarrassment. I slowly lowered myself into Dr. Byrne's place. I started replaying the phone conversation with Deenie in my head. She *had* invited me, hadn't she? Was I suffering from pregnancy brain already?

Everyone had resumed a kind of awkward chatter, too polite to ask what on earth was going on.

Deenie had definitely called me. Otherwise, how would I even know this dinner party was going on? Maybe she had told me about the dinner party, but had mentioned it in passing, and I misinterpreted it as an invite. Maybe she had told me, but had found some tactful middle-class way of asking me for catering help, and I thought that was an invite.

But I was sure, sure as the ten-week-old foetus in my stomach, that Deenie had phoned me to ask me to this dinner party. She'd even said I might make some contacts. She said I was part of the team that had made *Little Fire*. I had the book at home. It thanked me for policing the vibe.

Right now, I was murdering the vibe. Some advanced scallop mathematics went on in the kitchen, and I was passed a plate with one scallop on it, while everyone else had two.

The fishy odour mixed with the earthy smoke of the black pudding. My stomach turned over, and I took a long sip of water, wanting desperately to gag.

"Sorry," the woman next to me said. "I think that's my water glass."

"Sorry, sorry," I murmured, and grabbed for my own, the glass that was supposed to be Dr. Byrne's.

The drunk man started blithering away about how he thought he would be a great lecturer, and felt as though he had missed his chance. This eased the tension somewhat, and the group started talking about all the silly things they would teach.

"I can always get a pen to start working again after it's gone dry," Ciara said. "I could teach a course in that."

"I've seen every episode of *Keeping Up Appearances*," some-one else said. "I would do a course on class tensions in post-war Britain."

They had clearly thought about this before.

"What was the name of the brother-in-law again? Something weird. Otto."

"Onslow."

"Onslow!"

Deenie and Dr. Byrne were chatting politely to people on either side of them, but neither looked at me, or at each other. I wanted desperately to leave, but I had enough social sense to know that leaving was the only thing I could do that was worse than staying.

So I stayed, and I mashed up my scallop with a fork, and thought: *No matter how bad this is, it has to end. Dinners always end, eventually. That's the thing about dinners.*

The main course came out of the oven, and each of us was passed a clean warm plate. The fishy smell was replaced with the heavy odour of meat and onion and hot wine.

Ciara got up to help Deenie with the casserole dishes. It was clear they were very good friends, and had a kind of physical short-hand that I recognised. Ciara looked Deenie pointedly in the eyes, with an *are you okay?* expression. This seemed to revive Deenie's spirit.

"Coq au vin!" she said, coming to the table. "I know it's a cliché, very nineteen seventies, but you can make it in advance, so . . ."

"Divine!"

"Amazing!"

"Deenie, you're incredible."

"The *smell*, D, I can't get over it. I'm salivating."

Another casserole dish of mashed potato was revealed, and the chorus started up again.

"Mash!"

"Oh my God, *mash*."

"My favourite food, mash. Good hot, good cold. It's versatile."

"What's that Laurie Colwin line again . . . ? About people only wanting nursery food at dinner parties?"

"Yes, no one likes fiddly food. Not really."

"Mash!"

In the years since, I've always held my guests' reactions to the standard of Deenie Harrington's friends. No one has ever been quite as excited to see my mash. My husband actively dislikes it, and thinks mash is gloopy, like prison food. He will, however, go ape for my roast potatoes.

I have wondered a lot whether they were really that wild about her cooking, or whether they just saw she was suffering, and wanted her to feel good. I think it's the latter. They loved her so much.

22

A MAN WITH A BIG HEAD—like, physically large—finally spoke to me.

"I've been trying to think where I know you from," he said. "You work at O'Connor's, don't you?"

I smiled. It was the first time someone had asked me a question that didn't make me feel like a science experiment.

"Yeah, until recently. They've had to downsize massively, so I don't work there any more. Recession, you know."

He nodded. "Yes, that's it. And you were there at Fred's book launch, weren't you?"

Deenie dropped her fork and it clattered to the ground. Everyone looked up, and then back at me.

"Yes," I said. "Yes, I was still working there, around then."

"That was a good do," he said hurriedly, sensing he had made a faux pas. "We were in the pub until all hours, after that one."

Deenie had decided she'd had enough and left the room. It was all the excuse I needed. I followed, the silence trailing behind me. Deenie was sitting on her bed.

When she saw me in the doorway, she shrieked. Like I was a ghost, or a phantom.

"Get out of my bedroom," she said, her voice high and bitten with tears. "Get out of my *house*."

"Deenie, what is *going on*?" I tried to suppress my own cry. "You invited me here. You called me at work and invited me."

"That was before," she snarled. "That was before I knew."

"Knew what?"

She was appalled. Offended to be taken for an idiot.

"That you were *fucking* my husband."

"Deenie, why do you think that? I didn't have sex with Dr. Byrne."

"Oh, don't bother, Rachel." She started aggressively swiping at her tears, like she was trying to take off some of her skin. "We've had it out. He's told me everything. He tried to lie, too."

Dr. Byrne appeared in the doorway, and put his hand on my shoulder. "I think you'd better go, Rachel."

"No, I want to hear what she has to say." She looked like the wife from *The Shining*, all red-rimmed eyes and black hair. "God, is there any way of having this conversation that doesn't feel, like, so *boring*?" She went on, her voice fat with disgust. "It's so boring to be *this* character. This is the worst one to be, without question. Philandering husband, he gets to have loads of fun. Slutty young assistant, she has a brand-new life experience to write about in her diary. But I'm just fucking stuck here, feeling like an *idiot* for having let this person into my *home*."

"I don't understand." I was starting to blub. "Someone explain to me what is going *on*."

"I've seen the bills," she said fiercely. "The receipts. He sends things to your house, Rachel. He sends wine. And cheese."

Oh, no.

"I knew *something* was going on, but I never thought . . . You worked for me, Rachel. Then you made me drive you *home*. It was *your* address he was sending that stuff to. Rachel's address? *My* Rachel . . ."

"We're not having sex," I said, sticking to the truth. "Deenie, I'm not having sex with your husband."

"He's admitted it, Rachel; you might as well admit it, too."

This hit me like a battering ram. He *admitted* to sleeping with me?

Deenie looked at the duvet like she was considering getting under it. "Fred, call Ciara in."

He did as she said, and Ciara appeared.

"Are you all right, hun?" Gorgeous Ciara in her backless jumpsuit took one look around the room and stiffened, like a butler. "Do you want me to send people home?"

"Yes."

"Okay."

Then she disappeared.

"I'm going to have to tell her, now, too," Deenie said. "Although, everyone will have guessed. This'll be around Cork by tomorrow morning. Hope you're pleased."

Deenie wasn't being self-involved when she said this. It *would* be around Cork by tomorrow morning, because that is how small Cork is. She rubbed at her eyes. "Why didn't you ring her and tell her the jig was up, you prick? You could at least have saved me the humiliation of having her at my dad's book party."

I was startled to hear Deenie swear like this. "Prick" was not a word I expected to hear her say.

"I didn't know you had invited her in the first place," Dr. Byrne said lamely. "You never said."

"No, of course. She is my little friend after all. God, this is all so fucking . . . so fucking *Tudor*, Fred. You get me a lady-in-waiting so you can keep an eye on her?"

I wanted to scream: *It's not me; it's James he's fucking.* But would it make me any less guilty? I had still stood by while my best friend shagged her husband. I had drunk the infidelity wine, eaten the infidelity cheese. Plus, would she even believe it? She had no idea who James was.

"I have just one question, Rachel," she said, fixing her gaze on me. "Was Carey even real?"

"What?" The question knocked me sideways. "Of course Carey is real."

"All this sobbing you were doing on top of me," she carried on. "Were you crying about *my* husband? To *me*? That's all I could think about this week, you know. Did she make up a boyfriend? Is she that much of a sociopath?"

The beautiful strangeness of Carey, my sorrow, the bereft heart I had so openly showed her. Did she think I was just playing a game with her?

The lady-in-waiting analogy was oddly fitting, because Deenie did seem like a queen in those moments. Sitting cross-legged on her bed, offering pronouncements to the room. "When I first met you," she said, "with that stupid carry-on about how the shop wanted to put on the launch for his *awful* book. I knew something was off. It didn't make any sense. And then when I actually saw you . . ."

She allowed herself a dry cackle.

"I thought, *Oh God, how silly, she's just a chubby student with a crush.*"

Of all the things Deenie Harrington said that night, this is the line that I have come back to the most. On my worst days, on my bad dates, on the job interviews that didn't quite work out the way they should.

Just a chubby student with a crush.

Big blotches broke out on Deenie's neck and arms. There was no pearly glow left on her. She was rumpled, sweating, reddened. For once, her petite frame didn't seem feminine to me. It seemed childlike.

"Then suddenly . . . he knows all these *things* about you. Things I haven't told him. Things you don't know, if it's just . . . just a regular student. I know. It was me first, remember?"

I wanted so badly to leave, but I could still hear people filing out the front door, and I couldn't bear to face them. They had all put it together by now. I was afraid they would stone me to death.

Dr. Byrne was so still, like a painting of himself. He seemed to think if he just took the waves of abuse, it would eventually be over, and he would have his wife at the end of it. He had helped me with so much in the short time I had known him, but he would never help me again.

"I looked through his emails, after I dropped you off that day." Deenie scratched her arms, and the red marks grew redder. "He got you out of essays? He wrote letters to the department, and got you extensions? But you know this already."

She was scratching her fingers now. Her left hand working at the right, raking at the space between the knuckles and the joints.

"You know, there's a world where your degree isn't even *valid*, Rachel. I could call them up tomorrow and get him thrown out, and your grades are cancelled because you literally *fucked your way* into an extension. Did you even write your own essays? Or did he do those, too?"

The evidence was compelling. It seemed like every moment since Dr. Byrne walked into O'Connor's in January was leading up to this one. Fated from the instant I lied about the pre-orders of *The Kensington Diet*.

"Please don't do that," was all I said. "Please don't cancel my degree."

"She's not going to cancel your degree," Dr. Byrne said quietly. Turning me in would mean turning him in, and that would mean divorce, as well as him being fired. It appeared, on that night at least, that they had plans to stay married.

"The same night," Deenie went on, "the *same night* he emailed me about you. I remember. We were sitting on the couch, and he said, 'I have a student who needs an internship, that nice tall girl you met, I just emailed you about her.' Laptop open. Cool as a fucking cucumber."

She had spent days trying to metabolise this information, and it still wasn't going down. The facts, or what she believed to be the facts, kept coming up like bile.

In a way, I understood why Fred would prefer his wife to think that he was sleeping with a younger woman, rather than a younger man. He had been in the closet for a long time. I expect he is planning to die there.

But he would rather be an abusive and corrupt professor than be bisexual. He would prefer Deenie to think that he was a sociopath, acquiring jobs for his girlfriend with his wife, rather than be correctly identified as queer.

"I just wanted Rachel to have an opportunity," he said. "I didn't think . . ."

There was nowhere for the sentence to go. He looked at me with an expression that probably read as a lover's sorrow to Deenie, but whose real meaning I saw immediately. *Please, Rachel. Please don't say anything. I'm begging you.*

There was only one thing left for me to do.

"I'm pregnant."

It was one of those situations where the only way out was through.

The Harrington-Byrnes were silent.

"I'm pregnant," I said again.

"Rachel," Dr. Byrne said. "No, you aren't."

"I have an email from Marie Stopes."

Deenie looked as though she had been smacked across the face. "No," she echoed her husband. "No, no, you aren't."

"I am. Ten weeks."

I made a pact with myself that I would not lie to Deenie. Even now, I'm impressed with myself that I made it through this entire incident without really lying.

"There is a box for a pregnancy test in your bathroom," I said. "And it's empty. That's because I stole the test the last time I was here."

The house was empty now. I could feel the silence of the other rooms bearing down on this one, pushing at the walls.

Deenie got up from her bed, and took out her laptop. The rage had flown out the door with the remaining guests. She was now like a scientist in a film, one who has just discovered an asteroid is about to hit the earth.

"Show me," she said. "Show me the email."

It was crazy to be sitting with her on her bed, like being her assistant again. I logged in to my email account and showed her the appointment confirmation for the twenty-sixth.

"Well," Deenie said. "There it is."

I closed the laptop lid. "Two thousand," I said.

"What?" Deenie said.

Fred finally had the grace to appear shocked. "Rachel, what?"

"Two thousand euro." I clenched my fists so tight that I felt my fingernails embedding on my palms. "Two thousand euro, and you'll never see me, or hear about this, ever again."

"Two *thousand*?"

"For the abortion," I said. "For the flights, the procedure, the hotel. And I want a friend to come with me. I'm not doing it alone."

I cleared my throat. "My friend James."

They looked at each other, and I wondered if Dr. Byrne was grateful to be on the same team as his wife again. I was doing them a favour. Before, they were a struggling couple. Now they were going through something together, and that thing was extortion.

"I'm going to wait in the hallway," I said, my voice clear. "And you can discuss what you want to do."

I said, "I didn't want to do this. It wasn't my plan."

And I left them there.

I understand the instinct to judge me. Extorting Deenie Harrington for the termination of a baby that was not her husband's is the worst thing I have done, and I sincerely hope it is the worst thing I will do.

But while the gift of hindsight has changed much about this story, in my own head at least, it is still difficult to see what else I could have done.

I sat in a wooden chair in the hallway next to the post table and waited. After ten minutes, they came out of the bedroom. Deenie had a chequebook in her hands.

"How will we know that you haven't just kept the baby?" she said. Her hands were quivering.

I thought about this. "You won't."

By this point, Deenie Harrington had been glaring at me for almost an hour, but this was the first time she met my eyes. Her lips bitten, her nostrils tipped pink.

"Rachel," she whispered. "You weren't . . . you couldn't have been this person all along, could you?"

I examined each one of my teeth with my tongue. "I'm not evil," I said to her, and to myself. "I just . . . I don't have any money, Deenie."

She furrowed her brow. "It's not just that."

"But it is," I stressed. "I assure you, it is."

"Did I . . . ? Was I a bad boss, or something? Is this a revenge thing?"

She tore out the cheque and gave it to me.

"Deenie," I said, putting my hand on the front door, "I was your assistant."

Deenie looked even more confused. I hated her, then. Hated her friends, her daughter-of-a-poet beauty, her fake money worries. I hated him. Hated his cowardice, the way he pretended to love James, the way he was a tourist in our lives. I hated that he was spoiled, and that he always got what he wanted.

"And what?" Deenie said. "I was your assistant and what?"

"And you never fucking *paid* me."

23

WAS NOT PROUD of how I handled the dinner party. But I had managed to un-fuck myself in a situation that was profoundly fucked on all sides. Either way, I was destined to be alienated from the Harrington-Byrnes. Either way, I still had to pay for an abortion. It was prudent to compound those two problems, and it was a gift to them: they were now in cahoots together. They had paid for a problem to go away, and that problem was me.

I made a mistake, however. And that was in how I told James.

I burst through the door of our house, frothing and rabid. James was lying on the sofa, reading a magazine and smoking with the window open.

"You're home early," he said. Then he looked at my face. "Oh, fuck, what happened?"

"They think it's me," I exploded. "They thought it was *me* fucking him."

I began at the end: I told James that we had two grand, and then that we were never allowed to talk to the Harrington-Byrnes ever again. The rest of the story he had to prise from me through my tears, my hyperventilating, my sudden tense giggles that would end in me clutching my own arms, and then his. First he was confused, and asked hundreds of questions, made me tell the story again. I talked about the place settings, and Ciara, and the friends who had clearly never heard a thing about me, but who now would remember me for ever.

I gagged on my words as I made fresh realisations: that Dr. Sheehan and the other members of the English department would tell their colleagues, who would tell their Ph.D. students, who would tell their MA students, who would tell the BAs. That I would probably never walk through the UCC campus again without feeling as though I was being looked at. This fact, which might mean nothing if I lived in a bigger place, meant everything in Cork. The campus is almost part of the city. You attend art shows there, film screenings. You meet people.

Finally, my degree. My degree, while still valid, would always have a stain on it.

And that I would, too.

I sank into this. Drowned in it. The eradication of the past three years, which would now always feel like a prelude to this event. Every tutorial and lecture, every essay that Carey had called Chomsky, every casual coffee or beer in the students' union. It was all ruined for me now. I would always be That Girl.

I leaned so hard into this idea of myself as the scarlet woman of University College Cork that I didn't even see James's heart breaking right in front of me.

"He told her that he was shagging you," he said. "That he was sleeping with you. That he was in love with you."

I stalled. "He . . . he didn't say love. He didn't say anything, really."

He walked around the room in a circle and sat down. Then he got up and did the same thing again. He looked like a dog who couldn't settle.

"You told him that for two thousand euro he would never hear from you ever again."

"Yes."

"And he accepted that."

"I . . ."

How had I not thought of this? James had been holding my hand since the moment I found out I was pregnant. For almost a year we had been joined at the hip, and in the past week I had thought of him as merely extra storage for my own anxieties. I had not, for a single second, considered what this meant for him. That I had effectively broken up with Dr. Byrne for him.

I scrambled around. "There was nothing I could do. We were fucked, anyway. It was over, James. He hadn't called you in a week, remember? He was done. He was caught."

James moved his body away from me, his eyes haunted. He reached for his phone.

"I need to call him," he said. "I need to talk to him."

"James, don't." I tried to take his phone away, prising his fingers off of the case. "Don't call him. Definitely don't call him *tonight*."

"No," he snapped. He started dialling. "Fuck off, Rachel, this is nothing to do with you."

"Unfortunately it *is*," I said, still trying to grab the phone off of him. "He made me a part of it. He's a selfish, spoiled man who thought he could have it both ways, and when he was caught he took the most cowardly way out. You don't want to *talk* to him, James."

"I do," he growled. "Rachel, honestly, I need you to get out of my fucking face about this."

I leapt at my friend, and just like the day of our fight at the book-shop, I felt like an ogre towering over his impish frame. I didn't want James to humiliate himself. But I also didn't want him to ruin things. Deenie could still cancel the cheque. I wasn't about to ruin my reputation *and* lose the two thousand euro.

"Listen," I said, "on Monday we can cash the cheque. It will probably need two days to clear. That gives you until Wednesday to cool off and talk to him. Get closure or whatever. Call him at work. That way he won't be caught."

He made for the yard, still clutching the phone to his ear.

"You could probably still . . . I don't know, carry on, I guess? If you wanted to, but why would you want to? James. James. JAMES."

I lunged again. The phone flew out of his hand, hitting the yard wall, and smashing to the floor. The phone opened, the battery skittering across the flagstones. I grabbed the phone.

"Rachel. Give it back."

"No."

"I'm not fucking around here. Give it back."

I backed into the house, keeping my eyes wide and wary, like an animal you find in your bins.

"Rache, I swear to God."

I imagined a world where I had to go through everything I had just gone through, but I still had to deplete my savings to pay for my abortion. Not just deplete my savings, but tell my parents, and ask them for money that they didn't have for a procedure they were morally against. And with that horrifying thought, I took one step indoors, and threw James's phone into the toilet.

He looked at me, and then at the toilet, and then at me again.

"Rachel," he said quietly, "if I don't leave right now, I feel like I might hit you."

I moved out of the way. James walked in one straight line out the front door and didn't come back until the next day.

━━━━

I didn't sleep at all that night. I lay in bed with my phone next to my pillow, willing anyone in the world to reach out and say they loved me. It was the only time in the whole pregnancy where I thought seriously about keeping it. I thought: *Well, here's someone who couldn't leave, for eighteen years at least.* There were moments in that long night where I was absolutely certain that I was going to take the money and run. To start a new life as a single mother with the two thousand euro, our savings, and the few pennies left in my current account after emergency tax.

I thought about Carey. I even thought about calling him for phone sex. Anything for a bit of distraction. What would he think of all this? That I had just used our baby to scam a married couple out of two grand?

Our baby.

Our baby.

I rubbed my stomach again and again, like I had seen pregnant women do on TV. There was nothing to rub, really, except for the alcohol gut I had developed over the past year. It was now Saturday. In ten days I would be getting the plane to Manchester, a 6 a.m. flight for a 2 p.m. appointment.

For everything I had read about abortion, there wasn't very much about how it actually felt. People often described it as a Hoover for your insides. My insides.

James came back. It was just after seven, and I had given up on sleep. I sat with a blanket around me on the couch, *Frasier* once again on the TV.

"Hey."

"Hey."

He smelled of cigarettes, and like a drink had spilled on him.

"Did you go out?" I asked. "*Out* out?"

"I started walking to Fred's house," he said. "And then I realised that I didn't know his address."

"Oh."

James sat down next to me. I bunched my feet up to make room for him. He massaged his eye sockets, both palms flat to his face.

"I just . . . It was all pretend, wasn't it?"

"You and him?"

"Me and him."

"No, I don't think so. I don't think it was all pretend."

"It was like he was a tourist, wasn't he?"

It was funny that he found the word "tourist" so easily, because it was the one I had found the night before. Dr. Byrne wanted to visit our youth, our poverty, our liveliness. But he didn't want to live there.

He wiped at his face. "I had sex last night."

"With who?"

He shrugged. Not because he didn't know, but because it didn't matter. Tears trickled down his face, his big eyes wet and green like young grass.

"I'm sorry about your phone," I said.

"It's fine."

"I'll buy you a new one."

"With what money?" he said automatically. "Oh. Yeah. *That* money."

"I should have held out for more," I said, creeping my toes towards his leg. He nodded, swallowing his sadness down in big gulps.

"I'm worth five grand, at least."

"You're worth a million."

He smiled, grateful, even though it was corny.

"But they didn't have a million," I finished.

"Right."

We listened to Shandon Street wake up. There was a Nigerian food shop on the corner that got meat deliveries in the early morning, and we heard the sound of the van reversing, the metal shutter opening up, the boxes being handed from one person to another.

"I just don't think . . ." James said. "I don't think I'm one of those people that gets to be happy, in this area."

"What? What area?"

"Like"—he fiddled with the string edges of the blanket—"you know, people like me. I'm funny. I can write jokes. I can always get laid. I can always make a living. I can always get a job. That's a lot, you know?"

He braided the pieces of string together. "That's a lot for one person to have. I think it's okay if I never get to have, like, romantic love."

I was so insecure, then. I never thought that someone could have an insecurity that I myself hadn't thought of. James was sure he was an unlovable person. Maybe it was why he had decided to accept scraps of it from Dr. Byrne.

"I just think you're someone who wants a non-standard life, you know?" I began. "Like the TV stuff. Like the agent. I don't know anyone who chases after stuff the way you do. I think you just want this big huge exceptional life, and you're probably going to have a huge big exceptional love that goes with it."

He kissed my kneecap. "All I got was a huge big exceptional bastard."

24

WHENEVER I THINK ABOUT October 2010, I remember it as a month spent waiting. But there were movements and eras within that wait. The first few days of my pregnancy, the weekend where we waited for my first appointment, the days directly after where we thought about the abortion, that was one era. And the days after the dinner party was another.

James had been my support group and my parent during the first era; by the second, we were completely adrift. James was deep in grief for Dr. Byrne. I think he assumed that, because he and Dr. Byrne had already broken up once and got back together, they would go on uniting and parting for ever. It was dawning on him now that he and Dr. Byrne would never have a third act, and would never have a goodbye. His phone number had been blocked. He used my phone. My number was blocked also. The cheque cleared, and we now had close to three grand in our savings account.

I went to work. My performance was terrible, and I could tell that my manager was on the brink of firing me. I robotically went through the script that was provided for me, and I often went a full work day without committing anyone to increasing their direct debits. The worst days were the ones where I had to raise money for people in other countries. "Don't we have enough problems here?"

was the frequent answer, when I spoke about children walking miles to collect dirty water.

"You seem like an intelligent, compassionate sort of girl," said one woman. "Why don't you go work for something closer to home? Why don't you go work for the Deaf?"

My eyes started to brim, a combination of pregnancy hormones and being called "compassionate" when I had both deceived and extorted a reproductively challenged woman who—give or take a little exploitation—had never been anything but nice to me.

"We're not that sort of organisation," I said, the tears dripping onto my desk. "I have to take what's given to me. It's a new one every day."

The woman on the other end of the phone softened, moved by my lack of conviction. "Oh, pet. It's the recession, isn't it?"

"Yes."

"You should try to get a better job."

"Do you know of any?"

"No."

My manager, who was next to me, took the receiver out of my hand and finished the call. Then she brought me into her office and told me that if I didn't cop on I would lose my job.

James was working six days a week in the bookshop now. Almost everyone else had been let go by that point. We never understood why he was always kept on, except for an, as yet, unproved theory that Ben was closeted, too. When we came home in the evening we talked past one another, poor receptacles for the other's unhappiness because we were both so brimming with our own.

It was only a few days, I realise now, but it felt like a year.

I had made the choice not to tell Carey. I knew it would devastate him, and I suspected that—despite us never talking about it—he didn't have wholly positive things to say about abortion. There was something ancient and Catholic in him, a pure defiant streak of old Rome that had been strong in his family and kept alive by living in the North. He wore a miraculous medal. He knew his saints.

I didn't want to argue with Carey about abortion, but I didn't want to burden him with it either. It seemed like I had unwittingly ruined the lives of so many people, and I didn't want to ruin his, too. He was already going through so much.

And so I ignored phone calls. I gave curt responses to texts. I resolved that, after the abortion, and when the fog had cleared, I would resume being his long-distance girlfriend. But even then, I knew it was doomed. Carey could be at home for months, maybe years. I realised, with a stunning pain to the heart, that I might never see him again.

And then on Thursday I found the clot.

I was at work when it happened. I left my desk and walked across the by-pass to call the clinic. I was eventually passed on to the nurse who had spoken to James and me. I told her what I had found.

"Did you keep it?" she asked.

"No, I . . ." I was astounded by the question. "I was planning to get rid of it."

"The clot. Did you keep the clot?"

"Oh. No. I flushed it."

She tutted, like I had cut the tags off a dress I was trying to return.

"What did it look like? Liver?"

"Yes." I nodded, remembering the dark, shining substance. "Yeah, liver."

"All right. We better make you an appointment, then."

"At the clinic?"

"No, at the hospital."

She was moving through every step too quickly, and it frightened me. I kept begging her to slow down and explain things to me, but she had already moved on to the next phase of planning.

"I can get you in tomorrow morning? Ten a.m.?"

"I have work."

"Well, that's all I can do," she said.

"Am I miscarrying?"

"I can't diagnose that over the phone. You need to go to A&E, if you can't make an appointment."

"Is this what it would look like, though? If I were miscarrying?"

She took a moment to answer. "Yes. It would look quite like this. Do you want the appointment, or will you go to A&E?"

"I'll take the appointment," I said weakly, and hung up the phone. I stood at the side of the road, wearing a blazer over jeans, in a look that my mother described as "smart casual" but made me look like an estate agent.

I've tried not to stay angry at the nurse. Sexual health clinics have never been particularly well funded or well staffed in Ireland, and she was probably thinking of the abortion she had to cancel, and the other girl she could slide into my appointment's place.

There was a petrol station near the call centre. I bought a packet of the thickest Kotex pads I could find and went back to work.

I wish I had more to say about the clots, or the appointment the next day that confirmed the end of my pregnancy, or the days of heavy bleeding that felt like they might go on for ever. Those days have always been a strange, cold shadow in my memory. Years ago, I asked James what they were like, and what I was like during them.

"You were miles away," he said. "I was afraid your brain had broken for ever."

"In what way?"

"Like you'd butter some toast and walk away from it. Do up your buttons wrong. Be all chatty and hyper one minute, then all gloomy and distant the next."

"God."

"If you weren't looking closely, you would have seemed fine."

"Right."

"But I was looking closely, so."

There seemed no right way to feel. I was conscious that I had been let off the hook and that I should be grateful. I wouldn't have to go on a frightening trip to England, and I wouldn't have to bankrupt myself doing it. I knew that this was a net positive overall. But I could not shake the feeling that Carey's baby had died inside me because I was rotten, and did rotten things. I bled for so long that I started thinking of myself as a person who had made a bad bargain with the fairies. I had got my gold, and now I was paying for it.

Then my mother called.

"We really think you should reconsider this graduation thing, Rachel," she said sternly.

I felt like I was drowning and someone was asking about my tax return. "Oh?"

"It would mean a lot to your father," she continued. "He's very low. He needs a day out."

"It's too late anyway, Mum. All this stuff is arranged months in advance. Seating and gown rental or whatever."

"Don't mind all that," she said. "If you can sort the gown, I can sort the rest."

I didn't see how. My graduation was Monday, on what had once been the planned date of my abortion. "What do you mean, 'sort the gown,' Mum?" I said. "How on earth am I meant to 'sort the gown'? I don't have any connections at Big Gown. I have no idea where you even get them. It's all done through the college."

"You've gone very ratty," she said.

"I'm just trying to be realistic."

"Listen, I'll call the college. We'll pick up the degree, take a few photos, go for a nice lunch. We'll bring James. What's wrong with that?"

I had already taken two days off, for my appointment and for my miscarriage, and knew I was on thin ice at the call centre. I phoned my manager and asked for the time off. She sighed.

"Rachel, I think it's better if you don't come back in. I'm not sure if this is the right fit for you."

"Will I still get paid for my sick days?"

"What? No."

I hung up the phone.

My mother got her way. Well, most of her way.

She pestered the administration office all day to let me go. She invented various problems as to why I hadn't RSVP'd or booked my gown rental, hinting heavily at mental illness, financial ruin and general poor health. It was incredible how accurately she had nailed my situation while ostensibly lying about it. Eventually, she was allocated three guest passes to the ceremony, but was told that there was no scroll prepared for Rachel Murray, and that I would have to watch everyone else graduate. My mother thanked her, and then rang back an hour later. How could we get the scroll prepared? The woman said she had nothing to do with the scrolls. My mother asked for the phone number of the scroll people.

After a solid eight hours of pestering, bribery and exquisitely performed small talk, my mother called me to say that I would be collecting my scroll, after all. I had to sit in the guest section, and I would be permitted to collect it on stage after everyone else had picked up theirs. If I could not procure a gown, I had to wear "dark, loose-fitting formal wear."

"I have a black dress," Mum said triumphantly, and started talking about getting my hair blow-dried.

It seemed to me that this was the worst of all possible worlds. You could go to your graduation or you could not, but this in-between state was humiliating. It was too late to do anything about it. My mother had already worked too hard, and all I could do was wearily go along with it.

"How did you manage it?" I asked. "With the scroll people?"

"Oh, I promised everyone I spoke to a free teeth cleaning," she said.

I was in no position to complain about my fake graduation. Even if half the people my mother spoke to didn't accept the free teeth cleaning, it was still a huge expense that she couldn't afford.

My parents called to Shandon Street at 11 a.m. the next morning, my mother with her lipstick on, my father in a grey suit. The graduation had been sold to me as something my father desperately wanted and needed. That morning, however, he would have obviously rather been at home. He was utterly sullen, a mood that was in keeping with the tone of me and James's home at that time, and I began to wonder whether depression was coming out of the walls.

My dad sat down on the couch and seemed to sink right into it. "I'll just wait here," he said, "while you perform your ablutions."

Ever since Chris had shown up months before, I had thought about my father's depression as an errand that I must get around to. I didn't think about it as a thing that was happening to him, pushing on his shoulders, pinning him to chairs.

"Do you want a tea, Dad?"

He looked at a months-old magazine with Leona Lewis on the cover.

"All right."

I learned—later, of course—that my mother had insisted on celebrating my graduation day because the last of my father's investments—a shopping complex in Killarney—had just gone bust. All of my parents' money was in property and investments, and there were huge questions around what they were going to retire on.

I brought my father his tea and he spoke.

"You'll be going abroad, I suppose."

"Who told you that?"

"They all are," he said. "The youngies always go."

I thought about the three grand in our savings account and wondered if I should tell him about it. It might comfort him to know that someone had money.

"Just don't get up the duff, or anything stupid."

Despite everything, I laughed.

My mother and I went upstairs, and I put on the black wool dress she had brought from home, along with thick black tights and brogues. I looked like I was going to a funeral. She asked me how the job was going, and I told her that I had been fired again.

"Oh, never mind," she said, determined to put everyone in high spirits. "I don't think it's good for you to be sitting down all day, anyway."

We knew parking would be a nightmare so we walked to the college, which only added to the odd funereal tone of the day. It felt like we were following a hearse, and I was still so weak from the miscarriage. I felt eighty years old.

It was easiest, when I was living with James, to congratulate myself on my self-sufficiency and the fact that I was not a burden to my struggling parents. While that might have been part true, it didn't change the fact that I had done nothing to help them, either. My mother needed someone to talk to, my father needed someone to cheer him up. My brothers probably needed something, but their lives were too far away from mine to comprehend what that could be.

I said this to my mother, once. I apologised for being self-absorbed, for not asking more questions. It was years later, when she was sick, and although she did eventually get better it felt like a time for Big Truths. The statement startled her. "What could you have *done*?" she said. I told her that I could have been a better listener. She shook her head, and her reaction seemed to be: *What on earth would I have talked to you for?*

I stood next to my parents in the guest section, the rows and rows of empty seats in front of us, all awaiting graduates who had RSVP'd to the ceremony. It seemed like we waited for ever there, while various sets of parents and partners made polite chatter. I felt woozy, like my hands and feet were attached to my body with very loose string. "I've made a reservation at Isaacs," my mum said. "Do you remember, we used to always go there, back when you were in school?"

It was the kind of reliably chic mid-priced place that was famous for its crab cakes, and it was right near my secondary school. My mum often had lunch with her friends there, back in the old days, and I would sometimes join her.

My dad was gazing at a couple a few rows ahead of us.

"What's up, Dad?"

"I did his veneers," he said. "About five years ago."

"Ah."

My mother smiled, happy he had said something. The music started up, and the faculty began to walk in.

I had never been to a graduation ceremony before, and I haven't been to one since. It had not occurred to me that it's a big day for the faculty as well as for the students, and that they are usually in attendance.

There, cloaked in red robes and looking like a wizard, was Dr. Fred Byrne.

I gripped the side of my chair, and my bones began to vibrate. Everyone in the room stood up. I was the only one who remained seated. "Rachel," my mum prodded. "Stand."

I stood. My teeth clenched, a straight line going from my molars to my ears. Dr. Byrne looked perfectly relaxed, smiling widely as he took his seat behind the podium with the other members of the faculty. I recognised Dr. Sheehan, who had taught me about film noir and German expressionist painting.

Two thousand euro, and you'll never see me, or hear about this, ever again.

Was I breaking my promise by being here? It had never occurred to me, until that moment, to give back the money. The money was specifically for the termination, and when it turned out that I didn't need one, I thought of it as hush money. Money for what I had gone through. Money for the lie I had unwillingly taken part in. Seeing Dr. Byrne there made me feel like a fugitive. Like I should go to the cash machine, and slam the two grand into his fists.

The graduates entered in their black gowns and green bibs. The course had been too huge for me to recognise everyone, but I knew faces. People I had done tutorials with, borrowed pens from, given my notes to. They were part of the same moving amoeba, and I was sitting in a black wool dress with my parents at the back of the room. In a way, it was perfect. It was utterly in keeping with my university career. I felt lonely and beady-eyed and like life was a place that happened somewhere else.

The head of the department welcomed us to the ceremony in Irish, then in English, and spoke English for the rest of the service. It fell past me, like scenery outside a car window. All I could think about was the fact that I was in the same room as Dr. Byrne, who I had sworn to keep away from for the rest of my life.

Eventually, the graduates were told to turn around, and to give their families and loved ones a round of applause for supporting them in their education. They turned and clapped, their smiles wide, happy to be the centre of attention and to magnanimously give that attention away. A few of my classmates' gazes fell on me, and I saw some confused expressions, like they couldn't quite remember where they knew me from.

The scroll giving started. It went on for an hour, and I could see the boredom snatching at my parents. My mother looked as if she had realised this was a bad idea. We felt like charity cases, rejects from a world we had once occupied so easily. I held both of their hands. It was a terrible time, abysmal in every way, but I also felt very close to them. Like the three of us were on the same team, both as a family and as individuals. I never felt that way about my parents again, even on my wedding day.

Finally, when it felt like it had gone on for ever, when the bright beam of sunshine through the long windows had burned us all, when the department head was getting hoarse from name-calling, Rachel Murray was called. I shuffled out of my seat, past the confused, seated parents, and went to collect my scroll.

As I walked up the aisle, I couldn't help but find Dr. Byrne. His face filled with panic and confusion. He must, on some level, have expected to see me there. But not like that: apart from everyone, and not even wearing the gown.

If there had been nothing amiss with my university career, if I really was just a student who hadn't done the necessary admin to attend graduation and who had found a way to go anyway, I'm sure the whole room would have felt it. Everyone would have instinctively understood or assumed I was someone who had been sick, or *in absentia*, or had some other equally plausible and fine reason to be treated differently.

But there's a gut inside the body, and it metabolises the atmosphere quickly. Everyone knew that something was wrong, and that the graduation ceremony felt like a forced wedding between a child and a corpse. Like a horrible rite that they all had to sit through to ensure another safe harvest.

I took the scroll, and felt the eyes of every member of the department. How many of them knew about Rachel Murray and the terrible dinner party?

Afterwards, my father broke his silence. "Were you very close with your professors, Rachel?"

"No. Why?"

"Only, after you took your scroll, they couldn't seem to stop looking at you."

25

WE ARRIVED AT ISAACS, confused and awkward with one another, and I got a phone call from James. He was supposed to meet us there.

"Listen: I won't be able to make it. Ben can't spare me."

"What?!"

"I've sent a replacement."

"A replacement? Who? James, what are you playing at?"

"Just wait."

A minute later, James Carey arrived in a navy sports jacket and smiling like a talk-show host. "Hello, my darling," he said, his hands on my hips. "Christ, don't you look stunning? Congratulations."

My parents, desperate for something new to think about, became immediately excited.

"Rachel, who is *this*?"

I hadn't seen him since August, and in that time I had both carried and miscarried his baby. I was speechless, hard-blinking and jumpy.

"Hello," he said, sticking his hand out to my father. "My name is James."

"Another James?" Mum exclaimed.

"Well, Rachel calls me Carey, but she's the only one. I wouldn't dare try to replace the other James. No competition there, I'm afraid."

"Oh, don't we know it," Mum said, already charmed. "It's James this, James that since last Christmas. We've heard of nothing else."

All of a sudden, my parents and Carey were taking the piss out of me. My love affair with James Devlin, which had apparently tickled them, was being aired out for everyone to enjoy.

"He's great, though," Carey said. "He told me where you were today. I phoned him when Rachel said she didn't want to make a fuss over graduation. So I came down from Derry."

"From Derry?" Dad said. "Today?"

"Train to Dublin last night, train to Cork this morning."

"Aren't you great?" My mother was genuinely impressed. She had never liked Jonathan.

"Well, she worked so hard, didn't she? Have you read her essays?"

I am told that it was a lovely lunch. I can't remember if I said a word, or ate anything, or even smiled. All I knew was that I was glad he was there, but not enough to make me happy generally. Happiness felt very far away, and like something only the innocent were entitled to.

Carey turned the whole day around for my parents. He seemed to understand that they needed fun, and lightness, and crab cakes. He spoke reverently about his sick mother, but he didn't dwell on it. He had funny anecdotes about his father and the rest of his family. He said he didn't mind being back in Derry at all, and that it was very like Cork, really.

The lunch went on a long time, until the restaurant had to close for the dinner service. My parents kissed me goodbye outside, and my father handed me an envelope. "It's only a fifty," he said. "It's not much, but take yourselves out for a few more jars."

Carey and I walked down the street and discussed pubs. I leaned into him, my head on his shoulder. The further we were from my parents the more I slouched into him, less for love, and more to stay upright.

"Ey ey ey, what's going on? Are you legless already?"

I gripped him hard, like I was chaining myself to railings. His tone shifted.

"Are you all right, Rache?" he asked. "Oh God, I was right to come, wasn't I?"

"Yes," I murmured.

"What's wrong, then? Why have you gone all strange?"

"So much has happened, Carey. So much you don't even know about."

"Well, come on now, I can't find out if you won't tell me. How bad can it be?"

I took him to the pub, and I told him how bad it could be. How I realised I was pregnant after he had left for Derry. How I had not wanted to burden him with my problems, when he was dealing with so many of his own. How I had planned to get a termination, but in the end, didn't need to. I did not mention the Harrington-Byrnes. It was too complicated, and seemed irrelevant anyway.

It wasn't, of course. It was deeply relevant. I just wanted to save face where I could.

"I don't understand," he said finally. "Why didn't you say any of this to me? The baby, Rachel. How could you not say?"

"You've already got so much going on," I squeaked. "With your mum and your family and everything. I wanted you to think of me as, like, a fun person."

He looked appalled. "What does that mean? A fun person?"

"You know, whenever you called, we'd just flirt and talk shite, wouldn't we?" I said. "I didn't want to pile another thing on top of you. I didn't want to become another problem. Another dependent."

It came out all wrong. He looked more offended than ever. "I don't look after my mum because she's a problem or a dependent," he said. "I look after her because I love her."

This confused me. "I know."

"And I love you, too. When you love someone, you sign up for the whole thing. Even if they're grumpy or weird or sick or if they're *pregnant*, Rachel. It doesn't matter how many things you have on already. You love the whole person."

He looked at his full pint and sighed. "I don't think you ever got that."

Carey was speaking in the past tense already, and it terrified me. "I get that!" I said, my voice going up an octave. "I was always just afraid you might go off me again."

"Go off you?" he spluttered. "I've been mad about you for months. You've been the one ignoring *my* calls. My invites. My . . . feelings."

"You went off me once before," I hit back, more focused on winning the argument than being lovable. "Back in May. You fucked off with no warning."

"That was once."

"But it was for *weeks*."

"Well, I didn't think you were that arsed, did I?" he suddenly railed. "You were always running off to be with bloody James. And apparently nothing has changed. His is the only person's opinion you *actually* care about, Rachel. Everyone else is just fecking window dressing."

If only Carey knew the hours, days, I had spent lamenting his lack of interest in me to James. How I dissected his movements, his words, his gestures. I tried to tell him something like this: that I relied on James to decode Carey because Carey was so insistently undecipherable.

"I just don't believe it, Rachel. I've been clear," he said, shaking his head. "I've been clear about you the whole time. But you always want it to look a certain way, to get a certain number of texts, to have your little life with James always just so. I can see you, you know. I can see you watching me, noting down everything like the Gestapo, ready to report back so you can deconstruct it all. And it gets *irritating*. Sometimes I don't feel like providing you with the material."

I had spent so long building up Carey as this ungovernable mystery, and apparently I was the one who had been intangible and distant the entire time.

"This is stupid," he said, looking at his lap. "You didn't tell me you were having my baby. I feel like we're in a soap."

"Well, I wasn't going to *have* it, was I?" I spluttered.

He looked more wounded than ever. "You didn't even think about having it?"

I couldn't re-enter that world, the imagined playground of living in Derry with him and mothering one of many strawberry-blonde moppets. It was gone now, and it wasn't a fantasy any more, but a dead universe, collapsed in on itself. "No," I said. "I'm too young, Carey, you know that."

"I know," he said, his face twisting. "I just thought you would have at least considered it? You just booked an abortion straight away?"

"It's my body," I said limply. "My choice."

"Yes, I *know* it's your choice. But I should have had a consulting role, surely? In some sense?"

"It doesn't matter what I wanted, does it?" I snapped. "Because I lost it—I was always going to lose it, no matter what we talked or didn't talk about."

We went on like this, our moods and patter changing quickly and often. He would go from being remarkably tender to remembering that he was furious with me, and then go back to feeling sorry that I went through the whole thing alone. We exhausted ourselves. I wondered if he regretted coming down to Cork.

When we finally left the pub, he didn't touch me. "I'm trying to understand, Rache. I really am. I'm trying to get my head around it. But I feel like I don't know you at all. It's such a big thing to keep from someone you love. It's the biggest thing there is. And I could have helped."

"How?" I asked. "How could you have helped?"

"With the money. With, I don't know, comforting you."

He knew me well enough by that stage to know what I was thinking.

"But you had James for all that," he said.

"Well. I did."

He rolled his eyes.

"You can't *blame* me for that," I said. "He's my best friend."

"I know he's your best friend," he snapped. "This isn't about James."

"It feels like it is," I said. I was hoping to get Carey on a charge of homophobia, thus clearing me on the charge of being a selfish and stupid person.

"Don't you understand how condescending it is," he said, "for someone you love not to tell you about the biggest thing happening in their life, because they don't want to bother you? Because they think you can't handle it?"

"I just wanted to leave you out of it. Because I *do* love you. You know that. I'm always saying it."

"That's not an act of love, Rache. It's an act of . . . I don't know, ambivalence. It's an act of distance."

"Your mum was sick."

"I don't care if my entire family were thrown into a volcano, Rachel, I want to *fucking know* if I'm having a child with someone."

There is a parallel world where I said the right things to Carey that day. Made the right displays of affection, showed more signs of regret, wept and mourned the miscarriage in the way he wanted to. Perhaps in that world I got on the train to Dublin with him, and then to Derry. But I didn't have the strength or the character. My mind was still in the graduation ceremony, with Dr. Byrne and his red robes. With the eyes of hundreds of people, who all knew there was something wrong with me, but didn't quite know what.

I was a pretty cheerful person by nature. Emotionally dependable, like a good horse. Perhaps if I had been a more melancholy girl I would have been able to recognise that I was in the middle of a trauma, a word that still feels like it's for other people. But I was so far away from myself, and it didn't matter that a man I loved was trying to bring me back. He was too late, and it wasn't enough.

He came home with me. He sat on my bed, and I started to kiss him, feeling his face and chest with my hands. We couldn't have sex. I was still wearing the thick pads given to me by the doctor. I was desperate to get through to the part of Carey only I was able to reach, the sticky passionate silly place that transcended real life. I tried to convince him that my desperation was legitimate horniness, and for about three minutes, he was prepared to believe me.

I hid my face in his crotch, committing to an overly emotional blow job that we both knew was intended as an act of penance. I looked up at him, quickly, and saw that his face was tilted to the window. His cheekbones lit up by the street lamp, his eyes like an empty glass bowl.

He left for Dublin the next morning. I did not see him again.

Somehow, life went on.

I managed to get bar work, which didn't suit me as much as the bookshop but suited me much more than the call centre. There was a pub on Washington Street that took me on, near the small plates restaurant that had since closed. It was easy, and fun sometimes, although I never felt easy or fun any more.

I was rigid and off the pace. James wasn't all there, either. Our relationship had shifted its feet, adjusting for the amount of weight it was now holding. We still watched TV, and ate dinner, and checked in to see when the other person was coming home. But there was a change you could only see from the inside. Our conversations moved in the same directions—Why doesn't Glenn Close have an Oscar? Why don't they put crisps in the sandwiches at Subway?—but the flow, the sound, the echo, was different. I felt like we were playing cover songs of our own conversations. We just didn't enjoy each other in the same way.

Behind it all was anger, I think. We were both quietly suspicious that each of us had ruined the other's life. I would spend days angry that Dr. Byrne's affair with James had exploded my chances at a nice job, as well as my entire sense of self. I couldn't stop thinking about what Carey had said: that it was my co-dependence on James that had caused him to act distant.

James, I suspect, was brooding about how my pregnancy and subsequent scamming of the Harrington-Byrnes had severed his link to love for ever. I would be mean to James, make little digs about his not going to college, or engage in "playful" banter about his more feminine qualities. Things we would have laughed at before hit differently now that this new edge was here. He would become irritated by my messiness, and go on a patronising tirade about how I was useless, couldn't work a Hoover, couldn't fill an iron, couldn't do anything right, really.

Then the feelings would switch, and change their direction of flow. I would feel guilty about my part in James's sorrow, and suddenly lavish him with affection and treats from the shop. He would do the same: call me gorgeous, point at celebrities from the magazines he still compulsively bought, say, "You look a bit like her, don't you?"

We could never match up these moments. James was never in the mood to be loved when I wanted to love him, and vice versa. We started to spend more time with other people. James had a gang of three other gay boys, and they went to Chambers Bar together on the nights I was working. With college over, it was easier for me to meet up with secondary-school friends. People were moving back to Cork, having finished their own degrees elsewhere, with the exception of the Trinity students who we resented and who never came back. We played at adults, going for coffees and sandwiches during the day. They were feeling equally as hopeless about the future, and we lamented our useless degrees together.

My best friend from school was a girl called Gemma Dwyer. She was doing her first teaching placement in Cork, so was usually free in the afternoons. We fell into a pleasant, if somewhat dull, routine of meeting at a café on French Church Street at around 4 p.m., where I would eat a big sandwich before my shift started at six. She would tell me long stories that made her students sound like the Railway Children, and made her sound like a benevolent goddess that taught them about goodness and compassion.

One afternoon, Gemma leaned towards me.

"Rachel, there are two women behind you who won't stop looking at us."

I turned around. Two women in their forties had their heads together and were making no secret of the fact that they were discussing us.

"Oh. God."

"What shall we do?" Gem said.

"I don't know. Ignore them."

"They're still looking."

"Well, so?"

"It's rude."

"People are rude!"

When we got up to leave, Gemma marched up to them while I was putting on my coat.

"Excuse me—do we know each other?" she said.

"No, I don't think so," one of them responded.

"Well, you've been looking at me and my friend for this entire meal. I thought you might have something to say."

One of the women looked bashful, but the other met my gaze.

"You're Rachel Murray," she said.

"Yes," I replied. "Hello?"

"My husband works with Aideen Harrington." Her tone was a cold bare bulb in an interrogation room. The woman had not been at the party, which was the most terrifying thing. She just knew me, the way people often knew each other in Cork. She knew me by reputation. She knew me to see.

My stomach dropped into my hips. I waited for a few seconds for the blood to come back to my face, then walked out.

"What was that?" Gemma asked. "Who was that?"

I just said goodbye, and walked fast to my bar shift with my head down.

After that, I noticed strangers' reactions to me more and more. I felt naked, stripped of a shell, a soft baby-pink thing. It's hard, when you work behind a bar, to know who is looking at you and who is looking at the drinks lined up behind you. Intense eye contact is often just someone trying to focus on what tequila you carry. But it registered the same with me: the tequila gazers, and the people who knew who Rachel Murray was and what she had done.

Another night, a drunk girl came up to me and told me that we used to be in the same American Lit class.

"Cool," I said. "You have a good memory. That class was huge."

"Yeah," she said, then bent her head low, conspiratorial. I smelled the high synthetic sting of a vodka Red Bull on her breath. "You know, I always wondered if his dick was as big as he was."

She laughed and kissed me on the cheek. "You're a legend, girl," she said, and my gut sank as I noticed a table of her girl friends, looking over at our conversation like they had scripted the opening line.

These kinds of interactions didn't happen every day, or even every week. But I behaved as if they were about to. I was always conscious that I was minutes away from my next Dr. Byrne–related run-in, and held myself stiff. I didn't want to be caught doing something that would further cement me in the Cork consciousness as That Girl.

Round red circles, the size of coins, appeared on the tops of my breasts and arms.

"Oh my God," James said, smothering a laugh. "You actually *have* ringworm?"

Ringworm and scabies. The first thing we ever talked about, and we had just passed our first anniversary of it.

I did not have ringworm. I had something my family GP called "button psoriasis." I was asked if I had any new stresses in my life.

"Oh, I don't know," I lied. "The economy?"

Our savings were more important than ever. I never went out any more, because I worked nights, and I never spent during the day, because I was asleep or getting ready to work again. James was also vigilant, and we were both putting away fifty a week.

"We need to get out," I said to James.

"We need to get out," he confirmed.

———

A Google search, December 2021:

> Dr. Fred Byrne UCC cork
> Dr. Fred Byrne UCC cork sick
> Dr. Fred Byrne UCC cork sick coma
> Aideen Harrington
> Aideen Harrington sick husband coma
> Deenie Harrington sick husband coma

And finally:

> Alistair Harrington daughter husband sick coma

I search them all, like telegrams posted into the ether. Strangely enough, Alistair Harrington proves fruitful. A short interview in the *Evening Echo* had run at the beginning of October.

CORK POET TO RECEIVE RETROSPECTIVE
AT CRAWFORD ART GALLERY

My eyes skitter down the page, taking in nonsense phrases like "the homecoming Cork's poet laureate deserves" before finally landing on a quote from Deenie.

Speaking on behalf of her father's estate, Aideen
Byrne has said that she is "thrilled" the event will
finally be taking place, her archival work having
been delayed several times due to family illness.

"There's been a lot of renewed interest in Dad's
work over the years. Poetry is big again, and I think
younger audiences are beginning to realise how
resonant his work still is."

Alistair Harrington: Ashes to the Fire, Crawford
Art Gallery, 10 October–15 December, Tickets €8

My first thought is: I should book my flight right now, brave the
Christmas crowds at Stansted, and surprise my parents with a visit
from their heavily pregnant daughter. Stand in the Crawford, my
butt cheeks clenched, trying not to let out nervous pregnancy wind
while I stare at the letters and photos that I once touched in the
sun-drenched kitchen of the Harrington-Byrnes.

Or, the Byrnes.

She's going by just Byrne now. Why, Deenie, when you were so
comfortable with Harrington before, would you take your husband's name? After everything he did to me and James, after everything he must have continued to do after I evaporated from your
life completely? I circle back to the question I have asked myself
hundreds, if not thousands, of times over the years: How did she
make the marriage work? How much did she swallow and forgive?
How much did he change and promise?

I am good at a few things, but I am great at being married. As I
learned that year in Shandon Street, there is nothing that my personality or my humour thrives on more than being able to see the
same person at the same time every day. I thrive on over-exposure,
on elaborate jokes, on private mythology.

I am a huge advocate for marriage, and yet I still don't understand how Deenie kept hers going.

I should go, I think, looking at flight comparison websites, *to confirm to myself that it did all happen.* That there was a person called Rachel Murray, and she existed in the summer of 2010, full of sex and books, surrounded by the men she was in love with.

And then the baby kicks and it feels like an earthquake from the inside.

26

THE DISTANCE BETWEEN James and me, which was unpleasant yet organic, began to morph into something else.

I woke up one morning in November unusually early. I woke up with my neck crooked, my nose blocked, and beginning to wonder why on earth I lived in this house at all. The ants in summer, the frigid cold in the winter. Nothing fun had happened in Shandon Street since the exodus of Carey and Dr. Byrne. We drank but not joyously; ate junk food, but never with a sense of shared sin, always because it was the warmest, quickest thing to shove into our bodies. We were heartbroken. Every now and then we would inform one another that we had "really turned a corner" with our sadness, and that we were "over it" now. It wasn't true. We were not over it.

That early morning in November, I padded downstairs for a glass of water. It was 10 a.m., but it felt like dawn. I had got off work at three, and had stayed awake, wired, until well after four. James was awake, on his laptop, and talking on the phone.

When he saw me at the top of the stairs, he hung up like I had just caught him masturbating.

"Who was that?"

"Hmm?"

"On the phone. Who was that?"

"No one. What are you doing up?"

"Water."

"Ah."

"It's cold."

"I know."

"Can I take a heater?"

"In my bedroom. Take a hoodie, too, if you want."

I snuggled into bed and fell back to sleep. I would have forgotten about it, if the same thing didn't happen again a week later. Another dropped phone call, another smile and an offer of clothes, or food, or a drive out to the McDonald's. I kept catching James in the middle of something, but I didn't know what that something was.

I started to suspect that he was sleeping with Dr. Byrne again. There seemed no other explanation. Were they emailing? Hadn't Fred Byrne learned his lesson the first time?

James's absences from the house became longer, his speech more guarded, his body language more withdrawn. We were supposed to be emigrating together in January, just six weeks away. Was now really the time to be starting up with the man who had betrayed us so thoughtlessly?

I didn't want to ask about it. If I asked, then he would tell me, and because I couldn't ever say no or stay mad at James, I would end up tangled in their world again. I was already a fugitive in my own city. There was no way I was going to be an accomplice to Dr. Byrne's betrayal of Deenie again.

"Are you all right?" James asked one day. We were assembling a fake Christmas tree, gifted to us by his mother. Slotting branches into a green pole, the plastic leaves itching our faces.

"Yes," I said. "Are you?"

"You just seem . . ." He examined one of the branches. "Prickly."

"Good one. Is that going in the script?"

"Huh?"

"Branches. Prickly."

"Oh. Right. Hah. No." James looked queasy.

I thought about how I would feel if it was Carey who I was forbidden from seeing, even though he only lived a mile away. I felt a pang of loneliness for him, the desperate knowledge that he was off in the world, still living his life, not even having the common decency to be dead and therefore putting a graceful end to our relationship.

He had texted me only once, since arriving back in Derry, saying that he needed to think about us. I didn't hear from him again. I checked in, enquired about his mother's health, but no response.

I pretended to untangle fairy lights.

"Do you want to come over on Boxing Day?" he said.

"Stephen's Day," I corrected. He could still be so English sometimes. "Where? To Fermoy?"

"Yeah. Mum is having a party."

"Will you pick me up?"

"Sure."

"Sure."

We stepped back in surprise to see how lovely the whole room looked. I had always been brought up to think of plastic trees as tacky, that big dogs were better than small dogs, that potato waffles were common. So many of my beliefs about the world had been predicated on our once having had money. Now I knew that a real tree for forty euro is wasteful, especially as it can only be used once. That small dogs fare better in small houses. That potato waffles are useful stomach cladding when you don't have a lot else.

There, in our living room, fairy lights bouncing off the waxy green brush, I realised there was nothing at all wrong with a plastic tree.

"We should clean the house," I said. "Make it a bit more Christmassy."

We swept the floors, hoovered between the sofa cushions, salvaged candles from our bedrooms. There were some empty jars in the recycling and we put tealights in them. James went to the shop and brought back a bottle of mulled wine, some spiced rum and a packet of Cadbury Yule Logs.

We mixed the mulled wine and the rum together on the hob, the window on the back-porch door steaming up. James looked so gorgeous, so different to how he had looked a year before. It was like he had found his face, grown into his nose, found shades of grey for his green eyes.

He poured the wine mix into our best mug and gave it to me. Our order of mugs went like this: big *Flintstones* mug, ordinary grey mug, small mug with a map of Spain on it, pretty horse mug with a slow leak, and finally a mug that a KitKat Easter egg had once sat in, and burned your fingers when you held it too long. Carey always drank from the map of Spain. Dr. Byrne had the horse. Me and James took it in turns to alternate the *Flintstones* and the grey.

"I hate the Spanish one now," I said, blowing on the mixture. "Makes me sad."

"I hate the horse." He said it with such conviction that I began to doubt my theory that he was seeing Dr. Byrne again. We drank for a moment in silence.

"Let's throw them off the roof."

There was a hurley in James's room that seemed to exist so he could tell the people he slept with that he once played hurling in secondary school. We climbed out the window, him passing the hurl out to me, along with the entire saucepan of wine.

"I'll throw," he said. "You hit."

The hurl hit the Spanish mug in one clean slice, splitting it in half, so Gibraltar was on one side of the road and San Sebastian on the other.

"Fuck!" I screamed, the relief rattling through me. "Yes! Fuck!"

"Okay, I want a go," he said. I threw the horse mug up in the air and he belted the base of it, shattering it over our heads. I covered my face in my sleeve as the pieces came down.

"That felt good," he said. "*Shit.*"

"I feel so strong now. I wish we had more things to smash."

"We don't," he replied. "We have only so many mugs."

"I hate the KitKat one. Shall I get it?"

"Are you sure you want to do this? Then we'll only have two mugs," he said. "No more guests."

"Yes," I said. "No more guests, and no more cunts."

He threw, and I batted, just missing the mug, which bounced onto the footpath and smashed.

"Hmm," I said. "Bit of an anticlimax."

"Because the KitKat mug didn't stand for anything," he said sagely. "The KitKat mug was just minding its own business."

"Poor thing."

We drank on the roof until it became too cold, and when we came back into the house the candles were burning low and the whole kitchen smelled of spices. It felt like the lower decks of an old ship, rough and cosy and the only safety we had against the sea.

"I think we've exorcised them now," he said. "That's it. They're gone."

I hugged him, and we fell asleep under the blanket downstairs. I woke up a few hours later, a frightening new thought uncoiling like a snake.

If it wasn't Dr. Byrne he was hiding from me, then what was it?

———

I was glad that we had that night on the roof, because we saw little of each other for the rest of December. I worked every night until Christmas Eve, the party season getting more chaotic as we moved closer to the New Year. "Fairytale of New York" played constantly, and I was amazed that despite it being such a cliché, people still allowed themselves to be moved by it.

"Fucking done with twenty ten," people would tell me often, at the bar. "Fucking bring on twenty eleven. Death to this shit year."

I was relieved to go home for a few days. Chris was out most of the time. Kev, still only sixteen, was in. We watched *Buffy* re-runs together on the Syfy channel, ate cheese from the fridge, found a rhythm that had not been there before. A person was beginning to emerge, or perhaps had been emerging for a long time. He was funny, I realised. Softly spoken, but dry.

"What's your friend James doing, for Christmas?"

"At home, in Fermoy."

"He's gay, isn't he?"

"You know he is."

Kev went quiet. We carried on watching *Buffy*. James Marsters was furiously ranting about "the slayer" and what he would do to her, his bleached hair slicked back.

"Are *you* gay?" I asked.

"I don't know," he answered, eventually.

"Well, if you are," I said, feeling my big sisterhood very keenly, "you know that's completely cool, right? You don't need to hide it."

"I know," he said. And he did seem to know. "I'm still feeling it out."

We didn't talk much about it after that. I got the sense that he didn't want to discuss it with his big sister, and I didn't blame him. I had been checked out from his life for so long. But I was relieved he could talk about it. How he hadn't lied, or buckled in on himself. He wasn't going to end up leading Dr. Byrne's double life, or have to lie like James felt he had to lie. Maybe it really was getting easier.

"I'm going to bed," I said, and couldn't help kissing him on the temple.

James picked me up on Stephen's Day in his mum's car. The dress code, he said, was semi-formal. I wore a plunge-neck black sequin dress that I had bought second-hand but was originally from French Connection.

"My God," he said, beeping the horn in appreciation. "Rachel Murray, those legs go all the way up to your asshole!"

"Isn't that where legs usually end?"

"It's a figure of speech. Get in."

He talked non-stop all the way to Fermoy, about his Christmas presents (a pile of books on screenwriting, Comme des Garçons aftershave, a Hollister hoodie that he planned on returning) and his sisters' presents, and his mother's plan to get a dog. I couldn't tell if it was the days spent at home that had wound him up, but he seemed nervous.

When we got to the house, Nicola was handing out champagne flutes at the door with strawberries at the bottom of each. The kitchen island was filled with luxury hors d'oeuvres from Marks & Spencer, and I happily made my way around it, dipping crunchy prawn toasts into sweet chilli sauce. People filled the house quickly, and I enjoyed playing the role of Charming Young Woman who listens carefully and laughs easily.

I was surprised when I found Sabrina smoking outside with one of James's sisters. Sabrina, who had moved to New York that summer, and who James once thought was me.

"Hello!" I said, already a couple of drinks deep, and going in to hug her. "Gosh, fancy seeing you again. Are you home for Christmas?"

"Rachel!" She hugged me back. "Yeah, yeah, got back in on the twenty-third. How are you?"

I wondered how James ever thought Sabrina and I looked alike. She was smaller than me, for one. She had a short blonde bob, whereas my hair was long, and more of a fair dishwater colour. Sabrina had a sharp little face, a pointy chin, quick eyes. My face was fuller. "Like a classical painting," James said once, being kind.

The second thing that struck me was what Sabrina was doing here. We had hung around with her a little, when she worked with us, but we hung around with everyone who was vaguely our age. Our general consensus was that Sabrina was nice, if a little prissy. Truthfully, I had barely thought of her since she emigrated. Why on earth had she come out to Fermoy, miles away from anything, when Stephen's Day was the biggest night in town of the year?

"How's New York?" I asked, because what I really wanted to ask was *Why are you here?*

"Oh, you know. Freezing. But good. Americans are so friendly, I feel like there's something on every night."

"I always heard New Yorkers were rude."

"You hear that, but they're just rude compared to other Americans, I think. They're friendly compared to Europeans."

"People say Irish people are friendly. I don't think we are. I think we're just loud."

"Right!"

We chattered on like this, and after a while I got a funny feeling that the dynamic was off. We had always been friendly, and still were, but I had the itching sense that we were a present and former wife, fighting for territory. I saw her eyes flitting around, and I got the urge to prove my place in James's life by telling her that I had been to the house before as many times as I possibly could.

"Nicola breeds cats in that shed," I said. "Nicola is his mum's name."

"I know. I met her on the way in."

"She makes a great sandwich," I said, too enthusiastically, restating my longevity in the Devlin household. "She made me a ham sandwich, once."

Even though my reactions were strange, I knew my instincts were correct. There was something going on, with Sabrina at this party.

James came out into the garden with another tray of drinks. He smiled widely, showing all his teeth. A smile that I knew meant *fuck* and not *yay*.

"Hey, you two!" he said brightly.

"Hey!" we both said in unison.

Then I said, "You didn't say Sabrina was coming!"

"Yeah!" he said. Then a pause. "Rachel, do you want to help me with drinks inside? The pensioners are getting through the sherry very quickly, and Mum has me on top-up duty."

"Fine."

There was a utility room off the kitchen and I followed James in there.

"What's going on?"

"I'm moving to New York," he said.

His face was so serious that I actually laughed.

"You're not moving to New York," I said. "This is not a thing. This cannot be a thing."

"It can be, and is, a thing."

I crouched down, and held on to my guts. Unable to believe how in a year where everything had changed, things had somehow managed to change again.

"I'm sorry."

"This is what you've been so secretive about, isn't it?"

"Yes."

"I need to go home. I need to call a taxi."

"You can't call a taxi."

"I can."

"You won't get one, and even if you could, it would cost you fifty quid to get back to Douglas."

"Well, I can't stay here," I said, already crying.

"Come on," he said, holding my hand. "Follow me."

My face was streaked with tears, and I didn't want to see anyone. "No," I said, hanging back.

"Come on. We'll go for a walk."

He led me through the house and out the front door, hands clenched, both our heads bowed, like a married couple on the verge of divorce. We walked down his parents' driveway and through one field into another. Soon we were surrounded by nothing but grass and stars.

"Go on," he said.

"Go on, what?"

"Go on and scream at me, no one will hear you."

"I don't want to," I said, wanting very much to scream at him. "I just want to know why you've participated in this fucking *fiction* of London when you're moving to New York with Sabrina of all people? Do you even *like* her? Are you even *friends*?"

The field smelled of animals and moisture, and I felt swallowed by the vastness of it.

"I didn't think any of this would come off," he replied. "Look, I went round the houses with the London agents, and the production companies, and they're all saying that I should get my face out there as a comedian, do comedy festivals, get in the theatre, and, I don't know, that sounds okay, but not *me*. I started looking at other stuff, and I found this internship."

"An internship?" I scoffed. "You're moving to America for an internship?"

"It's a proper one. One of the late-night shows, the ones that shoot in New York, they do these internship programmes for people from under-represented groups trying to get into comedy. You start as a writing assistant, and they have all this infrastructure to help you work your way up."

I had never heard him use the word "infrastructure" before. I pictured him on phone interviews with a sleek TV person who must exist and yet had never been mentioned to me. Me, who was supposed to know everything about him.

"And that's you, is it?" I said. "You're an under-represented group?"

"I'm a gay man. And working class. So. Yes?"

I had never thought about the paper facts of our existence before. I was surprised by how much it upset me. I didn't want any more reminders that me and James were two different people.

"So, what? When did you apply for this?"

"June."

"June!"

"I never thought anything would come of it! It was more like a writing exercise. And then they called me, and I had an interview, and they said I was on the second stage, then the third stage, and then they called last month and said I had got it."

"Why didn't you tell me?"

"Oh, Rache, you were going through so much. Carey and . . . you know. And I didn't think in a million years that I'd get it."

"I can't believe you've been lying to me, James. We've been saving and talking about London for months. And you had already entered this fucking competition to live in New York."

It made me feel better, somehow, to call it a competition.

"I literally just filled out a form in June. I filled out a form to live in Paris back in February, but I never mentioned that either, because it never came to anything. I just, I don't know, you apply for things, don't you?"

"I don't!" I exploded. "I don't just *apply for* things!"

He kicked at a clod of dirt.

"Well, no, Rachel, because you don't have to, do you?"

"What the fuck is *that* supposed to mean?"

"You *know* what it means." He was bored of eating humble pie. "It means: your dad is a dentist and your grandad was a banker and you have a university degree. The playing field is not *level*, Rache."

Today, I would have probably accepted that retort lying down. I have read so many articles on middle-class privilege, and even written some. But this was 2010, and I had too much fight in me.

"Are you *high*, James?" I screeched. "Look *around* you."

I gestured back to the big house behind us, the fields of farmland his stepfather owned. He was the one who could get emergency cash off his mother. He was the one who got to borrow the family car. "You're better off than my family, and you know it."

This was supposed to be an argument about London and New York. About secrecy, and about lies. Why were we talking about class, and whose grandfather was a banker?

"Babe, I went from shitty estate to shitty estate until I was nine. I moved schools too much to learn long division properly. I *barely* got a Leaving Cert, no chance of uni, and I have no connections. Unless I want to get a job in a piggery, I'm fucked. I'm in retail for ever. *Maybe* I get a phone job and I work my way up to head office. But you can do anything, Rache. You can do any career. The real way. *That's* why you don't have to enter competitions."

I rolled my eyes. It was all melodrama to me, all tactics to distract from the real point, which was that James had lied to me.

"You think I'm talking shite," he said, his nostrils flaring. "But you'll see, pal. These little graces you've picked up from your family, from university, they mean something. Hearing 'Homer' and knowing when someone doesn't mean 'Simpson.' Knowing what part of the animal paté comes from. It all adds up. It all means something."

I don't know whether James's words were a prediction, or a spell, but he was right. It did, and would, mean something. After I moved to London, I found that my accent, my good manners and my vague ability to reference Trollope helped build a picture for my English peers that became more than the sum of its parts. "You have one of those *nice* Irish voices," someone once said to me. "Soft."

They thought I had a bohemian background, or perhaps was some distant cousin of the aristocracy. They all thought I went to Trinity, and knew lots of poets personally, and asked me for tips on racehorses. I was once invited to Ascot and was asked if I could introduce the group to any jockeys. I found it all hilarious, of course, and told James about it, but I rarely corrected anyone. The difference between the truth and the reality was so marginal. What's the difference between upper-middle and middle-middle, really?

"I just can't believe you're going to leave me," I said. "After everything."

James wrapped his arms around me and held on tightly, there, in the middle of his stepfather's field. "I don't want to leave you either," he said, starting to cry. "Rache, I'm so scared."

We held each other like that for a long time. I tried to imagine him walking down big New York streets, his scrawny body and his slightly too big head bobbing along as he fetched coffees and lunches and dry-cleaning. I thought about a world where I only saw him a few times a year. And I wondered about what I would do next.

We walked back to the party, arms draped at our waists, and I told him how proud I was of him, and how Michael and Alice were going to keep on living together even if we weren't. How Michael and Alice would sweep the Emmys one day, and we would be on the red carpet, collecting statues on their behalf.

The house was lit up, the party still in full swing. It's so hard to know what music to play at a Stephen's Day party, the Christmas music already feeling so tired out, so someone had put Elton John on. Elton, who is Christmas without being Christmas. I said this to James, and he laughed and told me it was funny.

He stopped at the front gate. "I'll have to go through our savings account," he said. "I'll just add up all my deposits and take that out."

The account was now tickling four grand. The two thousand the Harrington-Byrnes had paid me to go away was my money, I suppose. James would have never dreamed to claim it for his own. It was my pregnancy, my would-be abortion. My pound of flesh.

When I started writing this all down, I told you that me and James have only ever had one fight, officially speaking. The one in O'Connor's, where I shoved him against a wall. The one where he almost needed stitches. There have been two more, and they were the night I told him about blackmailing Dr. Byrne, and the night he told me about New York. All that said, though, I never remember St. Stephen's Night 2010 as a fight.

I remember it as the night we decided to split the money and run.

27

ARRIVED IN LONDON on 15 January 2011, on a day where the lift at Elephant & Castle tube station was not working.

I dragged my father's largest suitcase up 124 steps, breathless and fiercely hoping for a chivalry that did not come. When I emerged into the freezing air, I found that my new neighbourhood was a market street next to a roaring, busy road. There were snacks and clothes on rails and chicken bones on the ground. Everything smelled like popcorn, polyester clothing and car fumes.

I was moving in with strangers. There were other options available, of course. Just as James had fallen on Sabrina, his one New York contact, I could have searched my Facebook friends list for people who had moved to London and might have a spare bedroom. But the more I thought about it, the more I imagined my hometown like a creeping shadow. I was still getting girls coming up to me in the bar, asking me odd questions, glancing back at their friends. I was too frightened to go anywhere I thought the Harrington-Byrnes might be, and that included bookshops, live music venues and the English Market.

Was it really as bad as all that? It's hard to say. I was the centre of my world, so it felt natural to assume that everyone in Cork knew who I was and was talking about me. But could I have been imagining it all?

Whether the strange looks were real or not, they were real to me, and they affected every choice that came next. I never reached out to anyone from home: not before I moved, and not after.

I was, for the first time in my life, completely alone.

I had done a Skype interview for a flat share on the Old Kent Road. The landlord was odd. He insisted that he do a birth chart before I moved in, to check my harmony with the house, and I was asked my exact date of birth along with the time of day. I was very charmed by this, of course. It seemed exactly the kind of thing that would happen to a young heroine, moving to London alone. Plus I wanted anecdotes, for James. I couldn't bear the thought of him making stories and me having none.

The flat was eleven floors up, no lift, and so I dragged my suitcase once again. I arrived, knocked on the door, and found my new landlord in a string vest and boxers.

"Sun in Taurus!" he said, by way of greeting. "Moon in Scorpio! Hello!"

"Hello."

"Luxurious and hot-headed," he carried on. "Passionate. I hope you won't be keeping me awake, bringing boys in every hour of the day and night."

His name was Justin. He was not gay, as this kind of language might imply, but a pervert.

My room was the shape of an old fifty-pence piece. It had a rolled-out futon and a heavy wardrobe with no drawers. For three months, I hung what could be hung and kept all my knickers and socks in my suitcase.

My first morning in the flat, Justin followed me around constantly, like a dog with an anxiety disorder. He talked about his workout routine, his job selling electronics at the airport, his twenties as a dancer in Berlin, his dream to dance again in the London Olympics—which were holding auditions, and soon—and his general love of spiritualism and the occult. He talked about my birth chart, going into extensive patter about the alignment of planets, and then finishing with an Austin Powers impression: *"Does it make you horny, baby?"*

I had never met someone so odd who could simultaneously be so charmless. Even now I can feel myself failing to trap him with words. I had always assumed that I loved kooky people, but maybe now I hated them.

I went to shower and he followed me to the bathroom door, then sat outside and continued to talk while I washed myself.

"Justin!" I shouted, from under the weak spray of tepid water. "Can you please *fuck off*?"

He fucked off. When I came out of the shower he was gone, but he had left a little tortilla wrap with ham and lettuce in it on a plate on the floor. There was a Post-it stuck to it, stuck right onto the tortilla wrap. It said: *For you.*

I took the plate and ate the wrap on my futon, still dripping wet, and burst into tears. It was just the kind of thing James might have done—a version of it, anyway—and now a weirdo was doing it.

But, even through my tears, I could feel something happening within myself. I had told a stranger to fuck off, and I had meant it. I had drawn a line with someone. I had never really done that before.

———

England was not exempt from the recession, but London was. Or rather, it was responding to the recession by having the exact same number of jobs and just paying everyone less for them. This might have been a relief for some but was a mathematical puzzle to me. I didn't understand how an £18,000-a-year assistant job could require a first-class degree and over a year's experience.

A bigger riddle was my CV. I had done a solid five-month internship with Deenie Harrington. I had put a book out into the world with her. I was in the acknowledgements. But what if they called her?

"Just put 'references available upon request,'" James said, when we Skyped about it.

"But what happens when they request them?" I replied. "Whose name will I give them?"

"Mine. I'll pretend to be her."

"That will never work."

"Hang on," he said. He carried his laptop out into the hallway of his building. "Sorry. Sab is taking her seventh shower of the day and I can hear her singing."

"Any good?"

"*No.*"

To my delight, James and Sabrina were not getting along as housemates. He found her prim and judgemental, and despite selling him on the delights of New York's social scene, she wanted to spend every night doing craft projects.

"I'm watching her knit," he snapped. "I'm twenty-three years old in the greatest city on earth, and I'm watching this dumb bitch watch TV and *knit.*"

Nobody knew his name yet at the internship. They were briefly interested in him on his first day, when they attempted to locate their grandmothers' birthplaces by simply repeating the words "Louth?" and "No, Longford?" at him, but no one had talked to him since. His accent, which was strongly Cork with flecks of Mancunian in it, wasn't particularly hard to understand, but it was unusual and hard to place, so people were unable to focus on what he had to say when he spoke to them.

"Today someone said that it's a 'good thing' I don't want to be in front of the camera," he said. "What the fuck does that mean?"

"At least you have a real job."

I did not have a real job. I didn't have a National Insurance number either, which was why I was working at a pub that paid me cash in hand until I could legally work in the UK. I had got the job by walking down every street in central London and handing in my CV to bars, making sure I hammed up my accent as much as I could.

"Can you do the foam?" one bar manager asked.

"Excuse me?"

"The clover in the foam? In the Guinness?"

"Yes."

I could not do the clover in the foam in the Guinness. When the request to make a clover eventually came up, I looked sad and said that this keg of Guinness had "travelled badly" from Ireland and that the clover wouldn't settle. Amazingly, they seemed to believe me.

I passed a lot of landmarks on my way to work. I went over Tower Bridge on the bus, like a child in a cartoon about London, and saw the Tower of London and St. Paul's Cathedral. It helped. A landscape costs nothing, so it always helps. But more often, I wondered what exactly I was doing there. London wasn't my dream. It was James's. I had never even wanted to leave Cork very badly, until living in Cork felt like a panic attack waiting to happen.

James and I had talked about me moving to New York, but the visa was too complicated, and so James had suggested that I stay in Ireland and work on my application. It was obvious to me that this was the most pathetic option of all. The only dignified thing to do was to move to London and make a go of it on my own. I had already lost so much dignity in 2010. I needed to get some back.

My National Insurance number came through, eventually, and I found some office temp work. I still had no friends. No one talks to office temps. Justin was always there when I came home, talking endlessly.

The spring came. I still had no people I could hang around with on the weekend, and so I was taking myself on long walks of London, spending nothing, occasionally treating myself to a £2 pork bun in a Chinatown bakery. My money was running out. One day I was so exhausted from loneliness and worry that I sat down in the middle of Chinatown, next to a table offering fliers on pro-democracy protests. I hoped that people thought I was there in solidarity, a white girl who somehow "got it." A woman asked me for a donation, and when I said I didn't have one, she politely asked me to leave.

The same day, I found a bookshop. There are lots of bookshops near the Charing Cross Road. But this one was different, because it was mine.

It was huge and busy, but quiet, and it had a little café in the corner, with bar stools for sipping espresso on. It sold first-hand, and second-hand, and rare editions. You could buy music there, but only if it was jazz, and there was one man who ran the jazz section with astonishing enthusiasm. After I had browsed for an hour and bought nothing, I sat on one of the coffee stools in the window with the stirring realisation that I had found the first place in London that I liked. I made up my mind that I would get a job there.

It took a month. A month for them to accept that they needed someone to help cover the weekend shift, which I did in addition to my temp work, then another three months for the coffee guy to move on, so I took over his job, too. Then I was moved into fiction. I was young, and desperate for connection, and I treated everyone I worked with like a celebrity. I studied them like they were my master's degree. Sofia, who ate a smoked-salmon sandwich from Pret every day, even on the days when she wasn't working, and whose father worked with the Mayor of London. Who at that time, was, of course, Boris Johnson, and who, at the time, we found hilarious. Philippa, who drank Lilt, and was distantly connected to Princess Anne, through the Tindall side. Byron, who did the jazz, and ran a night in Shoreditch every Friday, which I now attended, every Friday. He was well into his forties, but loved a party, and was happy to introduce me to people that I would later befriend and/or sleep with. Radhika, who did rare editions, had a double first from Oxford, where she had also, in her own words, "caught" anorexia. She was over it now, she said. She told me never to envy anyone from Oxbridge because all of them were either egotistical bullies or trembling and frightened of themselves.

I became the girl who hated going home, who always asked

everyone for a drink after work, who took up every invitation, hunted them out. A few weeks in, Radhika admitted to me that they had never socialised as a group before I had shown up. I suppose they didn't need to. They were all from England. Had networks, old schoolmates, hobbies. But they were all lonely, in their own way. London eats at everyone. My loneliness became a galvanising force. It made people stay out, one more drink, another bar, Soho to the G-A-Y, then the horrible casinos in Leicester Square. Being Irish helped. People were ready to believe I was fun.

It was strange, because the people I now considered my best friends in London saw me, then, as a satellite friend. But those bookshop girls were everything to me. There was something ravishing about being back in the world of women again, and not schoolgirls or students, but women. They were posh and exotic, and had feminine English knowledge that felt secret and strange. I passed Rigby & Peller with Sofia one day, and she told me they were the official underwear suppliers for the Queen. I thought this was something only she was allowed to know, and then I found out the Queen had all kinds of suppliers. She laughed as she explained them to me, and linked her arm through mine, and said that no one had ever been so interested in what she had to say. She was just an ordinary sort of posh girl, and there are lots of them in London. I was probably supposed to dislike her, for political reasons, but the distance between us made me love her even more.

I was invited to her Christmas Eve party in Earl's Court, and when I told her that I would be going home for Christmas and couldn't, she wrapped her arms around me. "No, you can't," she moaned. "You have to come. Cancel it, won't you?"

I laughed into her hair and said I couldn't, and that my best friend was coming home, too, and that I had to see him. She let me go and agreed, although she was annoyed nonetheless.

When I packed my bags for Cork that Christmas, I looked around, and realised I had a life.

28

J AMES WAS IN NEW YORK, and was now a permanent member of staff on the late-night show that had given him the internship. He barely got to write at all, but he put his jokes on Twitter, and was developing a following. I joined Twitter to see what he was doing. I began tweeting on behalf of the bookshop. Then I reviewed books for the bookshop's blog. The bookshop is quite famous, in a London kind of way, and so I was eventually asked to submit book reviews to the kind of lifestyle magazines that are very thick and come out four times a year. An Irish woman wrote a book that did well, and *The Times* asked if I would like to interview her. Opportunities like this rolled in and out, never with great regularity, but I developed a CV all the same. I built a website, which the adverts said was easy but wasn't, and I cried three times while trying to make it go live.

I started hanging around Sofia's flat in Earl's Court. The flat belonged to her parents. She told me this timidly, afraid I was going to hate her for it, but I was too pleased to have a friend. If my parents had London properties I would live in them, too, so what was the point of being a bitch for no reason? She was delighted with this and asked me to move in.

She was tiny and delicate, which made me feel weird about

myself, so I cut off all my hair and bleached it. I decided to be an imposing, sexy sort of tall girl. I remembered what Carey said about me having a body like Wonder Woman. We didn't speak again, after I moved to London. Too much had happened. But the way he saw me left an impression. It changed how I saw myself.

Which didn't mean I wasn't insecure. There were so many beautiful women in London, and diets were useless. If I didn't have carbs three times a day I couldn't finish a sentence, and that was that. But men were never a problem. I dated a lot, had sex quite a bit, but my long spell of monogamy was broken. I dressed like I would have been afraid to dress in Ireland: big prints, loud colours, mad accessories. "Your clothes," a fashion editor once told me, "have a sense of humour, don't they?"

A newspaper back home let me write a fashion column for them for fifty euros a week, mostly taking the piss out of trends, and I still write the same column now. They have adjusted my rate for inflation; I now make seventy-five euros a week. But I have fun, and sometimes a brand will send me a scarf. So.

I left the bookshop two years after joining it, when the only person of my original set left was Byron. I was running fiction now, but I had too many responsibilities, the new hires were younger than me, and it felt like time to move on. I became a staff writer at a magazine called *The Chelsea Buyer*, which was run by a woman who ate mackerel straight from the packet and whose office was the basement in her Notting Hill townhouse.

James got his first joke on TV. It was about Obama's tan suit. I watched it on YouTube the next morning. I cried and left a voice-mail on his phone to say that I was proud of him.

That was the first year I had enough money to visit him in New York. He took me to a warehouse party in some district he was too poor to live in, showing me the cool things he knew about in New York. We rented bikes and rode over Brooklyn Bridge. I asked him if he did this with everyone who visited and he said yes. I knew he was tired, and would have preferred to be on the couch, but had spent so long complaining about Sabrina that he felt he had to prove he was fun.

"Do you ever miss Cork?" he asked, on my last night. "And knowing people?"

"I know people."

"I mean really knowing them."

I thought about them all the time. When I saw large men with dark-haired women, when I found second-hand anthologies of Irish poets, when someone asked me about university. I never told anyone about the Harrington-Byrnes. At first because the wound was too raw, and then because the story was too complicated, and eventually because the story was all so Irish that I felt embarrassed. There was no way of telling the story without paraphrasing it as a Maeve Binchy novel. Bright young girl. Insular little city. Life almost ruined by pregnancy, but not quite. It was humiliating. I did not like Ireland very much, once I got settled in England. I was angry about the abortion I had extorted my friends to almost-have, and livid that my country had put me in that position in the first place. I kept waiting to hear from them again. I was easy to get hold of. I had a website.

I started covering Irish abortion stories for the English press, did some holiday cover at *The Guardian*, got a job at another magazine, with a real office. I wasn't earning very much more than I was at the bookshop, but I was also not spending. There was always some event where you could drink for free.

A story about an Irish woman who had died after taking illegal abortion pills made it into our English newsroom.

"Why didn't she just fly over?" someone asked.

"Because it costs money," I replied.

"How much?"

I totted it up for them. I made it look like mental maths, and not a figure that had been living in my head for six years.

"Write it up," my editor said. " 'The True Cost of an Irish Abortion.' Hotels, trains, everything."

I went through each step again, the ones I had already completed with James years ago, stepping neatly into my old footprints. I wondered whether now was the time to talk about it. There were so many people adding their voices to the pro-choice debate, but they were all better women. Married women with fatal foetal abnormalities. That kind of thing. Even the women who were more like me, the girls in their teens and early twenties who simply were not adhering to their birth control schedule closely enough, at least their stories were all similar. The traditional abortion arc: going to the airport alone, shuffling past the protestors at the clinic, feeling tender and awkward in the hostel, and then on the plane back. It was bad, but it was familiar, like a fairy story at its most savage and transcribed from the original Danish.

Plus, my story was not an abortion story. My story was a miscarriage story, but I had no place with the miscarriage women either, who all seemed to want their babies.

Writing the "True Cost" piece gave me a headache so severe that I had to ask my boss if I could go home. Someone else did the piece instead.

One month before the Irish abortion referendum in 2018 my wrist began to seize up while I typed. I was still on staff for a newspaper, but freelancing in the evenings. Every UK newspaper wanted to have an upsetting piece about a woman who was sent her foetal remains in a jam jar, and it was my job to interview them. First my wrist froze, then my fingers would become temporarily stuck in a claw position. One day while washing my hair, I found that I could not create a lather with my fingers, and had to knead the shampoo with the heel of my hand. I bought a cast from the pharmacy, one with Velcro straps that wrapped around my knuckles. Food crumbs and lint stuck to it.

My editor saw me struggling to put my coat on one day, my Velcro hand sticking to the inside lining.

"Rachel, for fuck's sake," he said. "Go see a physio."

I was pretty sure that my injury had come from typing, on the kitchen counter, on the coffee table, and in my bed. I made an appointment for a physiotherapist, only after my editor confirmed that they would pay for it. I took myself and my Velcro hand to Pimlico and sat in a treatment room with a fibreglass model of the human spine.

"Rachel Murray?"

I looked up, still cradling my huge hand.

And there, eight years after he left me in Shandon Street, was James Carey.

James Carey, thirty-five years old, with lines on his forehead.

James Carey, built like a terrier and just as common, somehow wider and squarer than I had ever known him, the strawberry-blond hair shorter, but all him, all Carey.

James Carey, who once told me that I did not understand the point of loving people, who said that when you loved them you loved all of them.

James Carey, the first sexual partner I had legitimately orgasmed with. Here he was, holding a clipboard that said I was experiencing wrist trouble, had no history of blood clots, and was not allergic to penicillin.

"Carey," I said.

It was like the word had opened a portal, and he had to decide whether or not to step through it. I remembered that I was the only one to ever call him that. He stepped through the portal.

"Rachel," he said. "Your *hair*."

It was still short, a little longer than a pixie cut, and ashy blonde.

"I cut it," I said.

"When?"

"Um . . ." I thought about it carefully. "Twenty thirteen?"

He put his clipboard down, and started to laugh. I laughed, too, out of awkwardness. I wasn't really sure what we were laughing at, my hair or the year 2013.

"Well, give me a hug then, you silly cow."

He smelled like a person who showers every day, and like a man who puts a scent on, and both the cleanliness and the scent were so alien to me that I wondered if this really was the James Carey who broke my heart. But the hug went on, and my nose picked up on that faint earthiness living under the clean body. I wondered if he was doing the same, if that was the reason that the hug was going on six seconds longer than the hug of old friends. I wondered if he could find the Rachel underneath the patient who had just walked into his office.

When we parted, we could not stop laughing at each other. "What the fuck is this all about?" I spluttered. "Why are you pretending to be my physiotherapist?"

"Because I *am* your fucking physiotherapist."

"I'm sorry. Last time I saw James Carey, he worked in a bread shop."

I almost bit my lip in the lie. No, I thought. The last time I saw James Carey, he was gazing out the window of Shandon Street, wondering if there was anything left of the girl he thought he loved.

"I didn't even know you were interested in this . . ." I gestured to the model of the human spine. "Stuff."

"I know, I know. But it was either this or prison, wasn't it?"

"I actually imagined something more glamorous and squalid, like you'd end up drinking yourself to death under a bridge."

"Was I really such a fuck-up, then?"

"This from the man who shoplifted grains of salt from Paul Street Shopping Centre."

"God, Rache, even *as* I was doing that, I knew: this girl is going to put it in a book one day."

I grinned, overcome with happiness at seeing him.

"Carey," I said, "what are you *doing* here?"

"Well, according to this chart, I've got to see a woman with RSI."

"What's that?"

"Repetitive Strain Injury. From typing, I assume? Are you a writer now, something like that? Working in books, like you wanted?"

"Journalist," I answered. "I'm actually working overtime at the moment, covering Repeal."

He nodded. "My sisters are doing loads for that back home. Getting it in the North, you know."

"The women in the North tend to get ignored in this debate," I said, sounding like I was on a panel for women in media.

"Yes, and all they get told is how ignored they are." We both laughed again, amazed that we could sound so grown up with one another.

"Sorry, *how* are we talking about this?" I said.

"I know!

"Look," he said, "I need to look at your fucking wrist. I'm off at six. We could get a drink after?"

It was four o'clock. Could I wait around for two hours for James Carey? Was I still that Rachel Murray?

"I actually have to go back to work," I said. "But I could meet you this weekend? Proper catch-up?"

He looked disappointed. "Yeah. Yeah, yeah. The weekend. Look, I'll give you my number, and we can sort it. Let's look at the wrist, will we?" He gestured at my horrible Velcro glove. "Take off that thing."

I wondered if he was married, or had children, or a girlfriend. He was a man in his thirties, and men in their thirties are never single unless there's something wrong with them. I had heard this from many trusted sources.

He sat down on the chair opposite me, and took my wrist in his hands. The warm circle of his fingers like a bracelet.

"Now," he said, "tell me where the strain is."

I blundered my way through my various ailments. The freezing fingers, the wrist pain, the stuck thumb.

"You work too much," he said, and it was hard to tell whether it was a physiotherapist's opinion or the opinion of James Carey.

"Make your wrist go limp," he said, and I did, the fingers pointing down like a homophobic gesture. He put his hand flat in front of mine, his palm to my knuckles. "Now push against me."

I pushed my hand towards his, my fingertips grazing the lines of palm.

"Harder, go on. Hard as you can."

I flushed, and wondered whether I should ask for a different physiotherapist. This was too strange. Like a dream I would wake up and tell James about.

"Harder, go on, you're not trying."

My wrist was getting tired. "I *am* trying."

He took his other hand and worked his thumb up my arm, pressing hard, slightly massaging. "Here," he finally said, triumphantly. He rested his thumb in a spot below the elbow. "This muscle here. It's inflamed."

He dug his thumb deeper, rolling on the muscle he had found. I felt a strange release, of something being broken, kneaded, and then flooding into the rest of my body. Blood coursed up and down my arm and into my shoulder, my chest. I could not look at Carey, so instead I looked at the model of the human spine. *Kiss me*, I thought violently. *Fuck me in your weird office.*

"You'll need to do exercises," he said. "To strengthen your muscles there. And if you can do audio typing, that might help. Rest your hand as much as you can."

"No hand jobs for crack, then," I said, and immediately wanted to drown myself. It belonged to the time where I knew him last. It was a *South Park* joke, from a moment when *South Park* kind of mattered.

He laughed, this time out of bemusement, rather than from the cosmic coincidence that had brought us together again.

I have ruined it, I thought. *I have ruined it all, again.* He showed me the exercises, and I counted down the minutes until I could leave and phone James.

But as I got up to go, Carey the physiotherapist disappeared. "Go on then, Murray," he said. "Give us your phone number."

Carey suggested meeting on the South Bank on Saturday at noon, which told me that he had not been living in London very long. I met him by the book stall outside the BFI, where he was reading Cher's autobiography.

"Did you know she had an affair with Warren Beatty when she was still a teenager?" was the first thing he said.

"Didn't he have an affair with everyone?"

"I know, but *still*."

"Are you going to buy that?"

"No, let's go."

My physiotherapy appointment had been on Wednesday. It was a long time to wonder about James Carey. I had had other boyfriends in the years since, and it would be easy for me to say here that they never meant as much to me as Carey did, but of course they did. They meant all kinds of things to me, but now I couldn't remember what those things were. That Saturday, it seemed like my romantic life had been held on a screensaver for years. I was walking next to Carey, *the* Carey, and my heart was expanding and being crushed at the same time.

"I couldn't believe it when you walked into the practice," he said. Hands in his pockets, face to the ground. "Rachel. It was like . . . I don't know, some kind of lucid dream."

"You *must* have known I was in London," I countered. "I was the one surprised. You, who said you'd never live in England."

"I never said that."

"Oh yes you did. 'Come Out, Ye Black and Tans' on the Underground. You said that."

"I don't remember saying that."

"But you *did*," I stressed, a little too powerfully. "You *did*."

"Well, you're the journalist."

"And you're a physiotherapist?" I was still baffled by this development.

"You're a physiotherapist, full stop, Mr. Carey. Not 'You're a physiotherapist,' question mark. I know punctuation is everything to you types."

"Sorry. But. Since when?"

"You thought I was just sitting on my hole back in Derry, did you?"

"No," I said. He raised his eyebrows. "Sort of," I admitted.

"Sure, look. I don't blame you." We were walking up the South Bank now, a circle gathering around a man beatboxing into a microphone, both of us straining to hear each other.

"When did you start training? It must have taken a while?"

His mother had died a year after he had last seen me. He lived with his father after that. His father, who was generally "infirm" but not particularly unwell, though, needed a lot of attention to keep limber. Carey had gone to therapy with him, and drilled him on the movements at home. He found that his lupus symptoms were playing up less as a result of the physio, and started studying it at Ulster University, commuting from home several days a week. In three years, he was qualified. In four, he was working in Derry. After five, he started studying acupuncture, and after six, his father died, after complications following a stroke.

"I'm so sorry, Care," I said. "That's a lot."

"D'you know what?" he replied thoughtfully. "When you put it like that, it all sounds miserable. But it wasn't so bad, Rachel. Honestly. We were happy as two clams, living together, and we were never on top of each other. We had good craic together. And Derry is gorgeous. And I had the girls helping out, and my nieces and nephews are brilliant, and I had loads of my old mates around. I went out with a nice girl for a few years. A new profession. It was very . . ."

"Grounding?" I finished, my breath held on the nice girl, wondering where she was now.

"Grounding," he agreed. "Yes."

It was a cold spring day, and I had dressed to be fancied.

Leopard-print mini skirt, tight black funnel neck, leather jacket. I was freezing, next to the river. He could tell. "Shall we go in here?" he said, pointing at the Giraffe.

I laughed. "To *Giraffe*?"

"What? Is it no good?"

"No." I laughed again. "I don't know. I've never been. It's just . . . I don't know, it's a chain."

But Giraffe being a chain was not a good enough reason to say no to Giraffe, the way it would have been with my own friends.

"I cannot believe," I said, picking up my menu, "I am sitting inside the Giraffe on the South Bank with James Carey."

"Why not?"

"Because it's somewhere you go with your, like, distant cousin, who is visiting from home," I explained. "It is not where you go with your ex-boyfriend turned physiotherapist."

We had arrived in the middle of bottomless brunch and were surrounded by women in the early hours of a hen do or a thirtieth birthday party, high on Bloody Marys and mimosas.

"Well, Christ," he said, "if you can't beat 'em, join 'em. What do you think, Rache?"

"You haven't seen me in eight years and you want to do bottomless brunch with me?"

"Are you going to narrate everything we do today?" he asked, but nicely.

"No."

"Always taking notes," he said.

"Like the Gestapo?" I replied, a line which had been rolling around my head for approximately eight years.

He smiled, and I couldn't tell if he remembered saying it or not. "Like the Gestapo, yes."

We talked and ate and drank prosecco watered down with orange juice. Carey had been living in London for eight months. He did not know if he wanted to stay. It was so unfriendly, he thought. And pretentious.

"No, it isn't," I said fiercely. "London is great. It's fab."

"Yes, that's coming from you, though. You're too London to eat in Armadillo."

"What's Armadillo?"

"Is that not where we are?"

"Giraffe!"

I told him about what James was doing, and I was surprised that he needed filling in. I assumed everyone knew what James was doing. By now he was a senior producer at the show he started interning at, loyal to the end, even though he had offers elsewhere. The off-season was long enough that he could fly out to LA and work on scripts, including several big comedies that you have definitely heard of. He is often one of five writers behind a funny woman's big film, and has so many Instagram followers that he sometimes does adverts for PrEP.

"God," Carey said, leaning back into his plastic chair. "Well, he was always going to be famous, wasn't he?"

"Did you always think that?" I said, already phrasing this information in my head as though it were a text to James. "I suppose he was always very funny. And dedicated."

"And he gets people in his thrall very easy, doesn't he?" Carey said.

James, who has had countless lovers in the past decade, has never enthralled anyone on a permanent basis. Every few years he will make a half-hearted play towards a relationship, but usually gets tired of the person quickly. He has a huge friend group in New York, and is as dedicated to each of them as he is to me. He is always phoning me from a rental car, where he is invariably driving upstate for a wedding, a funeral or a millionaire's orgy.

"What do you mean?"

"Well, you."

"Was I 'in his thrall'?"

"Yes."

"That's a funny way of putting it," I said, swaying slightly from the sweet drinks. "I wouldn't say I was in his 'thrall.' Just that he was my best friend. Is."

Now I was certain Carey was thinking about our last pub trip, on the day of my graduation.

He looked at his menu. "I might have a beer, now, break up the sugar."

We talked about my life in London and what it had brought me, but his comment about James stuck to my back teeth like hard toffee.

With James now quite rich and famous, I sometimes convinced myself that he had outgrown me, and I was his needy little hanger-on, the kind of sad person who gets brought to parties as a treat and not because she belongs there. I would see James on social media, wearing a suit at a *GQ* party and talking to Jenny Slate, and think, *Oh, it's over.* I would mourn our friendship, privately, and decide to not be resentful. Then inevitably he would phone me and ask whether I thought Ben from the bookshop was queer all along, and I would realise how crazy I had been.

I once confessed to a friend of James's, a beautiful gay boy called Phil, that I often felt not good enough for my own best friend.

"Oh, none of us do," he said airily. "James secretly thinks he should be with a Harvard professor or something, doesn't he?"

This surprised me. I thought it meant Phil knew about Dr. Byrne, but he didn't. Phil had just witnessed Byrne's shadow: James's roaming sense that a boyfriend was supposed to be a big person who lectured you about books.

We stayed at Giraffe for a long time, until we got restless and released ourselves back onto the street. We still had not talked about the one thing the other person really cared about, which was whether we were both single.

"I'm not ready to go home yet," Carey said. "Are you?"

"No."

He put his arm around my shoulders. I had worn flats that day, so I wouldn't be too much taller than him. He never minded about that kind of thing, but maybe he had changed somehow, and become a man who minded. "Fucking hell," he said. "I can't believe you're here."

"I've always been here!" I said, laughing. "I've been here for years."

"Do you think I'm very different?" he asked, and he sounded almost anxious about it. I took the question seriously.

"I don't know. Yes. I think so. Or maybe I'm different. I don't know, I'm less afraid of you, now."

"*Afraid* of me? When were you afraid of me?"

"I was always terrified you were about to bolt."

He pushed me then, and I swayed, knocking against the rail of the river. "Oi! What was that about?"

"I never bolted. I was in it for the long run, Murray. I was obsessed with you."

"Care, you literally disappeared."

"That was the first time. Never the second time. If you take the entirety of our relationship, Rachel Murray, you'll find—rounding *up*—I was the one doing all the chasing."

I shook my head. "You can't just pretend the first time didn't happen. It destroyed me."

"How was I supposed to know that?" he retorted. "It was all 'me and James, me and James, me and James.' You didn't seem all that arsed about having a boyfriend. You already had a James. It was the first thing you ever said to me."

I had heard this before, or a version of it, but had never been in the position to believe it.

"Is that really how you felt?" I asked.

"I don't lie. Never to you."

I had often gone weeks at a time without thinking about James Carey, but never months. He was always in the background somewhere, a "what if" stacked on top of so many other "what ifs." What if I had never got pregnant; what if I had never lost the pregnancy; what if the Harrington-Byrnes had not chased me out of Cork with their money and their web of gossip, both real and imagined.

We walked through Parliament Square, and Carey gave his opinions on each of the statues. His opinion was pretty low, given how many of them had appalling track records in Ireland.

"Henry John Temple," he said. "He evicted a load of paddies off their land, you know, Rachel. In the famine."

"Really?" I said, looking up at the statue. "What a cunt."

"Dreadful man," he said. "Hey, can I kiss you?"

"You're asking?"

"I don't know, you might have a boyfriend, or something. I've been dying to know all day, and you haven't said a thing about it."

"Well, I don't."

"You haven't said if I can kiss you."

"Do you think it would anger Henry John Temple?" I said, looking at the statue.

"Oh, he'd be livid."

"Well, in that case."

He put his hands on my hips. He was shy, all of a sudden. There was a second of feeling like two teenagers who had been set up by their friends at the school disco. We exchanged a *well, look at us!* expression, and he tilted his head, very slightly, to kiss me.

And the kiss was like—what was it like?

It was like finding your favourite pair of boots under the bed. It was like finding them on the last day of your lease, the boxes already in the van, having assumed that they must have been left at an ex-lover's house, or simply vanished by your own carelessness. *Oh, these. Oh. Oh. I love these.*

When I finally stopped kissing him, I put my arms around his waist, and laid my head on his shoulder. My nose dug deep to find the old smell, my hands on the rough denim of his jacket. I had missed him so much, and I hadn't even known it.

"Carey," I said. "Carey, Carey, Carey."

"Darling," he replied. "I think you're a bit old to call me by my last name."

And so now, everyone I love is called James.

WE DIDN'T CALL THE BABY JAMES, even though James Devlin thought it was the only name that made sense.

"I just think," he said, "that there should be an endless continuum of Jameses looking out for you. A brotherhood. A pact."

"No."

"A pack of Jameses. A murder of Jameses. A *consortium* of Jameses."

We called him Shay, in the end, short for Séamus, which was James Carey's dad's name. As soon as I told James Devlin, I received the following screen grab from Wikipedia.

> Séamus (Irish pronunciation: [ˈʃeːmˠəsˠ]) is an Irish male given name, of Latin origin. It is the Irish equivalent of the name James. The name James is the English New Testament variant for the Hebrew name Jacob.

Alright, I texted back. You win.

The brotherhood of James welcomes yet another member, he replied.

I have practised telling him about Dr. Byrne in my head hundreds of times, and despite many revisions to how I would do it—complete with many careful, sensitive word choices—I still have not told him. I have told Carey, which marks a strange and important first in our history: the first time I have told him something that I have not told James. His advice is to wait. Wait until I know more, wait until James comes to visit in the summer. It's not the kind of thing you want to find out over the phone, he says, and I agree, mostly because it lets me off the hook.

And in the meantime I have written it all down. I am told that writing at night inflames my carpal tunnel syndrome, and I ignore this advice, because you're allowed to ignore your physiotherapist once you are married to him. I wrote at first for James, and then for Deenie, with some kind of impression in my mind that I would give it to either or both of them. I never will, of course—can you imagine? Your husband in a coma, and someone gives you a three-hundred-page confession?

I wonder what I did this for. And then I look at James Carey, a well-liked man nearing forty, and wonder: *Are you capable of the same kind of betrayal? And if you are—do I deserve it?* I am about the same age as Deenie Harrington-Byrne was when we first met, the age she will always be in my head. The impossible adulthood she and Dr. Byrne occupied, the easy sophistication that still feels alien to me but surely must be observed by the younger women at my office. Am I their Deenie? Am I anyone's?

I look at my baby and I am sure he is made of velvet. He has only just forgotten how to sleep, and so inevitably it is the two of us alone at night together. He clings on to bunches of my hair or jewellery or my bra strap. "Sssssshay," I say, both his name and a request for quiet. "Sssshay, Shay, Shay."

I think, quite a lot actually, about whether Shay is anything like the baby I would have had back in 2010, if either my brain or my body had been up to the task of keeping it.

I remember, with a kind of sharp clarity that evaded me for years, exactly what those days were like. When the beginnings of me and Carey's first pregnancy passed through me in clots, and I felt like an animal who had to take itself somewhere to die. The pain spread from my stomach and through to my back, working its way through to each notch on my spine, tapping on the base of my neck. The days in bed, the throwing the sheets away because they were ruined, the money taken off the house deposit because of the deep blood that seeped through the mattress, staining the box springs. James Devlin, coming in and out with potato waffles, chicken dippers, beans on toast. James with his own broken heart, looking after me.

You forget the pain of childbirth. But you forget other kinds of pain, too.

Shay is going to Cork for the first time. The sisters up in Derry are so used to new babies that, who cares, right? But for Mum and Dad, and Chris and Kev, this is new. The boys have both stayed in Cork, graduating just in time for the money to come back, and they both have jobs in tech. Kev is now gruffly bisexual, and has never come out to my parents. Nor has he hidden it. Everyone just seems to get it without being told, and, to be fair to my parents, I think they would cringe at having to discuss any of their children's sex lives.

I file a column about what to dress your baby in to meet your parents—do you resist the temptation to put a strange hat on him, or does that feel like you're compensating for something?—and we head to our flight, weighed down by plastic.

Dad meets us at the airport, and he cries when he sees Shay, saying, "Sure, God, would you look at him, look at the little fella, bold as brass, my God, Rachel, who would have thought?" He informs us that Mum has put out a big spread at home, and she's been to Dunnes, the posh bit of Dunnes, because wouldn't you get great stuff at Dunnes, these days?

They managed to keep the practice going in the end. They have done a great line in Botox, filler, Invisalign and tooth-whitening retainers that I should *really* consider getting into. "Wear it to bed, two weeks, Rachel," Dad says. "You won't believe the difference."

There is indeed a big spread at home. Mum cries when she sees

Shay. Kev and Chris are emotional, too. For some reason they are still allowed to call my husband Carey, whereas I must only call him James. He was serious about it, from the beginning.

"We can't do this," he said, "unless it's a completely new relationship. We need to get to know each other all over again, Rachel. We're different now."

"I'm not different. I don't think you are, either."

"You're very different, don't kid yourself. You'll only be disappointed."

"How am I different?"

He pointed to my scatter cushions, currently on the floor. "The Rachel Murray I knew did not have throw pillows."

"I won't be disappointed."

That worried look again. "This isn't a walk down memory lane, Rache. For me, anyway."

"I know."

"*Do* you?"

"James is very insecure. Carey was quite a cool customer, you know."

"You're so glamorous now, you see, I'll never keep up."

"Stop!" I said, then snuggled down into the sheets. "Go on."

I could not understand why he was single. At the same time, I could completely understand why he was single. He still had no concept of time. He was still filthy, deep down, though better at maintaining a front. He was still bad at sustaining interest in anything that he found remotely boring. He would suddenly leave parties, or conversations, sometimes conversations that I was still having with him. "Why did you walk away?" I would call after him. "Oh," he'd respond, "it sounded like you already knew what you thought."

He still has deep convictions on what love is, and how it functions.

We moved in together quickly, renting a place in Chalk Farm. We were better as live-in lovers than we ever were as daters. We were beans on toast people, two joints on a Saturday night people, keeping watch while the other person took a wild piss on a country walk people. It was instantly cosy, even if he could still be infuriating. One evening he didn't come home after work, and his phone was off. It was the kind of summer evening that should have been spent drinking wine in a pub garden, and he was spoiling it. I brimmed with anxiety that he had lost interest and was right now making a mockery of my fidelity. I walked miserably to the shop, ready to drown my sorrow in a bottle of Australian wine, and found Carey sitting on the street next to a free book box with an open can of Bulmers. It was almost 9 p.m.

"What the fuck are you doing here?" I asked.

"Reading?" he said simply, looking up from a book about octopuses.

"Just bring the books home, then? They're free? I've been worried!"

"We have enough books at home," he said. He lifted a black plastic bag of corner-shop cans. "Do you want one?"

So we sat on the pavement and drank cider and looked at the books from the free book box until it was too dark to read. Carey could be spacey and unreliable, but he didn't live with secrets. Not the way I did.

I told him the full story: the exile from Cork, the whole scenario with the Harrington-Byrnes, the abortion money we kept to emigrate. We were living together for six months before I found the courage to talk about it. Not because I thought he would leave me, but because I didn't want him to hate James.

"Christ," he said, marvelling, as if I were describing the finale of a TV show he had given up on watching. And then: "I wish I had known."

"I never really let you know anything."

"No," he agreed, pulling me close. "No, you didn't."

We are home for a week. We go out with the buggy, and we bump into all sorts of people. People who moved away and came back, people who insist that Ireland has the best primary schools and would not subject their children to the schools in England. What with the horrendous eleven plus exam, which is a surprisingly common talking point among the Irish.

It is my first trip home that I have not worried about running into the Harrington-Byrnes. He is sick. He is possibly even dead. Deenie will not be wandering the Cork streets. She is the wife of a sick person. They do different things.

Two days before we are due to leave for London, I receive an email.

> Dear Rachel,
>
> I hope you don't mind my getting in contact. I realise it has been a very long time, and the last time we saw each other it was not on pleasant terms. I also realise that this is an understatement.
>
> You may already know that Fred has not been well the past year. It has been a harrowing time for us both, and while I have been extremely busy with his care, there has been a lot of time—decidedly too much time—for reflection.
>
> I do not want to worry or bother you, but I would love to find a way to speak. I saw from your (very funny) column this week that you are planning a trip home— perhaps you would like to meet then?
>
> Congratulations on your career, which looks like it has been exciting. I read a lot of your pieces during the referendum. I feel proud to have known you.
>
> Hope this email finds you well,
> Deenie Byrne

When I first extorted the Harrington-Byrnes, I did so with the conviction that it was the only thing to do. Dr. Byrne had betrayed me and James terribly, and I needed the money for the abortion. But then I didn't need the money for the abortion. I just needed it, period.

It was this fundamental dishonesty that led me to believe that I deserved the weird looks on the street, the girls coming up to me in bars, the incident at my graduation. That I deserved the hate of the Harrington-Byrnes. And so I crawled out of the country with my head down. I avoided people from Cork and, just to be safe, from all of Munster. For years, there was no one in my circle who was Irish, and I believed this to be appropriate punishment for the way I had acted as a twenty-one-year-old girl in 2010.

And now I am an editor at a paper about the Irish in London, and Deenie Byrne wants to talk to me.

———

By the time I decide that I am definitely going to meet Deenie, my husband is at golf with my brothers, and my parents are at work. This means I have no choice but to bring Shay with me.

I do not know what Deenie Byrne's fertility journey has been like since I last met her, but something about her email says that she is still childless. She said she was "reflecting" a lot, which I suppose anyone could do at any time, but feels unlikely if she has a brood of children under ten.

I see her at a table, a manuscript plopped in front of her, and I am again jobless in 2010, and mad at her for not paying me more than fifty euros a week.

She is in her forties and looks broadly the same. Her roots a little grey, her Victorian eyes with a few lines, but still Deenie. Small and sturdy as a jewel. I'm still bulky from pregnancy, and the words *chubby student with a crush* come back to me.

"Hello," I say, reversing the buggy carefully next to the table.

"Rachel," she says, standing. "Oh my God, you're so grown up."

"Thanks."

She is startled by Shay, and I can see the fear and confusion pass over her pretty face. Even though she knows I have a child now, for about three seconds, she is back in 2010, too. I have kept the baby that belongs to her, and this is him. She blinks hard. Snaps herself out of it.

"And who is *this* little man?"

"This is Shay."

"How old . . . ?"

"Ten weeks!"

"Oh my goodness. He's so long."

"I know, I know, he's the longest in his class."

I sit down while Deenie politely engages with my son, who is asleep.

"Congratulations, Rachel. He's gorgeous."

"Thanks," I say. "I was sorry to hear about Fred."

The last time I saw this woman, she was handing me a cheque for two thousand euros, and I promised she would never have to see me ever again.

"Yes," she says, used to sympathy by now. "It's been hard. Do you want a coffee?"

"I'll just have a sparkling water, or something."

"I'll get it for you."

She shoots up quickly and sits back down with my water.

"I didn't let myself google you for years," she says. "But then I saw your piece in *The Irish Times*, during the referendum. Interviewing the English abortion providers about Irish women."

I nod. "That was a hard one."

She nods, too. "It was really well done. I'm so glad it has worked out for you."

I want to be patient with Deenie Byrne, but I am not going to compare LinkedIns with her.

"It would have been easier if I could have used any of my publishing experience," I say flatly. Then I feel bad. She thought I was having an affair with her husband, after all. And who knows how helpful that experience would have even been? Would Deenie's name have meant anything to an English publisher, when so few Irish things mean anything to English people?

She nods again, her eyes flicking to her manuscript.

"Did you . . . ?" she says, then stops. "Did you cover all the abortion stuff, because of your own . . . experience?"

"What? Oh. No. It was just, you know. It was important."

"Of course."

"And I'm an Irish journalist in England. There's only a few beats they really want you on."

"The abortion beat?"

"The abortion beat, the child molesting beat, the occasional 'Ten Reasons Irish Women Are Hot Right Now' beat. Those are the main beats."

She laughs.

"How is he doing?" I ask.

"Um, well, he's awake."

"Oh, wow!"

"Yes. Since January."

"And how is he . . . ?"

"He's very different." She says it like a mother explaining her shy child to a new teacher. "You wouldn't know him, I don't think."

"I'm sorry, I don't really know what happened."

"Of course. It's, ah, it's quite a rare thing. We were swimming."

"*Swimming?*"

"We were in South Carolina last year. For our anniversary, you know. Fifteen years married. We did a tour of the Southern states. And we were in this beautiful creek, in this big national park. Later we got back to the hotel, and he started vomiting, and we thought it was sun stroke."

"Oh my God."

"I know." She had obviously told this story many times. The next few lines came out in a big rush.

"And well, there's a kind of amoeba that lives in water, all water really, South Carolina wasn't special, and it enters your bloodstream through your ears and nose, and it can lead to a brain infection, and that's what he got. He was hospitalised, and we were stuck in South Carolina for weeks, and we thought he was going to die, and being sick in America is like staying at the Ritz Carlton and ordering everything on room service every night, money wise, but he didn't die. We somehow got him back to Ireland, and he had moments of being awake, but then he would fall back in again. And he would fade, and then do better, and then fade again. And now he's awake."

In all the many punishments I had dreamed up for the Harrington-Byrnes over the years, I would never have allowed this to enter even my darkest fantasies. It was too cruel, too unusual.

"Deenie," I said, "I'm so sorry."

Sensing the agony in the room, Shay wakes up and begins to moan. I wait a minute, and hope he is just squeaking, looking for a more comfortable way to sleep. But he doesn't want to sleep. He wants to be with me. He gets louder, and I take him out.

"Oh," Deenie says. "He's so small."

"No," I laugh, glad that he's cutting the tension. "He's very long, remember?"

His hands start to ball into fists, and I realise he wants to eat.

Can I really get my tit out in front of Deenie Byrne?

"Sorry," I say, wrestling with my top, my annoying maternity bra. "Do you mind if I . . . ?"

"No, please, Rachel. Go ahead."

I always said that I would not be one of those mothers that puts a tea towel over her child's head while he feeds. I found it prudish and weird. *We all know what's happening under there!* Now, I hated myself for not being a tea-towel mother. Deenie Harrington could see my enormous purple nipple.

His lips smack against me. It's embarrassingly noisy, and I can feel my face going crimson. "You're so natural," she says. "Such an earth mother."

No one ever says "earth mother" to petite women.

"You must be wondering why I wanted to speak to you."

"A little."

She allows herself full eye contact with Shay, and with my boob. "I've wondered a lot, about you."

"I've thought a lot about you, too."

"It never happened, did it, Rachel?"

My arms freeze. Shay can feel me stiffening, and moves his arms and legs around in protest.

"What do you mean?"

"You never slept with him, did you?"

"Why would you say that?"

I am, yet again, in another impossible situation with Deenie Byrne. How can I admit it now, without telling her everything? Did she know about James Devlin already?

"I cheated," she says. "Years later, I cheated. With a man I worked with. You actually met him, I think. Sandy hair?"

"Yes, I remember. That dinner party."

She gives a hollow laugh. "Yes, that terrible dinner party." She continues. "But Fred knew right away because the way I spoke about Dominic changed. It was right there, in the texture or something, like every sentence had new bumps and grooves on it. He said to me, a month in—*Deenie, you're sleeping with him, aren't you?* And I broke completely, and said yes."

"Wow. All right. So you were kind of even."

"Kind of," she says. "Fred wasn't a psychopath. Isn't. The way he spoke about you, Rachel, when we were at home alone together. All those months when you were hanging around. He was obviously very fond of you, but it wasn't how someone talks about their lover, even their secret lover."

"How?" I ask.

"It was *because* he was so fond of you, that was the giveaway. He was always saying, *Rachel is a great girl, Rachel is going places. Rachel should be given a chance. Rachel picks the wrong men.* It was too wholesome. If he was sleeping with you, he would never talk to me like that, would he?"

"No," I say. "I suppose not."

I feel like someone who has been on death row for years, and am experiencing a strange release at finally having my number called.

"We went to therapy. We worked on our marriage. We were better for it, in the end. He was so good with my mother, Rachel. You wouldn't believe." Her voice cracked slightly, overwhelmed by her husband in his former role as carer, and not as patient. "But all those years after, being open, and talking about our fears, not once did I get any clarity on The Rachel Incident."

"The Rachel Incident?" I ask. "That's what you called it?"

"That's what I called it." She shrugs. "It's been like my Bermuda Triangle, Rachel. I know that he disappeared inside there for a while, but I don't know how, or why, or what it meant to him."

I nod again.

"And now I can't ask him. So many of those memories are just gone. So much language. I might never know. I hate that I'm asking you, but I'm asking you."

"Asking me what?"

Deenie runs her finger around the circumference of her coffee saucer. "Did you sleep with my husband, and were you his mistress?"

I have no intention of lying to Deenie, but I don't have the strength to deconstruct this alternate reality that I accepted to protect Dr. Byrne's queerness and my friend's anonymity.

"No, I never slept with him."

"But you were pregnant."

"Yes. I was."

"With . . . who was that boy? The one I accused you of making up?"

"Carey," I say. Then I remember the rules, about not calling him that any more. "James Carey. He's my husband, now."

She looks to Shay. "And him . . . ?"

"Yes. He's Shay's dad."

"You stayed together? All that time? After . . . ?"

"No, we reconnected, a few years ago. It's a long story. But I was never pregnant with Fred's kid. I was just . . . I was backed into a corner, and he wanted you to believe that we were sleeping together, so I decided to make the best out of it."

Her body sways forward, like she is trying to nod but can only bow. A whole world, shattered in one breath. Thank God, her phone rings. The letters DOM appear on her screen. She frowns at it, mutes the call.

"Dom," I say. "Is that . . . ?"

"Yes," she answers. "Dominic. The one you met."

"So he's still . . . ?"

"Yes. We're sort of. We're together."

I want to maintain a look of zero judgement. After all, her lying cheating husband was in a coma for some time, and would not be returning to his original personality. I had no idea what she was dealing with.

"He loves me. You know? He did then, too. He was married before but he's not any more. We found each other again, a bit like you and your Carey."

"And what about Dr. Byrne?" I was in no position to ask the question, but we had been through too much together. I needed to know.

"Well, we're still married. And I'm his carer, officially. But Dominic and I live together now."

I can't resist digging more.

"Kids?" I say, without much tact.

"He has two." She smiles. "Boy and a girl. They're lovely."

She looks, for a moment, genuinely happy. Relief floods my guts, because what a good stepmother Deenie must be. And God, how terrible it would be if she had nothing.

"I need to know, Rachel."

She waits for me to volunteer information.

"Rachel, please."

The Rachel Incident. The idea of being a figure in their lives, the same way they were phantoms in mine.

"The receipts," she urges. "They were to your house."

"Yes. But it wasn't me," I respond uncertainly. "It was . . . it was someone else."

The slow, rocking bow again. Whatever colour Deenie had in her white face has drained out of it. "Who?"

It is twelve years ago again, and I am sitting on the couch in Shandon Street, weeping for my broken heart. My old professor amiably accepts my rage that he had dared to dock me for late essays when he was using my house for sex. James leans against the living-room wall, sternly telling Dr. Byrne to be kinder to me. *Why can't anyone love me like this?* I had thought. *Why are they making it work, when I can't?*

But that wasn't making it work. Whatever came after was. Whatever Deenie and Dr. Byrne did or said or promised in the long marriage that followed me and James. A story I won't ever know.

I put Shay back in his buggy. Fiddle with the straps, the clips, the little hat.

"I can't tell you that," I say. I unzip my handbag, take out my pen and paper. "It's not my story."

I write down his name and his email address. I know about making things work, too.

I say the same sentence that I have been saying for years now, each time with more pride. I tear the piece of paper from my note-pad, and fold it in a square.

"My best friend is called James Devlin," I say, sliding the piece of paper to her. "And he's a writer who lives in New York."

Acknowledgements

This book was written during the coldest and saddest part of the 2021 lockdown, and while I was on deadline for another book entirely. They tell you that you should never abandon a half-finished project in favour of a new one. Well. Sometimes you should. This is one such example.

Ryan Farrell is not James Devlin, but they have a few things in common: thank you for letting me write about those things.

Thank you to Natasha Hodgson for her expert screenwriting on *Discs*. You are the artist that James aspires to be.

Thank you to Ella Risbridger, who read every single draft of this thing, even when it was called *Frogger*. I truly don't know how I would finish a book without you.

Thank you to Dolly Alderton, who taught me that the smallest moments can be cinematic.

Thank you to the only two WhatsApp groups I will ever respond to: The Tub and Monica's Ass.

Thank you to Sarah Savitt, for letting me write this book instead of the other one that I promised to write, but didn't. Thank you Bryony Woods and Andrew Mills for representing this book like it was their own firstborn. Thank you to Clare Gordon for being this book's eleventh-hour midwife. Thank you to Jenny Jackson for seeing its potential.

Thank you, as always, to the whole team at Virago. Thank you also to Page Boy, whose intelligent notes always helped me see my own work more clearly, and sometimes resulted in a few last-minute changes.

Thank you to my family for always being there. Thank you to everyone who made those Cork years worth it: everyone who worked at HMV, everyone who visited our stupid little house, everyone who worked at The Bróg, everyone I stole a drink off.

Thank you to Gavin Day, for always taking the time to tell me what is in a whale's head.

The acknowledgements are a part of the book where you must observe everything that went into the creation of the story. A sad fact of this book is that it revolves around the access—or lack thereof—of reproductive healthcare. With this in mind, please consider donating your time or money to Planned Parenthood, BPAS, or any charity that aids this cause.